TO THE READER:

This book was written sometime between 1985 and 1990 if I remember correctly. Technology described in this story is based on what I knew of what was then current or my best speculation of what was current at the time. This being a work of fiction I also added speculative technology in some instances. I have decided not to update or change anything prior to publication in that respect.

One note about some of the naming conventions used: My current understanding is that the US Navy designates unknown contacts as 'Uniform' and known contacts as 'Sierra' with numbers assigned as they show up. I used 'Bravo' in this story because in this case they knew darn well who was coming after them and had signatures for some of the adversary units in their records already. I suppose I should have designated the Russian Sierra as Romeo One but at the time I wrote this it seemed best to do it like I did. So I'll let all that stand as is.

The usual disclaimers about characters in this book apply. I did not mold any character in totality or even near to it to fit anyone I knew, personally or however distantly or historically, at the time of its writing. I think writers always pull specific and individual characteristics and mannerisms from people they're exposed to for use in character construction, but hardly ever do they cast a character from the same mold as any real person anywhere (historical fiction excepted, of course).

As far as the governments and the countries used in the book and their actions and attitudes as expressed in this story—keep in mind that this is, after all, a work of fiction. Which means that at the time I wrote all this I was making it up. That should be obvious given the fact that nothing happened like it was written in the story.

All that said, it seems best at this time to get out of your way and let you read like you want to. I wish you well.

CR Williams

PRESENT

"Ground in which the army survives only if it fights with the courage of desperation is called Death."

Sun Tzu

"Conn, Sonar."

Cruising.

"Conn aye."

If you could call it that. It was really more like floating. They were moving just enough to maintain stability—a submarine can hover if it's trimmed properly, but it can be a nuisance to keep up—and to keep the towed array stretched out, since towed arrays are useless under other circumstances. They weren't moving very fast, in other words. Most people could walk faster than Alabama (Mod-Ohio-class, 18,700 tons, give or take ten or twenty, 560 feet long, 95 officers and crewmen, the pride of the fleet in the completely objective eyes of her crew) was moving. It was part of what made her hard to find, and being hard to find was something that American nuclear submarines did better than anyone else. It mostly was a matter of greater experience. Americans had been doing this kind of thing, building submarines, moving slowly, being quiet, and waiting under water like they were doing more or longer, sometimes both, than anyone else.

"Tell the Captain we've got 'em again."

"Captain, Sonar reports the Bravo contacts are back."

J.T. decided against the headset. He picked up a phone and pressed one button. "This is the Captain."

"Johnson, skipper. We've got 'em again, and more besides. At the outer edge of the first zone this time. I still can't give you much, though. You want to see it?"

It was true that his initials were J.T. It was true that his last name started with a K. It was also true that he was the captain of this vessel. Other than that, many things were different. The ship he commanded was called a boat, the boat was named after a state and not a town in that state, and there was no one on board named Sulu, Scott, or McCoy. That didn't mean that jokes weren't made, of course, but it did cut down on the number and type thereof. There was also the fact that, by now, J.T. had learned how to either (most often) ignore the jokes or else (almost never in practice) beat hell out of anyone who made them. He didn't get that many jokes nowadays, anyway, so it wasn't much of a problem.

"I'll come in and take a look. I want it on the repeaters also." Many operational-test modifications had been combined with the UPDATE program that gave every boat some incremental improvements every couple of years during the intensive maintenance cycle. They lost crewmen and gained some interesting-looking gadgets that J.T. was still thinking about in some cases, even if fewer bodies did mean more room for the rest (even on an Ohio, extra space was never turned down). One of the results of the last round of work was the addition of repeater screens in Ops, so that the officers didn't have to requisition somebody else's multifunction display when they wanted to look over someone's shoulder by remote control. It also meant less crowding in the wardroom when there was a good movie on, but no one mentioned that to the higher-ups. Some things were best left unsaid. "I'll want opinions on this, Ed," J.T. said to his executive officer, "I'll be around the comer getting it out of the horse's mouth. You have the conn."

"I have the conn, aye."

J.T.'s name had not been given to him capriciously. His parents had, at the time, no idea that a certain other purely fictional commander with the same initials in his name was about to become so famous. And to be fair, the coincidence had probably helped him as much as it had hurt him. A very fine wife and certain marvelous children had resulted from a conversation about his name, for example. Unfortunately, though, it was human to remember mostly the bad things— jokes and needling and a few outright brawls—more than you did the good things. But then, even the bad things had been of some benefit in the long run. They had helped drive J.T. to be more competent, better at what he did. And he had been, therefore he commanded. So maybe having that particular name wasn't so bad after all.

"Good morning, gentlemen," J.T. said as he entered Sonar. For him it was, though for Srully Johnson it was nearer the end of the watch, while Roland Tullibee was in the middle of his. The Navy had adopted this somewhat complicated scheduling system to cut down the chance that everyone on watch would "fade" at the same time, and so that everyone on a crew would have a chance to work with everyone else in their department. This was supposed to enhance teamwork and cut down on any friction between personnel, as the theory went. It also required a computer to set up and keep track of the duty schedules, but that was no problem. If there was one thing that any U.S. Navy unit or platform had plenty of, and wanted still more of, it was computers of any kind.

"What have you got for me, Srully?"

Johnson had split one of his displays and was backing up a recorder when J.T. came in, preparing to divide himself between past history and the here- and-now. Next to Johnson, Tullibee concentrated exclusively on the current readings coming in through Alabama's several sonars. Behind the two primary operator positions and offset so that everybody could look over everybody else's shoulders were the T/K, Trainee/Kibitzer, positions, one of which was being occupied by a real trainee—actually, the newest member of the crew who would be there for most of the patrol while the more senior operators helped him to properly mix training with reality. It was a relatively new layout, peculiar so far only to Alabama and Georgia, which supposedly increased efficiency and productivity while it cut down on manpower requirements. That it had cut manpower was evident enough—there would normally have been two other men in the compartment, before the UPDATE—but it would take more than one-and-a-half very average patrols before anyone could say that it was more efficient and productive. J.T. was willing to give the changes a chance, but he would also admit that it made him uneasy to see this particular compartment with so relatively few people in it.

Johnson was in the process of splitting one of his major screens—one of four displays, two large and two smaller, that each man had—into pieces so he could show J.T. what he wanted make a point of. The other men had their monitors split in the standard way, between the waterfall frequency readouts that J.T. was more familiar with and the newer-style graphic position-and-bearing readouts that more powerful computers on Navy platforms had been making possible for almost eighteen months now. As for most of the other changes that were being made, opinions on the new forms of information-display were also mixed. This was one change that J.T. definitely liked, however—the graphic display gave him needed information more quickly and understandably than a talker could, and he didn't have to wait for a chart to be marked to get it. It made his job easier. He was always for anything that did that.

"Aren't you supposed to be off-watch, Mr. Wilson?" J.T. asked the new man.

Wilson allowed a guilty look to get loose. "Yes sir. But I don't have anything else I want to do for a while, and I couldn't see that some extra time here would hurt me, sir."

J.T. acted as if he were seriously considering the notion for a few seconds. "Very good. You'll get some points for that." Before Wilson could react, he turned his attention back to Johnson. "Go ahead, Srully. What have you got?"

"A little bit from the second zone, sir, right here." He nodded toward a split portion of the left-hand display. "And this from the inner zone." Johnson's fingers ran across a keyboard. The past-history part of the display split again into a bearing-only indicator at the top and several graphic representations of sound waves at the bottom.

"Topmost wave is from the outer zone, just a few seconds here and there. This—" He moused a pip onto a wave line. "—is probably a surface unit. We've cleaned it up quite a bit. I'll take that out--" A tap on a key erased the extra line. "—to get this here."

J.T. studied the broken waves that remained on the screen. They didn't look good to him. "I forget things sometimes. Pressure of command and all that. What do make out of this, Mr. Wilson?"

"Sir?" Wilson had started to relax when J.T. had turned away. "Uh, well, sir, I—" He started to scratch his head, decided that the gesture wasn't appropriate to the time, and turned it into a smooth-the-hair-down motion. "The contact is pretty spotty, sir," he said, "of course. But what I'd guess—"

"Estimates," Tullibee growled without taking his eyes off his own screens, "We don't give guesses, we offer estimates."

"Ah, right," Wilson said, instantly re-flustered, "I mean, yes sir, I mean, okay." He paused again, acutely aware that J.T. was waiting for him to say something.

"Take your time, Mr. Wilson," J.T. said, "Mr. Tullibee has a habit of doing that to people who don't yet know how lovable he really is."

"Yes sir. Thank you sir." Wilson took a slow breath. "My estimate, Captain, is that at least two other units were close by that surface contact." He eyed the traces again, carefully. "I would have said small surface units at first, but I'm less sure of that now. But there are definitely more diesels there than one ship would be running."

"Thank you, Mr. Wilson. Srully?"

"He did as well as I could for what we got, Skipper," Johnson said, "I'll stick my neck out further because I've got more data, and say we got several shallow subsurface contacts that were trying to mask themselves by running close to a surface unit."

"Snorkeling diesel-electrics," J.T. said.

"Yessir. That's the most I'm going to gamble on that outer-zone stuff." Johnson nodded toward a bearing indicator. "Here's what we got from that then."

There were two bearings indicated, which J.T. assumed were the first and last contacts from the outermost convergence zone. For Alabama that was about eighty-one nautical miles, one-hundred-sixty-two thousand yards, away. For anyone with a sonar that could reach that far the narrow ring of sound reception was four nautical miles, eight thousand yards, wide. You couldn't get much from that range. The trick of physics that bent sound from those narrow bands to where they could receive it also cut their sensitivity, thus their ability to get information from what they heard, in half. That was still more than nearly everyone else in the world could get, though, and J.T. was thankful for it. Alabama's sonars were almost the best in the world, and the computers that analyzed and the men who interpreted the signals that those sonars received <u>were</u> the best in the world.

That's why J.T. knew he could be troubled by what Srully Johnson was showing him. It wasn't a ghost or a false echo or somebody's too-vivid imagination on the display. Not only that, but there was little doubt about the line of the contact's movement. He didn't need a good range indicator, which was practically impossible to get under those conditions, to know that most of the possibilities suggested by the contacts they had were very close to Alabama's firing point. A place that they were going to have to be at all too soon.

"Okay," he said, "what's the rest of it?"

"By the time we get something in the first zone, everybody's lost their shade," Johnson said, "We're all moving slow here, so there's plenty of time. But they're also running electric, which cuts our efficiency. It balances out, except that we have more time this time, so we get more information."

The first zone for J.T.'s submarine was centered fifty-four nautical miles out, starting at fifty-two and ending at fifty-six. A submarine at three knots would take over an hour to cross it. *We're less than that—cut it by a third*. There were three contacts coming almost directly at them, spread in a line across their path.

"Are they in clear water yet?"

"No sir," Tullibee answered, "We'll have them five, maybe ten minutes more. Readings are intermittent." He didn't have to say why. Submerged diesel-electrics are very quiet submarines.

"We've designated them as Bravo One, Two, Three," Johnson said, adding the markers to each one.

"How long before direct-path?" J.T. asked. That was sixty thousand yards under ideal conditions.

Johnson considered it. "That depends, Skipper. Our effective range is down just 'cause they're so quiet now. We haven't lived long enough in this water, either." Every area of water was different to a sonar operator. There were different temperature variants, different sea life, different currents, even geologic activity in some places, all making noise or changing the way that noise acted when it was made. It took time for operators and computers to understand what was or was not normal in a given region.

For this part of the Atlantic Ocean, there had not been enough time. This was just their second patrol since Alabama and Georgia had completed two major modification-sets in addition to their regular UPDATES. Both boats were now optimized for their D-X missiles, the new Tridents that had been nicknamed Thorshammers by the designers. There had also been modifications to allow for under-ice operations, an operational-trials program required by the shorter range of the D-X. Besides some structural work and upgrades to navigation systems and the under-ice sonar, Alabama had gotten her hydroplanes moved from the conning tower to her bow. It was still a little strange to J.T. to see smooth sides where he expected 'planes like most other American submarines had.

"Nobody's moving very fast," Johnson said, "I'd estimate six to eight hours on this heading before we hear them directly."

J.T. didn't say anything for a few seconds. He was very conscious of the printout in his pocket, an eyes-only transmission from King's Bay courtesy of LIGHTCOMSAT II. The silence was louder than a shout to men accustomed to interpreting both sound and silence.

"I see," he said. His voice was normal. His thoughts were not. "Do you have anything else?"

"Well," Johnson said, matching his captain's tone of voice, "I do think you should look at this, sir." *Something is up*. He eliminated two of the wave patterns from the outer-zone trace on his display. "That's the best we've got on Bravo Two." *Thank God for dedicated processors*. It was actually pieces of a wave representing engine and propeller noise of the indicated submarine. Johnson grabbed the trace with a pip and moused it down on top of the inner-zone trace. "This is the best record we've got so far for the same boat." He cleared the other Bravo-traces away. "See this?"

J.T. leaned closer to the screen. "That is interesting." He checked to see that the intercom was green. "Ed?"

"I see it," the X-0 answered, "I'm not sure what to do with it, though."

The wave-form, in both the waterfall and graphic representations, was the same, even though the boat in question had been supposedly snorkeling while it was at long range. The telltale trace of a running diesel was nowhere to be seen. If the record was accurate—and there was no reason to believe otherwise—Bravo Two had been running on electric motors the entire time they were in contact with it.

"Anybody think it's a nuke?" There had been some rumors that Brazil was working on a nuclear attack submarine.

"No sir," Johnson answered.

"I go with that," Simmons said, "Even if they've got one, it's not going to look like that."

"All right," J.T. said, straightening up, "We'll keep going until we get to direct-path range. That will tell us more. There shouldn't be a problem staying out of their way while we get a better look." *We have to go that way anyway.* "Let's try to find out more about what we're dealing with."

Information is of extreme importance to the military. What you don't know can defeat you. The problem was getting it. Submarines had an especially tough time because they could usually only get their information one way, through sonar. Passive sonar, the kind that Alabama was limited to using, required a lot of processing power, intelligent operators, and enough time to make use of the computers and their heads. In general, the more time you had to listen, the more you knew. It was as simple as that. What Alabama had that any possible hunter didn't have was enough range and processing power so that she could listen longer and get more out of what she heard, attended to by men who were the best in the world at what they did. That was how her captain and crew could expect to know more than the other guy.

Sometimes. Maybe. It was not called the 'fog of war' for nothing.

"We've got a fire order, haven't we, sir?" Tullibee asked.

A submarine, even as big a one as the Ohio-class boats, was still not a very large area to let a cat out of a bag into. Furthermore, it was a logical assumption. Tullibee knew that they would already be turning away from any contact unless they had received the order to launch their missiles.

"They set off the demonstrator a few hours ago."

"Damn."

"It took them longer than that to get here," Johnson said, "They knew what's going on before we did."

"Looks that way," J.T. said, staring at the monitors. All the Bravo boats were in clear water now, outside the convergence zone. Across their path. How did they know? "Good job so far, gentlemen. Keep me informed."

"Sure thing, Skipper," Johnson said, "And how's the wife doing?"

J.T.'s smile was automatic. "She's very fine, Srully, as are the children. Why do you ask?"

"Just thought I'd break you away from the problem, you know? Sometimes it helps to get lost for a few seconds. You can maybe get some better perspective, come back at it with a fresh angle. Helps me sometimes that way." *And those Bravos out there are Problems, capital P, rhymes with T, stands for Serious Trouble. Mamas, don't let your babies grow up to be submariners.*

"I see." The smile dropped away as the present reasserted itself in J.T.'s mind. "I'll remember that. Thank you, Srully. Carry on." He left them to their headphones and multiple multifunction displays.

"What did I tell you?" Tullibee asked Wilson when the Captain was gone. He didn't take his eyes off the displays. "Now tell me how long he's been married."

"If it was easy you wouldn't ask me," Wilson said while he watched Johnson reformat screens. *They make it look so casual.* "Still and all, I haven't known three men my whole life who smiled like that after they'd been married more than two years, and my daddy wasn't one of them. Unless maybe he's got something on the side."

"Skipper? Uhn-uhn." Johnson added a head shake to the negation. "He don't preach, but what you got working here for us is a real live man-of-God, man. Besides, his wife is a stone fox."

"He's right," Tullibee said, "I've seen centerfolds didn't look as good. Modify the response?"

"Maybe. Children, he said, right?"

"Yes. That important?"

"That's a trick question." Wilson watched his waterfall display change and tried to match it to what he was hearing in his headphones. He had been through sonar school so he would be able to do that already, but two weeks on station had taught him how much there still was to pick up on. Fortunately, everyone had been patient with him so far. "Even stone foxes get tiresome, but they might stay together for the kids, right?"

"Man's too intelligent for that, even if he are an ossifer," Tullibee said, "And that still wouldn't explain what he's smiling about."

"Mighta just come up with a good way to dump the woman, for all I know."

"He does, I want to know about it."

"About the kids. How many and how old?"

"Picky son-of-a-bitch, isn't he?" Johnson said to Tullibee, "I got a— hold on." He put a hand up to his headphone. "You hear that?"

All three listened to noise and looked at displays for almost a full minute. There was nothing else.

"Natural transient," Tullibee said to break the silence, "Some whale passing gas or similar."

"I guess so," Johnson said. But he didn't completely relax.

"Real show doesn't start for a while yet, anyway."

"You really think they're coming after us?" Wilson asked.

"You think somebody in South America just suddenly decided to send their whole submarine force out into the South Atlantic on a short-notice exercise? I bet they're farther out than they've ever been in their lives and it's not for fun. But don't worry about your education benefits yet. They still haven't found us, and they've got to do that before they do anything else." Tullibee tapped the self-noise monitor. "Only boat that's quiet as us is Sea Wolf, or maybe a Mod El-Ay. And we still got a lot of water to hide in."

"Yeah, but we also got to be some place specific pretty soon," Johnson said, "The least they could have done was wait for the Block Three mods before they set off the nuke." Having those missiles would have meant that they could be on the way home by now, if the technoids were up to their advertising. Instead, they were still staring at empty displays, and Srully Johnson was watching bearing tracks change directions and converge in his mind. Why did they decide to come in this direction?

* * *

"We have the beacon, Capitao. It is faint, but it is there."

"Excellent. The others are in place?"

"Pulling slightly ahead now, sir."

That was according to plan.

"Very good, very good. Continue the watch."

"Aye, sir."

* * *

"Oh, damn," Simmons had said when J.T. handed him the fire order.

"Oh, damn," he said now as they watched the position display firm up on one of the Ops repeaters.

"They know more than we thought," J.T. said.

Bravo One, Two, and Three were now inside the practical edge of Alabama's direct-sonar range, proceeding slowly almost directly opposite their direction of travel. They had been in contact long enough to use movement- over-time plus Alabama's length combined with an eighteen-hundred-foot towed array sonar to triangulate their positions and headings with disturbing accuracy.

Those positions formed a triangle, the open end almost fifty miles wide and pointed toward the missile submarine. Their movement was taking that triangle like a giant mouth toward a place where it could swallow them whole.

"Sonar, Conn. Are there any, any other contacts, at <u>all</u>, around us?"

"Negative, Captain," Tullibee answered. He and Johnson were back in the hot seats after an enforced rest period, backed up by two other experienced sonar operators. It played havoc with watch schedules, but it put the best men where J.T. needed them. "Water is clear all the way around."

J.T. debated sounding General Quarters. They were practically in that condition now—the officer's slow-growing tension had spread to the crew—but he hadn't made it official yet. He decided it would be premature. But something was making him nervous, like his old kali teacher used to do with his sneak attacks. That old man could make anybody jumpy, and regularly did. What was bothering him now, other than the obvious thing?

"Helm, steer—" he made sure of their current heading, "three-four-five, and ease us up to five knots. We'll work in behind Three, then back around them."

Simmons studied the plot. "Maybe a little close, assuming everybody's got a tail." Without a towed array, a submarine was blind throughout a sixty degree arc to its rear. Towed arrays were also the best sonars that any given platform deployed, and the sensors that J.T. was planning to run them within range of.

"A chance either way," J.T. said, "Hull sets are good on them too, from what we know." The alternative was a very long end-around that would make them late for the firing point. The National Command Authority, i.e. the President, wanted a quick response to the Brazilian action. The best way to get it was for them to slip through a hole in the net that was in front of them. "I don't like it either, but we're under time constraints."

"Agreed." Simmons stopped talking and let J.T. think.

Not about submarines, though. For a moment, J.T. allowed himself to think about Diana—or more specifically why it seemed so unusual to so many that he still smiled like he did after eight years of marriage to a beautiful, intelligent, sexy, generally wonderful woman who was certainly more than he deserved to have.

Their first meeting had been unfortuitously normal. It had been at a church, in fact, in as low-key an environment as J.T. could find back then. He had been the executive officer on Alaska. She was just turning the comer on an earlier marriage that had been based more on rebellion than on love. Her first husband had in fact died in a shootout during a robbery attempt at a restaurant. J.T. had simply been looking for a small congregation like he remembered from his childhood, somewhere away from the city and the base. But he was honest enough with himself to admit that he had gone back to that particular place because of her. There had been a bit of irrational guilt about that for a while, until he understood that God apparently didn't mind about his less-than-spiritual reasons for attending that particular church. J.T. wasn't stupid enough to continue to be bothered by something that didn't bother God.

The courtship had proceeded in almost an old-world fashion. The underlying passion they had for each other had not exploded after they were married so much as it had started building, like a slow fire that changed continuously in intensity according to conditions. The only steady thing about this particular flame was that it had actually grown stronger and brighter over time as each partner consciously sought out new and different fuels to feed it with. J.T. thought that even now they had only begun to explore all the possibilities, erotic, romantic, and otherwise, that were open to imaginative and committed partners. The commitment to continued exploration had certainly made married life much more interesting than he had thought it could be.

"You're smiling," Simmons said.

"I'm taking Johnson's advice," J.T. said, "Getting my mind off the problem for a second. Review what we know about the Brazilian boats with me."

"Not as much as we want to," Simmons said. Like a loaded supertanker, American intelligence operations were hard-pressed to turn on anything resembling a dime. Even so relatively-long after the end of the Cold War and the Soviet Union, shifting significant assets away from Eastern Europe and the still-unsettled Commonwealth of Independent States in order to focus on South America's first declared nuclear power was not something that could be done quickly. Agents had to be retrained and oriented toward new environments and then given time to insinuate themselves properly into new operating areas. A bit over a year was not enough time to do that, even for a CIA that was the most efficient organization of its size in the world. Military intelligence organizations had been caught even more off-balance by the sudden revelations of a nuclear weapons program that an earlier democratic government had ended back in '91.

The regular intelligence organizations had at first tried to compensate for their oversights by "borrowing" agents from the Drug Enforcement Administration. This had been a mistake quickly realized, but difficult to correct. The only beneficiary of the stop-gap arrangement, if there was a beneficiary at all, was the DEA, which now could call on a large number of favors owed to it by various other agencies. This didn't make the DEA feel that good about it, however—field agents had been labelled as spies whether they were or not, and operatives had to be shifted, moved, and removed by the dozens. Several ongoing investigations were completely disrupted. Man-years of effort were traded for marginal amounts of information. The DEA agent/informer network, though it was the largest on the continent at the time, was not at all placed to provide the kind of military and strategic- political intelligence that had been needed. It showed in the results.

In other words, a good time had not been had by all.

"They had eight boats, replaced them with six," Simmons said, "Four two-oh-nine-fourteen-hundreds, two old Zvaardis-class."

"The old Dutch boats, yes. They still got their tails?"

"Jane's says yes. Nobody official seams sure. I go with Jane's. Hell, our people act mystified about how they got the boats to begin with."

"They took a left at the third arms dealer. Those tails could be a problem." The old Royal Netherlands Navy submarines, modelled on the old US Albacore hull design, carried British-made towed arrays with two-thirds the range of Alabama's unit on a smaller hull. And because they were diesel- electric, they were still very quiet submerged, old or not. "For that matter, the two-oh-nines are too." The German designs carried hull sonars with the same range as the towed arrays. Or was it too pessimistic to think that Germany would sell her best? *Depends on how bad they needed the money. Don't be cynical*. He considered the worst case, reasonable range on their sonars balanced somewhat by small, naturally quieter designs. We'll find them, but they'll be closer by the time we do that. The United States Navy had a dirty little secret of sorts: They didn't like submarines in shallow water, "shallow" in this case being between a thousand and fifteen hundred feet depending on the coastline. Diesel-electrics, with their superior ability to operate closer to shore, were the main reason why.

Once we decide who's who, the Zvaardis-is should be closely followed. OK, we know that five of the six are operational."

"Maybe not. What about the Argentines?" There were some agreements between Brazil and Argentina about missiles and maybe warheads, but the strength and scope of those were part of an ongoing political/military strategy debate that had been going on ever since Alabama had left port.

"Loaners? You and Bearkiller are the only ones who think they would do that. And if they're committed enough to do that, I hope the Brits are committed enough to sink them when they go around south." The

British had regularly operated attack submarines out of the Falklands since the war in 1982.

"Well, I would if I were them. But you never know." While it was improper to say that they were scared about the thought of nuclear warheads on Argentine missiles, it was not too inaccurate to call the British attitude one of concern. The Argentine government was still relatively stable and still nominally democratic, however, so the chances of Britain risking a "war shot" were admittedly slim. *On the other hand, there's that missile-site-thing that nobody admits ever happened.* "Okay, scratch the loaners. That means that we're dealing with some serious intentions, here." Normally, a navy that could keep even half of its units at sea was considered abnormally competent. Surging this many units, even if it were only a specific group in that navy, required something close to a war footing combined with a willingness to ignore any minor operating or maintenance problems in the platforms involved.

"The next question is, how operational are they? Unless they've kept them in continuous refit, somebody should be having some problems."

"I hear the thought. But we've got nothing to show for it so far." Simmons nodded at a repeater, which had a graphic from Sonar on it. "We may not have had long enough to hear it, true, but there's no sign of a problem with anybody so far. They could have kept them tied up until they knew they were committed. Why not? And we know they've done a lot of work on some of those boats. One of the two-oh-nines just finished a major refit, remember."

"Yeah. Somebody in Intelligence was expecting the world's smallest nuke conversion, as I recall." Such a program, if it were true, might have resulted in a nuclear submarine almost a thousand tons lighter than the French Rubis-class attack boats.

"It still could be, in a way. You familiar with the Canadian system? They sold a prototype to Brazil before the IMF breakdown."

"I didn't know that. I've heard of the system, of course." A Canadian corporation marketed a self-contained nuclear power system designed specifically for marine operations that was small enough to be dropped into a conventional submarine's hull. The result was a 'tribrid', a diesel/electric/nuclear submarine that could run from six to eight knots submerged without tapping battery power for its motors. That meant more endurance at speed when it was needed, which was rarely during normal submarine operations. Even nuclear submarines seldom went very fast because most reactor system required coolant pumps that made too much noise at anything above a fast crawl. Some boats could be identified by name just from those kinds of noise signatures. This was much more than simply an embarrassment to the maintenance crews. It was a death sentence in combat. Since the Canadian system employed natural circulation to cool the reactor, any submarine that had still moved about as quietly as a normal diesel- electric, but it gained the endurance capability of a fully nuclear-powered boat, and much more inexpensively. So far only the Canadians themselves had put the concept to the test, as far as anyone knew. Two tribrid submarines were patrolling under Arctic ice now. A third would be joining them soon.

Had Brazil already gotten into the club?

"You buying pizza for the spies or something? You seem to know quite a bit about this."

"I read a lot. I'm not as distracted by the wife as much as you are."

"Liar. You just read faster than me. She's not a distraction, anyway. Anything you voluntarily pay attention to is not a distraction. And what about the kids? Funny how nobody mentions them."

"That's because the average male focuses more on the above-average female than he does on children. They're also too proud to admit that they don't have a clue as to how you maintain as close a relationship with the girls running around as you do. But if they're a problem, let me know. Mary wants them to come live with us anyway."

"No thank you. We made 'em, we gon' keep 'em." J.T. kept his eyes on the repeater. "What do you think?"

"I think a working standoff weapon and looser rules of engagement would be useful right now." The Sea Lance program to develop a non-nuclear successor to SUBROC had been canceled years ago. A follow-on program was not doing a lot better. The Pentagon was still learning how not to spend good money on useless add-ons to developing systems. "I think Sea Wolf in a blocking position would be nice, too."

"Atlanta is on the way," J.T. said, "but it's another twenty-four hours at least before she gets here." They were supposed to have had an attack submarine with them this time, but Louisville had developed a coolant pump problem and turned back, and everybody else was a long way north tracking an unexpected and unexplained surge of Russian units. "We have to fire before then. NCA wants a fast response to this one." He took another sheet of paper out of his pocket and handed it to Simmons. It was another eyes-only message.

"J.T.: Late word - One Brazilian in port, apparent mechanical problem. Three at sea, one still unaccounted for. Best we can do. Also: Something is very wrong in several places. We've gotten short-time word of some leaks. Latest word is that they have some idea of where you are, enough to narrow a search area. We don't know how, maybe never will at this end. Something else too, something "different" out there. No details. Sorry. Best I can give you. Be very careful, repeat very careful. Good luck. Brad."

Bradley Jefferson was deputy commander of the group that included Alabama and Georgia.

"That's why we were supposed to have the attacker," Simmons said, "Whatever it is, it's enough to make them worried. Something 'different.' That all-electric trace qualifies for that."

"One unaccounted for," J.T. said, "We have the three, one is out, one is a mystery."

"Screening north, maybe, or backstopping at the firing point. Worst case is, if they know the area they also know the position."

"How could they know? No, that's irrelevant. What's the defensive load?"

"They gave us an extra MOSS. Both of them are up the tubes with two torpedoes, and eight reloads. Expendable countermeasures are plus twenty percent, and we have two Nixies, one streamed on standby and one in the hole. Fish are all Block Fours."

"That's a better than usual." The Navy had finally gotten all of their torpedoes through the ADCAP, the ADvanced CAPability upgrade program, just a couple of years ago. The newest attack boats were already getting

Block Sixes, incorporating further incremental improvements. "I'd rather have the escort."

"Agreed." Pause. "They must have known something before we left. They wouldn't have stuffed us this way otherwise."

"Something bothered them, but not enough to tell us." He had a flash of insight. "They wanted to make sure we could survive until the attacker killed it, whatever it is." *Were they, are they, planning for us to be attacked? How? By what? But that doesn't make sense.* They could see further and better than anyone else in the world who wasn't on the same side. How was anyone going to get close enough to launch on than? But it explained the overload of countermeasures and the additional Mobile Submarine Simulator in their tubes. The mobile, programmable decoys were expensive. Not every submarine had even one in its weapons load. *Forget the timing, maybe. Cut and run until Atlanta gets down.* "You have the conn. I'm going to inspect the torpedo room. I'll be back shortly."

"Aye sir, boss." Simmons watched J.T. leave. *The man is concerned.* Simmons was too. "The torpedo room? Oooooo, damn," he said to himself. He decided to run through a few fire control simulations as soon as possible. "Atlanta is still a day off. Oooooo, damn."

* * *

"Tullibee?"

"Intermittent readings, Captain. Evewybody's bewing vewy kwiet. They're firming up, though."

"Keep me posted."

"It's what they hired me to do, sir."

They were one hour and ten thousand yards into a plan to sneak through a leg of the triangle. J.T. had been asking Sonar the same question at two to five minute intervals all during that time. He was trying to be patient. He was not succeeding.

Depending on what Bravo was picked, Alabama was between eighteen and twenty-five nautical miles away. And they were entering the direct-path range of at least one towed array.

"Conn, Sonar, faint contact between one-eight-zero and three-four-zero."

"Behind us?" Simmons said, "Sonar, confirm that contact!"

"We can't, sir," Jeb Kinsey, the third man in that compartment with Johnson and

Tullibee, said, "It was there and not it's—damn! Transient! That's a transient! Conn, we got tubes flooding, about one-eight-zero or one-nine-zero relative."

On the bridge repeaters a bearing indicator went on and off.

"Gone now, Conn."

"No problem," J.T. said to no one in particular, "There'll be another one." He felt very certain about it. The old kali man had taught him too well. "It's official, gentlemen. Sound General Quarters, Battle Stations Torpedo." They didn't have very far to go for that—as tension spread outward from the bridge, men had begun to drift toward their stations during the last two hours. Everything was almost fully manned already. "Clocks and recorders on now." Telemetry, voice, and visual recordings, tied to a Zulu-time clock and an elapsed-time indicator, would now be fed to four separate storage points on the boat including a special disaster-marker buoy that incorporated its own decision-release software. The Navy had gotten very serious about keeping track of what was happening on its ships and submarines in the last few years.

"Helm, go to one-five-zero. Diving officer, take us down three hundred, level at six."

"Heading one-five-zero degrees, aye. Sir, I'm turning to one-five-zero."

"Down three hundred, level at six, aye. Planes, give me five degrees down, down three hundred, level at six," Atcheson said to the planesman.

"Aye sir, five degrees down, down three hundred level at six." The planesman pushed his half-wheel forward a half-inch.

"Conn-Sonar-transient-transient!" It was Johnson this time. "I got tube doors opening behind us. On the hull repeat on the hull." That meant that Alabama's bow- and hull-mounted sonar systems had picked up the new contact. "This is very weird."

"That puts him inside twelve," Simmons said. Any time a submarine with a towed array turned, the towed array became useless until it had straightened out again. The hull sonars had a much shorter range than the array, so if the contact was detectable "on the hull," it was a lot closer than anybody wanted it to be. "But that — damn!"

"Flood the tubes," J.T. ordered, "Open the doors and set number three up for bearing-only launch." The torpedo would have to search and attack on its own unless they got better information about what was sure to be coming now.

"Conn, we got increased screw noises," Kinsey reported, "two-nine-five relative."

"Somebody getting anxious," Simmons said.

"Captain, we're level at six hundred, steady on one-five-zero."

"Acknowledged." *Only one more thing to look for, then.*

PING.

Doesn't quite sound like it does in the movies.

"Damn it," the planesman meant to whisper.

PING.

"Damn it to hell!" He didn't manage to whisper that, either.

"Don't have a cow, my man," the diving officer said, "yet."

PING.

"That's the range confirmation," Simmons said.

"Took them long enough," J.T. said. He was surprised at how calm they sounded. "One of ours could have done it in two even on a bad day."

In Sonar, Tullibee's expression changed to one of shocked surprise. "Hell! It worked! Conn, Captain! I've got a range estimate on the aft contact! Sonofabitch!" He had listened for a re-echo of the active sonar pulse as it bounced off the broadcasting submarine's hull on the return. "Sixteen, not more than nineteen thousand!" Alabama had no active sonar except for a very short range unit for under-ice work, and ranging was difficult to do fast on passive sets. He had successfully borrowed the other's unit. "I got—"

J.T. had set an earphone to monitor some sonar, so he didn't need a report. He understood the burst of noise as well as they did. It was another transient, a specific one that indicated the use of high-pressure air to expel a certain roughly four-thousand-pound, twenty-odd foot long object away from the other submarine and toward them.

"Say it," he whispered.

"Conn, we got launch transients, launch transients." A pause. "And high-speed screws."

"You can have that cow now," Atcheson told the planesman. "Conn, fast screws confirmed, bearing one-eight-five relative."

"A torpedo is in the water."

PAST

"What is called 'foreknowledge' cannot be defined from spirits, nor from gods, nor by analogy with past events, nor from calculations. It must be obtained from men who know about the enemy situation."

Sun Tzu

The information trail for Michael Eggert started in a cafeteria in a different building with an overheard snippet of conversation that was itself brought about by another Post break. He didn't know at the time that it was significant —he had been concentrating on something else at the time--but something must have made the words bury themselves in his mind, waiting for Maria to trigger the memory. He wondered now if she had done it deliberately. Probably not. He couldn't see how what they had been doing at the time that had started those memories toward his consciousness could have possibly been deliberate.

She had been on top, moving long and high, her hands squeezing his forearms, tightening convulsively, harder with each thrust, squeezing the muscles on his arm like she squeezed the other muscle that she was so tightly wrapped around, sliding up and down along his full length every inch with every stroke mouth open head back body arched upward panting gasping sweating despite air conditioning so beautiful so marvelous so good...

"You getting off, Lieutenant?"

It took him a moment to focus on the open doors and the other person in the elevator. An office worker like he was, like they all were. Uniform or not, they were just office workers, clerks and bureaucrats all. They were just more organized and formal about it. The ones like her, like him, carried rank but no power. They were a faceless legion of cogs in a machine whose major components were supposed to be human beings, a group of typists and messengers who earned their rank and higher pay grade by being used by captains, commodores, and admirals. Lesser mortals were only bent over by mere lieutenants and commanders.

"Oh, yes," Michael said, still coming down from the memory. "Excuse me, sorry."

She had started calling out to him at the end, not so much out of her head, he thought now, as she wanted him to believe. She had called out as she gasped and shuddered and made her last convulsive movements just before he had to let go. It was a rephrasing of the end of a conversation they'd had before.

"Help me, Michael!"

She always called him Michael.

"Help me! Help me!"

It wasn't the way she had said it in the conversation before. It was more direct this time, more personal. Much more personal.

"Help me, Michael! Help me!"

In time with her final short movements and his own short, bursting rhythm.

"Help me!"

He couldn't, then. He didn't know how...where...what to look for...what to access. He didn't know what could be done then.

"Help me!"

He'd had no power then. He hadn't known then what he knew now.

"Help me!"

Like the other poor schmuck in the elevator. No power. Then.

"Help me!"

He had power now. She had driven him to that. Because of her he had learned how much power the clerks and secretaries and typists of the world could really have if they wanted to. She had shown him, given him, power.

"Help me!"

He could. He would. Now.

"A shit-eating grin if I ever saw one," the sergeant checking his badge and briefcase said, "Got a hot one lined up, Lieutenant?"

Michael smiled, because he was expected to and because the sergeant was right anyway. "If I don't come back, tell than I went down in line of duty."

"Oh, hell, Lieutenant, I'd be happy to pull you out before it came to that."

"Sounds a little too kinky for me, Sergeant, thanks for the consideration anyway. I think I can handle this one okay by myself. Goodnight."

"Goodnight, sir," the sergeant said aloud, and finished with a whisper, "Stupid geek. Fuckin' officers get the best ones. Hell, probably just the tags. Stupid bitches go for the gold. That's what I need, 'coupla bars. Hell, I could get some at the PX..."

You stupid jarhead son of a bitch. Fuck you! Fuck all your badge checks and searches! What the Marine had been looking for was not in the briefcase. It didn't need to be. That information, that power, was now in his mind. Until they could crack human consciousness open like they did portfolios and briefcases, he would keep that power. For himself. For Maria.

Four numbers locked in his mind. Four two-digit numbers, eight symbols whose generation had started long before the Brazilians had become a problem. At first it had seemed like a solution without a problem, simply Navy maneuvering to hang on to a few more ballistic missile submarines. Converting selected Poseidon and Trident boats into "non-nuclear precision strike tactical ballistic bombardment platforms" had seemed like an odd idea even to a lot of diehard Navy Men. It didn't quite fit anywhere in to the standard submarine-vs.-aircraft carrier-vs.-surface combatant debates. And why this particular response to this particular problem had been chosen was far from clear to Michael. Perhaps simply because it needed a problem to be a solution to.

Not that the why of it was especially important to him. It had been difficult enough to cross property lines and go over the fences into other pastures just to find a particular cow. The reason why the farmer had put it there was irrelevant to what Michael wanted. That overheard piece of conversation in the cafeteria had been a very bare beginning. Months of digging had produced a jigsaw puzzle that had only been completed—no, not completed. The other Post leak had simply directed and affirmed his search direction. He had been unsure of his track until then. Several strategies for dealing with the Brazilians had seemed equally plausible until that story had been printed.

But that was then, and this was now, and he had what he needed. And he would act with it and damn the foreign policy of the United States. Why shouldn't Brazil have nukes? The Israelis had them. Why shouldn't anybody—well, almost anybody have them that wanted them?

He was being extreme. He knew that. Just like he knew that Maria wasn't going to turn his information over to any activist environmental group like she implied that she would. It wouldn't be Greenpeace going after that Trident submarine. So be it. Michael didn't care who pinged the damn boat. He didn't care if the boat got pinged at all. He didn't care whether Brazil set off a nuke demonstrator successfully, either. Did he?

Then what did he care about?

The question held him at his coffee stop longer than was usual. (It was just as well. Rush hour seemed more insane than it normally was today.) He didn't have a good answer. He didn't care about America much—well, he did care about same parts of it, but certainly not about everything about the country. That was probably true of most people. On the other hand, most people weren't about to commit treason, either (he had to call it like he saw it). He for sure didn't care about the Navy, or the military in general, any more. Being All You Can Be while Reaching for the Sky with The Few and the Proud wasn't all it was cracked up to be, John Wayne and Tom Cruise notwithstanding. But he didn't care about the Brazilians, either, even if he was going to help them try to embarrass the United States.

So, again: What did he care about?

He cared about himself, of course. He cared about his immediate family to some degree as well. Actually, he was ambivalent-but-dutiful about his family. He cared about Mar—

It was not a shocking self-revelation, but it was a somewhat surprising one. He had thought himself past the point of caring after what Brenda had done to him. But Brenda was three years ago. He hardly thought about her, or that, any more. Still, even though Maria was almost a year "old," he hadn't until now thought that he really cared much about her. Time must heal even the very bad things, given enough of it.

Love? Maybe. What else would drive him to "espionage?" Michael smiled at the thought the he was some kind of spy. That made Maria a South American Mata Hari. She would love that one. Silly thought. Not a spy. No, not her. The worst she would be was nationalistic, or maybe regionalistic was a better word. She wanted the US completely out of South and Central America in anything approaching a military sense, and an end to any "untoward influences" in the region. Michael wasn't sure what that meant, and he couldn't think of an area in the world that had less American military power than the South, but he was willing to nod and smile when she talked about it. He got more than enough in return for the attention he gave her small rantings.

But don't call it love. Not yet. Call it something else, like yet another joke pulled on US foreign policy. Or can you pull a joke on something that was already a joke? Whatever it was, he was going to play it.

Such thoughts occupied him until he reached her apartment. It was not a long drive, for Washington. But it was, after all, Washington, and he had not quite managed to work past rush hour this time. Still, it seemed to even out in the end somehow. He was on schedule when he arrived.

"Who's there?" Maria asked in her playing-games voice as soon as he knocked.

"You know who it is," Michael said, hovering now between anticipation and guilt about what he was about to do, "You're expecting me. Open up—I've got something for you."

Maria opened the door, but only as far as a heavy chain allowed. "Oh yes," she said, "Michael." Her dark eyes travelled downward. "You do have something for me, I see. Give it to me." She put a hand out, reaching low.

"Yes, I—what are you—"

"Something small," she said, and unzipped him, "but very nice." Her hand started trying to do two things at once, stroking a very sudden erection while trying to get his shorts down. "I want to see it."

The available space for both maneuvers was getting smaller with every movement of her hand.

"Maria! Damn!" Michael looked around without turning, at the other door that let out onto this second-floor balcony and then around the courtyard and its surrounding buildings. How many could see this if they looked? "Stop! Cut it out!" Was anyone going by? He let her pull him against the door frame, turning a little to further block an outside view. Her hand was very active. "You can't do this! Let me in!" The sergeant would love this. He sweated from more than the heat.

"Not until you deliver," she said from where she was kneeling.

"I will! But not—I —please!" His "package" popped out of his pants seemingly of its own volition. Maria's hand still stroked and squeezed it, getting it harder and harder as she pulled it in through the gap in the door. "Maria, please!"

"You can come in now, Michael," she said, and giggled, and put her head down.

He wasn't small, but he wasn't oversize either. Her mouth met her hand about half an inch past the base of the tip.

Later, it would occur to him that he had not once used his hands to push her away or hold her off. He had not even thought about trying. For the moment, however, memory, logic, and a goodly portion of conscious thought was lost to him. He stood against the door frame, pinned as much by the boldness and novelty of the act as he was by the warm/wet pleasure of it. She was so very, very good at what she was doing.

So he stood and tried to turn himself so that what was happening was out of sight, and hoped that nobody was pulling a class job—a routine check by a student of one of the intelligence or police schools that the government ran in and around Washington, done as part of the training program— on him. Michael had never detected such a shadow, but that could simply mean that the person assigned was at the top of the class in surveillance technique. This would not be a good notation to find in somebody's notebook.

Ahhhh, but she is so goooooood, so goooooood, so goooooood...

She wouldn't let go, she wouldn't pause, she wouldn't stop. Tongue and teeth and lips, working on him, working at him, working around and up and down and over all over oh God oh God—the numbers! Where—

harder, harder, please fifteen, thirty, please, fifteen, oh, thirty, ah please ah—

He surrendered. It was either let go or misplace digits, and he had gone too far to allow the numbers to escape like that. He couldn't resist her anyway. That's why he had done this and everything else she wanted him to do, even things she didn't ask about. From obtaining classified information to letting her suck him off through the door, it was what Maria wanted from him, and it was what Maria got from him.

She finished him neatly (not good form to leave anything on the carpet), carefully tucked everything away and zipped him up, giggling throughout. He let her do it her way, amused because she was amused, happy because...well, because he'd just gotten a marvelous blow job, for one thing. But also because she was finally letting him in, pressing full-length against him and kissing him hard.

He was going to recover fast today. He knew he was.

"I've got something else to give you," he said when she let go, "something important."

"But not as much fun, I bet." She led him to the couch and put a drink in his hand. Then she sat and listened while he told her what the numbers were and what they meant. He had to concentrate to avoid further distraction from what Maria was wearing. It was a short robe. Period. Maria had a wonderful body—it was what had originally drawn his attention to her. That was odd, in a way. That is, lots of women have great bodies, but Michael never approached them in shopping malls because of it. It was very fortunate that he had made an exception in Maria's case.

She didn't say anything for a long time after he stopped talking. He took this as a sign that she understood the implications of what he had told her. She was normally more playful and talkative.

"This is very serious," she finally said, voice tone and facial expression totally at odds with the rest of her appearance. "Are you going to get into trouble if this comes out?"

"No." Her concern for him was touching. "I mean, I'd get into trouble, but the chance of it being traced to me is very small. I crossed some lines to get most of it, but I was very careful. There's too many separate pieces for them to be able to trace every path to me." He hoped he wasn't being stupid about that. "It's not anywhere near my job area, anyway. They wouldn't search there without a reason, and they won't find anything if they do." Any and all paper he had used, anywhere, that was connected to this had been already converted to powder. "It's all in my head. Can you do anything with it? Maybe pass it on to somebody who can use it?" The media would have a field day with this!

Maria considered it. "There are one or two people who I think might be able to do something with it," she said, "They might know who to pass it on to, or what to do with it somehow. I will contact them and see, tomorrow." She leaned toward him and smiled. The normal Maria was back. "You went to a lot of trouble for me. For a fanatic." Her robe fell open.

"Maybe I don't think you're a fanatic. Maybe I think you're right." He had trouble keeping his eyes up to look into hers. "Maybe I've become a fanatic too." He hadn't, but if saying it made her happy he would convert to Catholicism and swear on the Pope's ring that he was.

"You're being silly. But you deserve something for the risk you've taken for me. Hmmrnrmin? I know—how about I pin you down and fuck your brains out? Just my way of saying thanks. Now!" And she pushed him down onto the couch and did exactly that.

He knew by the time he left that he really was in love with her.

* * *

After he had gone she sat cross-legged on the couch, still naked, and thought about what he had said.

It was important. That meant it was valuable. Very important. Very valuable. But not for the reasons that anyone else thought, except perhaps Papai. He, at least, would be able to understand. This bit would be more than enough, added to the rest, to finance the breakaway. Thirteen years as a whore was long enough.

Granted, she was a very special kind of whore. Papai (not his real name, just as Maria was not hers) had very carefully and clearly pointed this out during her training. She had known from the first day after her sale that her destiny would not be played out on her back in a simple brothel. Flower—the English translation of her real name—was intelligent enough to know that. She was too intelligent and too beautiful to be allowed to remain in the Amazonian village she had been born in. This had been evident to her parents as well as to Papai, who made periodic trips to the out-country in search of girls for his businesses. When he found her he knew that she was just the thing for a special commission he had received from the moneyed ones. He told her parents that only the most special girls would be suitable for the task they had given him, and that Flower was certainly such a girl. And they believed him because Papai, whatever else he was, was an honorable man who always did well for his women and his girls. He considered it good business practice and the major source of his success. By keeping his women happy he could guarantee quality service to his clients, who would in turn provide him quality profits. It was something he believed, and it worked well for him.

Fifteen years old and still a virgin (somewhat remarkable given the circumstances—her beauty was already evident to everyone who saw her), she was sold to a man to be taken and trained and given to other men for their pleasure. Flower didn't blame her parents for that any more. They were poor, and Papai had offered an astounding price for her. She would not have survived for long at the farthest edges of civilization. It was better for all of them that he took her away.

She did not remain a virgin for long, but neither was her virginity sold or traded away for money. Instead a day after her sixteenth birthday, Papai took her himself, not only because she was desirable but because inexperience was going to be a drawback to the task she was being trained for. So he erased a certain problem at the same time that he started educating her in the ways of sex and of men. He was a wonderful teacher, able to draw upon years of experience with the hundreds of women he had handled in his life. Flower still thought him to be the best she'd ever had, more fully satisfying at one encounter than others she had known for a year or more.

He did not remain the only one, of course. Her special task was centered around men. She would be required to please them, to give them what they wanted, to do what any prostitute was required to do. Accordingly, at irregular intervals, she was presented with and to various men. Papai carefully orchestrated a range of personalities ranging from caring and gentle to callous and selfish for her to experience as lovers. None of these were too deviant or extreme in nature, however. Others in Flower's small and select group were being trained for such as those.

She didn't know about the others at first, but her training stretched over many months, over more than a year, and her world was very small and insular for that time. Eventually, during classes in English and training in tradecraft and working on blending into American life and culture, she met them all, learning just a little about each one and about the task they were all being prepared for.

Papai had found eight girls, all young and malleable and intelligent, who could easily learn second and third languages, who were intelligent enough to learn quickly and completely and who were attractive enough to gain access to the information sources that they would be learning from. Two of the eight were specially trained to satisfy less-than-usual needs: Bondage, domination, certain fetishes, the giving and receiving of pain. Three others, and the first two, were further trained to function in high-level society, to draw in and satisfy members of the upper classes of finance and politics both male and female. Not to blackmail them, but simply to make them happy. And trusting.

The last three, Flower among them, were aimed at different targets: Office workers, clerks, secretaries of all types. These people were the wheels upon which a government or corporation rolled. "These seeming low ones will have the small details that my clients desire to hear," Papai told than, "The great ones they serve think high thoughts, and let such servants handle smaller matters of execution and planning. It is a kind of arrogance that only a few special ones can avoid. We will exploit it, and know their plans even before they themselves do."

Papai even went so far as to select the most beautiful and intelligent of the eight solely for the seduction of these "servants." "They see the great ones with their wives and mistresses and they are jealous," he said, "Beautiful women pass them over, seeking instead those powerful ones with whom they want to link themselves with. You will make them feel blessed, you will make them happy that you have chosen them. They will feel the equal of their commanders and bosses when they are with you. To impress you, they will tell you important things. To keep you, they will tell you everything."

He was right. A very wise man, Papai. She would miss him, a little.

"Never write anything," he told them all, "Do not take documents, do not ask for papers, do not ask anything but the questions that show your concern for them. How was your day? Was the work hard? How are you? Be concerned not for information from them, but for them. And listen, and remember. Remember everything."

A smart man, intelligent far beyond his level of education, and a lover without equal. Even as old as he was, even now, Flower would match him against anyone she had known—against Michael, against Paul, against Tony, anyone—and he would win. She was sure of it.

They had trained for almost seven years to operate in America, and then they were dispatched, placed, and provided tor while they built a base of contacts. The operation actually began before the moneyed ones had formalized their secret agreements and moved fully into Amazonia. The moneyed ones had learned from the Columbia. They were prepared to take a longer view, now. For that, certain information was required. Certain special information.

They got it. Some members of her group were feeding information to than in less than a year, but for most of them it took two or three to find and fix the sources the moneyed ones needed. Flower didn't know directly what the others did—no contact between them was allowed. But she saw the ripples of their successes in the news and in the gossip her men provided. They had given advance warning of the IMF and World Bank actions, and had provided details of DEA and military plans concerning most of the northern regions of the continent. They had furnished names and places for contacts, useful for the military programs, specifically the no-longer-secret nuclear weapons development plan. They had assisted the Leadership in making economic adjustments to counter the cutoffs. And she was sure that they had a hand (and other parts as well) in the secret agreements with Argentina.

Now this. Specifics of the method the United States would use to disable the nuclear program if the demonstration device were actually detonated. This would tell the Leadership how they might be stopped, if the Leadership chose to take such action. This was important. Would it lead to war? She ran the things she knew through her mind, sorting, sifting, comparing, adding to and subtracting from. Flower was very intelligent, as any good spy had to be. There would probably not be any overt conflict, she decided. But there would probably be a fight of some kind, at some level. She was sure of that much.

But a fight between politicians or diplomats or even generals was not her concern now. Now she had to pass the numbers and their meaning through as soon as possible. Then she would collect a bonus (She would get one for this and it would be large. She had a feel for such things.), complete her preparations, and disappear. She knew how she would do this. She had been trained in the method of it, and she knew how the networks of the moneyed ones operated. They were extensive, yes, but on the whole not professional and certainly not omniscient. She had been preparing for this from the very first day of her arrival in the United States, preparing quietly, carefully, gradually. She was light-skinned enough to pass as Caucasian, and voice training allowed her to erase her accent at will. There were towns in the mid- and southwest that were large enough to hide in yet small enough so that she could be warned of anyone who came looking for her. Her new identity was the best that could be found, and it had been carefully built up and reinforced. Funds had been accumulated. It was time for her to go.

First, she would pass the information on. The regular channel was too slow for this bit, however. She would use the critical-message route, through Alderone. He was a level above her, in another department of the business lobby group that she was supposedly attached to. Their contacts had been intermittent, but there had been enough of than to avoid suspicion if she were to visit him in his office.

She would go early tomorrow and start the information on its way, and the bonus on its way back. She might even let Alderone fuck her while she was there. He would enjoy that. It might even be interesting. He was handsome and distinguished-looking, and he had always been courteous to her, though she knew that he lusted for her. It was not hard to see. Most of the men in the office were more overt in their desire for her, and less polite in their attempts to satisfy that desire. He deserved a reward for his courtesy and control. It might even be fun, and it could be her last act as a whore. It would mark the beginning of the end, the start of her transition to freedom. Then, when the bonus was hers, she would go. New identity, new location, new life—how many people got a chance to start over like that? She would be "normal" for the first time in her life. She would find a good man, and marry, and spend the rest of her life raising children and teaching him how to please her. She would hope for happiness, and settle for contentment and stability.

And she would kill anyone who tried to link her to what had been.

* * *

Alderone did nothing but sit for almost twenty minutes after Maria had left his office, caught up in the afterglow of an exquisite conquest.

She was magnificent. Off all the women that had been his, she was the best by so very far. *Where had she learned such things? And so—innocent—looking.* He would, must, find a way to see her again. *Yes.*

First, however, there was the disposition of the information she had given him. It was important. He had known this before she had spoken, by the way she had moved coming in and the way she had set herself before the special recorder to make the report. There was also, of course, the code-phrase she had used, the one requiring him to make the information transfer personally. Only one other time had such a phrase entered his ears, from someone else, another woman that he had never seen before. But the special words had commanded him, and he had gone. That had been some time ago, before the link between the government and the moneyed ones had become fully known in America. That other one had been beautiful too, like Maria was. But there was something in her eyes that made him glad that he never saw her again. Something abnormal. Twisted...

Back to the recording. Something so timely, so important, was valuable. The *others* would undoubtedly want to know about it. He would ask for a large advance, thus indicating the importance of the information. He would have to give it to them verbally, of course. The recorded report would erase itself unless played back on a specific machine. It would, in fact, erase itself period, once it was played back. But that would be another's concern. His was to get the wire spool to the contact in Rio, and to get word to The Others before he left. He wanted to report while the memory was fresh and the information current. Some extra pocket money would be welcome, also. His handler would have cash, or he would have nothing at all.

It was good to have such a life, and such income sources. He was paid as a lobbyist, a courier, and as a sort of double agent. He could finish his time here with enough to handle even Brazilian inflation rates, should he decide to return home. He would not. The Leadership was being stupid, challenging America like this, like the Argentines did Britain. Look what happened there. No, not home. No "major power respect" and no South American empire or coalition for Alderone, no. Rather, a quiet place somewhere else, away from agitation and confrontation. Perhaps one of his out-country holdings. Or he could immigrate, become a U.S. citizen.

He laughed at that one and summoned his secretary. The flight home could be delayed no longer than a few hours. He would have to contact The Others and arrange to make his report. No calls could go out from this office, either. He did not think for a moment that the place was bugged, but tensions were up, and his outside employers did not pay him to take stupid risks. The start would have to be made from outside.

He sighed. The best part of the day, wasted, not to mention the flight home and back. It would be worth it, though. He would reward himself when he returned—yes, he would. He would see that woman, that exquisite woman, again. She would be perfect. Reward enough and more.

Alderone was smiling as he left the office.

PRESENT

"When you are on death ground, *fight*."

Sun Tzu

For the briefest of instants, in just the time it took it took for everyone's attention to focus on him in expectation of orders to come, J.T.'s mind went somewhere else, to another time and place, and to a question.

There had been a limousine waiting for him outside the secure zone, a long time before Alabama had been shifted to the Atlantic side, eons before she had received her special Tridents. They had returned from a two-week run with some engineers who were checking things out for what would be the under-ice modifications, and there had been a limousine waiting for him. As was his habit, J.T. had been the last one off. He was still in transition, a mental adjustment from sea-thinking to shore-thinking, when the chauffeur had called his name. The man was dressed for the part, cap and white gloves and everything, and J.T. had been properly confused by him and the stretch limo he was standing beside. Because she had done similar, but not so elaborate, things before, J.T. assumed that Diana was behind it. There was also the matter of an anniversary that was two days away. They were in the habit of surprising each other with unusual things during those times. So J.T. was at the same time bemused and a bit embarrassed by it (some of the crew, seeing the limo, had stayed behind to see who it was for). But he let the man load his bags into a garage-sized trunk and open the door for him. He did find himself hoping that there wasn't an admiral watching somewhere as he got in.

The passenger compartment seemed to be as big as their living room. It was so dark because of the window tints that the lights were on. As he suspected, Diana was inside, lounging in the opposite comer wrapped in a full-length coat with an I've-got-a-secret look in her eye. J.T., waiting for her scheme to play itself out, held himself in the seat across from his wife and waited to see what else would happen.

Nothing happened until the limousine had been rolling, by his estimation, long enough to have nearly cleared the base perimeter. At that point Diana said, "We're paid up for two hours," and threw the coat open.

The—call it a negligee—she was mostly not wearing didn't look like it had enough material in it to make a decent bikini panty. Where it wasn't transparent or nearly so, it was baby-blue, all the way from the choker it was attached to at the top to where two strips of stretched-tight material ran over wonderfully firm breasts, molding itself around nipples that were already invitingly hard, and finally met in a very open V at Diana's—very far below her navel. The outfit, if you could call such a single, so-very-stretched-out piece of material could be called an outfit, was complemented (more accurately set off, activated, fired up, accentuated, and more fully eroticized) by thigh-high stockings with lace tops and high heels that were the same baby-blue shade as the top.

J.T. came instantly to full alert state.

"Command decision, Captain," Diana purred then, and stretched out a stockinged leg so that a high-heeled foot was in his lap. It was funny that he hadn't noticed the shoes. She didn't wear heels that often. That didn't bother J.T.—he wasn't sure how any woman managed it without crippling themselves. But oh, what an effect it could have when they did...

"Well, Captain?" his wife asked him after he'd had a few seconds to recover from the shock, "What-'cha-gon-na-do?"

* * *

J.T. had paid for more time in the limousine, among other things. The most important thing he had done at the time, though, was to answer Diana's question, by words and by actions that he felt sure had resulted in the birth of his second daughter about nine months after that particular anniversary celebration.

Now the millisecond memory was gone, but the question she had asked then was the same one that the people around him and the situation he was presented with was asking him.

And he would have to answer it not only correctly, but for as long as the situation lasted he had to answer it continuously, so that life would result for all of them as it had resulted for him and Diana on that wonderful day. It was, in fact, his job to answer that question, every day of his command and of his life, whether there was a torpedo coming at him or not.

"Helm, come around to two-seven-zero. Give me revolutions for ten knots." His words came out more quietly and firmly than he thought they would.

The helmsman threw the aircraft-style yoke over and held it. "Steer to two-seven-zero and ten knots aye, sir, my wheel is hard over, we are making revolutions for ten knots." He lowered his voice. "We're getting behind it, right?" The question was directed at the diving officer, who was tightening the restraint on his seat.

"Sonar, I need your best estimate," J.T. said, "Is the fish at high or low speed?" Every modem torpedo had two speed settings they could be set to run at depending on the target's range and speed and on whether you wanted the torpedo to make much noise or not. Some could have their speed as well as their course varied by the launching submarine, as long as the control wires stayed connected. What J.T. could do about this one depended in part on what the torpedo was capable of doing.

"That's right," Atcheson was answering, "Fastest way out of the seeker cone before it goes active." He was careful to speak more calmly than he was feeling. It was his job to do that. "We'll slow down in a little while to see if we can help them break the trace, so they don't turn the sucker around behind us. All they can do is go to where we were." He hoped. "Naturally, we won't be there then."

"It's running slow, Skipper," Johnson answered, "They started it high and then cranked it down. They've lost us for now, I'd say."

"For now."

"Sir, we are at two-seven-zero and ten knots."

"Acknowledged. Maintain course and speed. Sonar—any idea if it's a Tigerfish or not?" It was another piece of the puzzle about what he could and couldn't do.

"Unless the Germans sold them some of theirs with those new boats, it has to be," Simmons said, "They've got a large number of ours from back before the arms-sale restrictions."

"My money's on it being a Four-Eight, Captain," Tullibee answered.

J.T. made rough calculations. A slow Mark Forty-Eight ran at forty knots...*for thirteen, maybe fourteen minutes from launch...Alabama was running ten knots, which puts us...three, more likely four thousand yards behind it when it starts pinging.* There was very little chance of a hit.

But there would be others. There had to be.

"Jim," J.T. said to his weapons officer, "make sure that countermeasures are optimized for those parameters. Do we have anything on the German, uh-"

"Seeals."

"Thank you. Have we got what we need on them?"

"I think we have enough." There had been a scramble to refit the threat profile libraries when the two missile submarines had been assigned their new mission. South American weapon-system performance had proven to be harder to find out about than anyone had thought. The fact that they could be running several different systems—American, British and German were the top candidates but had the money to buy from anybody anywhere—had only complicated things. "I'll set it up on a separate channel."

Jim Bearkiller turned to his brand new Integrated Weapons Control System panel and set to work. There was hesitation only when he considered between various options—he had been living on system simulators when he wasn't participating in the installation and testing of the actual system on both boats. The pauses were nonetheless important. Choices had to be made.

Alabama's sonar jammers were of course capable of broadband output, but broadband jamming was good for only two-thirds of the range of a jamming or deception solution that was tailored to the seeker of a specific weapon. The expendable countermeasures presented a different question. The decoy and jammer canisters could be set for either broadband or specific-system output, and they could be reprogrammed as necessary. But the pea-brain processors that ran the expendables didn't allow for fast switchover between settings, and there were only so many ejectors to launch them from. Ten or fifteen seconds to reset might well be too long for a torpedo that was close enough to require countermeasures.

He set the majority of the expendables up to fit the parameters of an American-designed Mark Forty Eight, while keeping a small reserve tuned for the German-made Seeals. For desperation, a handful could be kept on the general purpose setting. He also made sure that resets were "on the board" where he could transmit a setting change with the flick of a switch. Fortunately, the new rotary-launcher system didn't need to be told what kind of canister to launch in what order, a major advantage over the old manually-fed countermeasure launchers.

"Captain, expendables and jammers are set, and we are prepared for remote broadcasting through the Nixie. They're ready when we need them."

"I hope we don't," J.T. said, "Sonar, what's status on the fish?"

"Still running slow, still running straight, Skipper, heading for where we used to be. Hasn't gone active, hasn't turned."

"Other Bravos?"

"They're still coming toward us, but slower. There was a scramble when the fish was fired, but everybody's stopped running now."

"Saving their batteries for later. They want us to thrash around same more so they can know where to shoot," Simmons said, "Gentlemen, it is now officially serious."

"Indeed," J.T. said, "Okay, Sonar. Tell me how a torpedo can come out of empty water. And while we're at it, can you tell me what the empty water is doing now?"

There was a moment of silence. Then Tullibee said slowly, "Captain, that empty water went back to being empty after it let go the torpedo. We've got a localization that's getting worse as time passes, and we're working on a theory as to how it happened. Without an active set, unless you want to see if a fish will find it for us, it's the best we can do until something else happens." Pause. "It does little good to say, sir, but we're sorry."

J.T. smiled. "I know you're working on it. If we can get clear you can send somebody over to tell me what you know later. Can you maintain any kind of trace on it now that you have some idea of what's happening?"

There was a long pause, probably a fast conference. "The way we figure it, Skipper," Johnson answered, "it depends on whether the idea is right about what it is and on the range. We've only got a good guess now, and when we lose it reacquisition will be a bitch if it's possible at all."

"They've fired," Simmons said, "They've made their intentions clear, and we have standing authorization to defend ourselves. Let's pop them now while we can guide one in."

"But if we do that, we'll announce ourselves to his friends out there," Bearkiller said, "and we'll get more coming back. We could end up in a dogfight." It was not an argument, it was a comment. J.T. encouraged such exchanges. "We'd be the biggest dog on the block, but that's not much when the rest of them are pit bulls."

J.T. looked at the repeater, which was showing position/bearing graphics from Sonar.
"Sonar, does it look like anybody knows where we are now?"

"Negative, Skipper. All Bravos seem to be returning to the previous pattern."

"Okay," J.T. said, "We seem to have slipped them for the moment, so we'll try to get completely away first. That's what we're built to do best. At least we'll buy some time for Atlanta." It was entirely feasible that Alabama could evade long enough for the attack submarine to arrive and bail them out. Submarine warfare could be a very slow process even under the best conditions. "Helm go to two-five-zero. Diving officer, ease us down to one thousand feet."

"Two-five-zero degrees aye," the helmsman said, "Coming around to two-five-zero, sir." That heading pointed them at the largest gap in the ragged pattern that the Bravo submarines had settled back into.

"One thousand feet, aye," Atcheson said, "Planes, give me five degrees down-angle, watch your trim. Level at one thousand."

"Five degrees down-angle level at one thousand." The planesman pushed the yoke forward, switching his attention between the depth indicator and the trim monitors.

"You have the conn, Ed," J.T. said, and started out, "I'm going to see what Sonar has to say about that empty water. Try not to let it heat up again, will you? I hate anything that's overcooked."

* * *

Delamadrid watched the target's trace disappear from his screens. Only the torpedo still showed, running mindlessly to where he knew the American would no longer be.

One wasted. No matter. There are more than enough to spare.

"I'm sorry, Capitao," the senior sonar operator said, "we've lost him again. The best I can say now is that he is in front of us, somewhere."

"It is of little consequence," Delamadrid said, "We will find him in the end. It's just a matter of time." He put a hand on the lieutenant's shoulder. "Don't worry. You are doing your best. These Americans are very good, as they should be. They are worthy opponents. Continue the watch, and keep me informed."

"Aye, sir."

He returned to the attack center and his first officer. "We've lost them, of course. Return to the search pattern," he ordered the helmsman, "The rabbit has awakened to the hounds," he said to Corte', "Their captain shows intelligence. He did not react to the provocation as I thought he might." It would be a better hunt than he had expected.

"That's not good. They know of our intentions now," Corte' said. He looked worried, but it was normal for him to look worried.

"I don't think we've surprised them there. They probably guessed what we had in mind as soon as they detected us coming." He shrugged. "All we have erased in their minds are doubts about the seriousness of our intentions."

"They'll call for help now," Corte' said, "One of their attack submarines, perhaps even their Seawolf." He suppressed a shudder. Seawolf was big, fast, and quiet. A match, more than a match probably, for everything they had. "How will we deal with that?"

"The way we deal with everything else," Delamadrid answered, "the best way we can. But I am not certain that help will come as you say. They are not anxious to have their presence here revealed. Others would be kept well away, lest attention be drawn here."

"They must know of us by now!"

"What—you believe the myth of their omniscience, their global satellites with their cameras that photograph license plates from above? Not here. They have too long been superior in their attitudes toward us. When we finally demand our rightful place in the world, when we finally begin to take the position we deserve, they are surprised. Their 'assets' here are too pitiful to adequately monitor us. They were too focused on their effort to drive the moneyed ones out of Columbia and Peru and Bolivia. Lucky for us they have mostly succeeded, is it not? They have not truly seen us until it is not too late. And they are overconfident, these

Americans we so quietly struggle with." Delamadrid did not refer to the men in the submarine his flotilla hunted. He meant their leaders, the commanders and politicians who had sent them here to be destroyed. "Why should they guard something that will never, has never, been found? We waste our time hunting a shadow, Corte'. That is what they believe. Even if we find them, we won't hold them, they think. They will slip away from us. They are of course wrong. They don't know about Sombra. They don't know about our other special systems. We are about to show them how solid their shadows have become. We are going to take away their invisibility. And we will do it by showing them something that is even more invisible."

"We already have, Captain," Corte' said. He was referring to the boat that had fired the first shot, the one that was named Shadow. "They did not seem overly awed by it."

"I do not expect them to be, Corte'. Surprised, yes, but not awed. They will adapt to this soon enough. But there are the other things we have, things they are not aware of yet. They won't adapt to them as quickly or easily, I assure you. We have led the way, Corte'. We will show other countries how to make the nuclear navies afraid. They will turn to us for tools and leadership to do the same thing, and we will forge alliances that will set the so-called major powers back on their heels."

"Well and good, Captain," Corte' said, "but first we must find the American again."

Delamadrid laughed and clapped Corte' on the shoulder. "Ever the practical one, you are. It's good that I have you to pull me down from the clouds. You are right, of course. But we will find them, don't worry."

"I still wish we could have brought surface units in," Corte' grumbled quietly. But he knew why they had not. Besides the risk that someone above would fire on the wrong submarine, which was a very real one, there was the need to keep this action out of the eyes of spectators official and not. With just submarines involved there would be nothing seen or stumbled upon by someone else. The American would simply disappear. It would not return to base. There would be a search, and it would be declared lost at sea. Everything would be handled quietly.

For the time being.

But first, they had to find the American again.

"Captain!" It was the sonar technician.

"So. Here we go again," Corte' muttered. Even this far in to it, he was still not sure whether he supported what his country was doing. But he would continue to follow his orders.

His duty allowed him no other alternative.

Delamadrid picked up a microphone. "What do you have for me?"

"The American, sir! I think we have him! But the traces are bare, very bare." There was a long pause. "I can give you a rough bearing, but little else."

"Excellent!" The engineers had done better than he'd hoped, refurbishing the used British-made towed-array on his very used and very modified formerly-Dutch submarine. "Can you tell me whether he goes away or comes toward us?"

"A moment, Captain." It was a long one. "He goes away, I think. Angling away from Sombra, now." The laser beacon on the masked submarine told them exactly where the "Shadow" was falling. "Bearing is somewhere around two-six-zero or two-five-zero. That's the nearest I can narrow it to, and that is uncertain."

"But that's still very good, Lieutenant," Delamadrid said, "a very good job indeed. Carry on." He put down the microphone. "They are trying to sneak away from our little encirclement. Sombra's attack must have pulled the others out of position as it did us." The other two submarines were out of direct-path range and convergence zones both, and only Sombra and Triunfante had lasers with which to mark their positions. Almirante and Cacador could track them without sonar, if they were close enough, by using the laser recievers, but they couldn't be tracked except by conventional means. If the lieutenant was correct, a turn to two-fifty degrees would put Triunfante almost directly behind the American. It would also break the formation, dissolving the noose that they were trying to put around the missile submarine's neck.

"Helm, starboard to two-five-zero. Increase speed to fifteen knots. Corte', please assist the diving officer. Make your depth four hundred meters." The diving officer was the least-experienced man he had on board. A pity.

"That is below our operating depth."

If the men in the attack center had been cats, their ears would have straightened and swiveled toward their commanders.

"But still well above crush depth," Delamadrid said matter-of-factly. The safety factor built into Triunfante's hull allowed them to go, if necessary, over a hundred and fifty meters below the recommended maximum of three hundred. Delamadrid felt it to be necessary. "We were below that in test dives."

"Yes, Captain, but—"

"The depth will suppress cavitation noise. It will cut their detection range. We need every edge we can develop if we are to effectively hunt them."

"The course change will break the pattern," Corte' said then, "It means changing the plan." It was Corte's way of coming around to agreement.

Delamadrid's scheme was simple enough. It relied heavily on the new developments and cutting-edge technologies that had been installed in two of Brazil's submarines so far.

Sombra, with its special masking system, tribrid drive, the prototype detection and tracking system, and a reduced crew, had been sent out first, to search the area around the firing position and find the American. It had then released a communications buoy and settled in to follow the missile submarine for as long as it was able, using a laser as a beacon so that the others could find it. The rest of the flotilla had scrambled once the message was received, running to the last reported position and then using their sensitive laser detectors to home in on Sombra. The sweep formation had then been established and the American had been almost, but not quite, cornered. The plan, as most such plans do, had worked only to a point.

But Sombra had fired too early, probably in an effort to run the target toward the cordon. They were probably anxious to end their very long stalk. The crew of that submarine had been cut to increase their time on station. There had been no illusions about finding the American fast. The men on board had also been required to maintain a higher than normal level of noise discipline despite the new masking system. There was no telling what their current state of mind was. Only the Americans and perhaps the British routinely kept submarines out as long as this. If Delamadrid's force could not end the hunt very soon, in fact, they would all be breaking records for patrol duration.

So—the American knew what was happening now, knew that they were not out simply to embarrass the United States with a few pings from an active sonar. They had not chosen to engage in combat, however, and this was in line with Delamadrid's estimation of how they would be thinking. Their strength was stealth and endurance—no, had been stealth and endurance up till now. But they didn't know that yet, so they would try to use those perceived strengths, knowing (quite correctly) that they were not an attack submarine.

They were running for the gap that their computers told than would be there. That was another strength of theirs, the most difficult one to neutralize. There were a number of sonar units in the world that had the raw sensitivity of the American sets—Delamadrid had a couple of than in his flotilla. But raw sensitivity was nothing without the ability to filter out the ambient noises and irrelevant background sounds. The Americans could do that better than anyone else.

Still, there were ways to counter even that. The prototype system on Sombra was one. The laser-based non-acoustic detection systems there and on Triunfante was another. Both systems had their limitations, but they also offered the hope of a way to break the superiority of Western naval technology. The major problem was affording it. The German laser systems were very expensive for what they could do—the Northern navies still considered them developmental systems, only a step removed from the experimental stage for now. Only the riches of the moneyed ones had enabled Brazil to acquire just the two they had. But there might be hope there too. The Japanese had gotten certain parts of the German design, and they had a talent for inexpensive copying and improvements. A way was coming. Delamadrid could feel it. In fact, he was riding the cutting edge of it right now.

"I think we must take the chance, Corte'. We must take away their stealth, which is their best weapon. It is important to bring them to battle while our conventional units are still able to help." The batteries on Almirante and Cacador would last less than an hour if high-speed maneuvering was required, and Sombra's minireactor allowed only six knots of speed—her batteries were fully charged, but that was worth an hour of speed at best. Only Triunfante was capable of a sustained high-speed chase. Its high-output fuel cells would easily carry them long enough to run the American down if they had to. It would be better, though, to use a pack of dogs to run down this particular fox.

"We knew that the plan would not survive long after first contact," he said, "Typical of military plans, is it not? Take us down, Corte'. Make fifteen—no, wait a moment." He picked up the microphone. "Sonar. How badly would twenty knots degrade our capability?" They had the proper aspect on the American to use the laser, but he didn't think they were in range yet. For the moment, it was an expensive deadweight that had lost them a torpedo tube.

"We would lose range, Captain. A third, at worst, I would say. We are quieter than most." Triunfante was all-electric now, and insulation had been added during the rebuild. That would compensate somewhat for the sound of water running past their hydrophones at speed. "There is also, of course, the loss of sensitivity to consider." This would be true at anything beyond a creep, however.

"We will take that risk also," Delamadrid said after a moment's thought, "Corte', make our speed twenty knots. Let's see if we can end this quickly."

"Yes, Captain," Corte' answered, quietly, and went to assist the diving officer. He felt more sad than worried. This was not going to end quickly, he knew. Even if they succeeded.

* * *

"This," Johnson said, putting a blinking X on the chart table, "is our hole-in-the-water. Maybe, we think."

The three of them stood over a self-illuminating liquid-crystal display that was still called a chart, which was mounted on a solid base containing a computer, some fiber optics, and an independent power supply. It was still called a chart table.

"Think?" Simmons asked.

Currently centered on the display was a tiny top view of Alabama. Numbers beside it indicated course, speed, and position according to the inertial navigators. Around that marker were four others. They were either solid, or solid with a circle around them (which indicated a very good contact). Three of them had numbers also, but fewer than Alabama had. One of those was about ten degrees portside of their stern. The fourth marker was the blinking X.

"We lost it pretty quickly as we moved away. We're not too happy about it either, sir."

J.T. had started his last tour as executive officer just as the Navy decided to install the electronic chart tables on its submarines and surface combatants. The test that had convinced them most was been code-named Eggshell. Two decommissioned attack boats had their reactor cores removed and a number of experimental systems fitted on them. Hundreds of sensors had been installed on each boat, to monitor what would happen—there were even sophisticated dummies on board one, mimicking human crewmen—and then the boats had been towed to deep water and hit with live torpedoes. One had been hit with Mark Fifties, the air-droppable Barracudas, and the other had taken a live Forty-Eight almost dead on the attack center.

"If the theory's right, then we're all going to have problems for a while," J.T. said,

"Explain it, Srully."

When the robot cameras went down to examine the punctured hulls, the liquid-crystal chart table on one had still been in operation, ticking away on its internal power supply. The one that had taken the Forty-Eight didn't have a chart table left to examine. It disappeared with the rest of the attack center when the heavyweight torpedo detonated. The film of that event was said to be spectacular.

"Our guess. Commander, is that they've developed a workable application of basic physics," Johnson said, "If you know the amplitude and frequency of a sound wave, you can generate a wave with the same frequency but opposite amplitude that will cancel the first one out. You just got to fix it so the trough of one wave meets the crest of the other and vice versa. That's what's supposed to happen with some white-noise generators, but even the best of than still give you a loud hiss. But total silence was always possible." Johnson looked down at the blinking X. "As of now, I'd say it's been made practical too."

Somewhere around the UPDATE after next, Alabama would be getting a holographic display that would project a three-dimensional image that would show relative depth and that you could walk around. It was already undergoing operational testing on one Improved Los Angeles boat and on Seawolf.

J.T. wasn't sure how completely he would trust that one, either.

"SILENT SENTRY," Simmons said.

"What?" J.T. and Johnson asked.

There was also a mechanical-feed wide-paper printer in the table which would print a paper chart on demand, which could then be marked on in the old-fashioned way. It made J.T. comfortable to think that maybe the Navy didn't quite completely trust the electronics, either.

"I can't remember where I heard it," Simmons said, "It was a program like this, late sixties or mid-seventies. They couldn't make it work at the time so they dropped it."

"Probably didn't have enough processing capability," Johnson said, "You have to process an extremely complex noise environment and vary your counter harmonics on the fly to cancel it out. You're talking mini-mainframe at the least, more probably parallel processors."

"So they solved that problem," J.T. said, "and presented us with it, in a manner of speaking. How do we solve it?"

"There's a bare possibility," Johnson said, "depending on how much flexibility the programmers gave us in the sonar control set. The system knows how to strip the background stuff out of whatever it hears. But with this masker they're running, if it works like this, there's nothing left to hear. The computer has been told to look for anything left over after it strips the background, but we're going to have to tell it now to look for <u>nothing</u> after it strips the background."

"They knew what we want," Simmons said, "and they gave it to us."

"Right," Johnson said, "<u>Nothing</u> is supposed to be safe. Now we've got to tell the system that what's been safe isn't. I don't know if the software filters will do that. If I ever find the son-of-a-bitch that came up with this, I don't know whether to shake his hand or kill him."

"You shake his hand," J.T. said, "I'll kill him. Do we have any kind of handle on it?"

"The best we can do quickly is to tag this for the processor so that it'll bring the same conditions to our attention. But they have to be pretty similar to notice. And he'll have to be close, Skipper, real close, before we have a chance of finding him."

"Maybe closer than he wants to get."

"Yessir. There's something else you want to know about, too."

"Bravo Two?" That was the one most nearly astern of them.

"He's been making about twenty knots for over forty-five minutes now, by our calculations. The other two are just loitering. Two should be dead in the water or very near to it by now, sir."

"Ed? Could it be that tribrid you were talking about?"

"Tribrid?" Johnson asked.

"It could be. They could keep the batteries topped off with it. On the other hand, those Zvaardis boats have got pretty long legs on batteries. Even a two-oh-nine's good for an hour if it's fresh."

"Tribrid?"

"We'll explain later, Srully. Giving them the benefit of a fresh start, if it's a two-oh-nine, it'll die in about fifteen minutes. If it's a Zvaardis, it has thirty minutes plus to run us down." J.T. looked at the chart table. "But it won't have to do that, because it's thinking to herd us. The anvil is here, gentlemen." He indicated the Bravo that was closest to their current heading. "The hammer is coming at us at twenty knots. We're in range for a long shot now, but he doesn't want that." A Mark Forty-Eight could go forty thousand yards at forty knots.

"From behind, it would probably run out of fuel first," Simmons said, "or it would lose us. He wants it up-close-and-personal, and he thinks he can get it."

"One way or the other," J.T. said, "Very well, Srully. Keep working on it. Very good job so far. Just see if you can keep us alive a while longer. Tube load, Ed?"

"Two Four-Eights, two MOSSes." And the Forty-Eights were all ADCAPs, ADvanced CAPability torpedoes. They were faster, smarter, and more destructive than the older models the Brazilians were using. "Countermeasures are prepped, Nixie is in trail and warm. Tubes have been flooded for over an hour."

"We'll hold them a while longer. The loads are supposed to be waterproof." J.T. picked up a microphone. "All hands, this is the Captain. In twenty minutes we will go superquiet. Repeat, rig for superquiet in twenty minutes. That is all. Chief," he said to Atcheson, "repeat the warning in ten minutes."

"Superquiet in twenty minutes, repeat warning at ten minutes, aye sir." "Ed, you and the Chief check the prep. Leave him in Engineering. I want just a half-knot or so, Chief, just enough to keep the tail stretched. But I may need anything up to max power any moment. Keep them ready for me."

"No problem, sir. I'll make sure the hamsters are watered and keep some extra men on the bicycles."

"A little weird sometimes, but he works," Simmons said after the Chief was gone.

"For which small favor I would consider signing on a witch doctor. I don't expect any problems, Ed, but take an especially hard look at things when you go through. When we go quiet, I want us to go vewy, vewy kwiet indeed." J.T. nodded at the chart table. "It's time to show the Elmers here that it's not wabbit season anymore."

* * *

"He's gone, Captain," Corte' said.

Delamadrid's head jerked around, toward the Sonar compartment. This was not at all what he'd been expecting.

"Slow to five knots." Had he been too aggressive? "Sonar, what is your last reading?"

"A probable, sir, a little over a minute ago. I thought I had just reacquired him after a loss of signal."

"Was it the speed?" Delamadrid suppressed panic.

"I don't believe so, Captain," the operator said, "I think it was something else. Something is different now, but I don't know what."

Where was he? Had he doubled back while their sensitivity was reduced? Angled off somewhere? Or was he sitting, quiet and patient, listening to them run past?

"Can you detect the others?"

"I can pinpoint Sombra by the laser, of course. She is closest to where I think the American is, or was. Almirante is out of range, but somewhere in front of us. Cacador is running almost parallel to us at three-four-five relative, around medium direct range."

"What is your last indication of the target?"

"We were closing, sir, and near to the correct bearing. I cannot, of course, give a range." Unless the bearing changed over time, allowing for triangulation, range could not be calculated using passive sonar.

"The others might have heard the American move or stop. Raise them on the underwater telephone!"

"It will reveal our position!" Corte' said.

"He already knows it! Their equipment is the best in the world, and we have been running at speed for them!" *I've made a mistake. I was too anxious.* "Contact the others!" *It may still be correctable. It has to be.*

* * *

"They're talking," Tullibee said, "Gertrudes all around."

"I dare say we have no idea what's being said?"

J.T. was sitting in the Trainee/Kibitzer position behind the two main sonar operators. Anyone who didn't absolutely have to move was either sitting or lying down. Anyone who absolutely had to move was doing so very carefully and very quietly. Alabama was acting like clear water, but without the help of a masking system like at least one of her hunters had. That's why J.T. was wearing the headset.

"Even if it was clear, Skipper, it would be in Portuguese," Johnson said, "All I can tell you is that everybody's talking, except for our shadow. Positions are marked." The underwater communication system the

Brazilians were using marked them like beacons. "We got solutions on almost everybody except for the hole-in-the-water."

The headset was another new concept. The earphones and wraparound voice-activated microphone weren't new, of course, but the voice-commanded, semi-intelligent switching network it was tied to was. The system worked like a cellular telephone, with small transmitter/receivers in each compartment that automatically followed the wearer as he moved through the boat. The computer would switch the speaker to any person or area named with almost no perceptible delay, and it recognized priority of access according to preset hierarchies or by spoken command. J.T., for example, could break in on anybody he wanted to, but not everyone could break in on J.T. The headset could also be set so that it would feed different kinds of information into each ear, though most users found that a distraction. J.T.'s headset was currently tied to the sonar system with an automatic voice-communications override on a stepped-priority basis.

"Jim," J.T. said, just barely pausing for the computer to recognize the designation and switch channels, "set tubes two and four, one each to nearest contacts."

Tullibee and Johnson only had an override in one ear. They couldn't talk to as many people as the command crew could, either. As a backup to the voice-command system and for those who didn't like talking with machines, there was a hand controller that clipped to the belt or pocket. J.T. had never felt insecure enough to use his.

The Navy could take silence very seriously when it wanted to.

"After you've done that, program MOSS one to drop behind and follow us. Understood?"

"Acknowledged."

Since their introduction, the Mobile Submarine Simulators had been vastly improved.

The simple torpedo-with-a-noisemaker had been replaced by a purpose-built, programmable, semi-intelligent decoy that could perform complex maneuvers, change the signature it was broadcasting to imitate a maneuvering submarine, and use its sonar system to make the parent submarine a base point around which it would maneuver. It could also function as an RPV with much finer maneuverability than a torpedo, for as long as control wires could stay connected. That would be impossible in this case, so the wires would be cut as soon as the MOSS was fired, allowing immediate reloading of the torpedo tube.

"They've stopped talking," Johnson said, adjusting volume and sensitivity. The strength of the Bravo Two signal faded to the same level as the Bravo Three signature, though Three was much farther away. "That's a quiet boat they've got behind us, Skipper."

"They've been very busy underneath that shed at the boatyard, Srully. Do we still have solutions?"

Tullibee checked the panel that monitored the information feed to Bearkiller's fire control panel. "No problem so far, Captain."

"Then let's see if they figured us out."

* * *

"The last signal we can be sure of was at least ten minutes ago," Corte' reported.

"What did our sonar hear, then?" Delamadrid spoke calmly, but he was much closer to panic than he appeared to be. If they lost them now they would have to re-establish the closure pattern, even if Sombra still had them. The others would undoubtedly have to snorkel to restore their batteries. The American would most likely escape them then, perhaps even slip past the final guard and launch its missiles. They couldn't allow that to happen.

"A ghost," Corte' said, "A biological. Perhaps even a result of our own movement." He made a notation on the chart. "This is the last bearing that anyone could claim as a contact, and even that is rated a possible only."

Delamadrid stared at the lines on the chart. "He stopped running." *They are in front of me. They were running away.* The big bronze propeller would be pointed at Triunfante. The range was probably right. "Search with the laser!" The parameters were satisfied. Delamadrid had not really expected to have to use the prototype system himself. He mistrusted it a little, in fact, even with Sombra's apparent success. He had grumbled over the loss of a torpedo tube. But if it worked now, he would sacrifice a virgin in its honor!

The system was made active. Power flowed to the continuous-wave laser, which sent out a narrow blue-green beam at a frequency that would carry it well through sea water but that wouldn't be detected by the receivers on the American that their strategic communications satellites sent messages to. The Germans were still trying to work various weaknesses out of the system, such as the relatively short range. Against the dark-painted surface of a submerged hull, for example, it was less than two thousand yards: a bounce off the propeller was worth five times that. It was also, because of the way it was mounted, capable of search and detection over just the forward sixty-degree cone. But it could instantly provide the range to a target, and it could be used at high speed, unlike passive sonars. And unlike active sonars it was absolutely silent. It gave nothing away to the victim.

The beam went out at the speed of light in water—slower than in air or space but still impossibly fast. For most of the cone of water it covered, it kept going and never came back. There was, however, one small part of the cone, one area, that didn't send the beam away. That was the area that was occupied by a seven-bladed propeller, the barely-turning propeller of an Ohio-class nuclear ballistic missile submarine.

The beam swept, it bounced, and it came back to Triunfante's receivers, telling them where and how far away the American was trying to hide from then. Laser radar, Ladar, had come into the sea. And it had found a violent new home there.

"I have them, Captain!" the lieutenant said, surprised even though he had the most faith in the system of anyone aboard, "Bearing zero one-three, range seven-seven-five-zero! Amazing!"

Delamadrid smiled, and promised the god of light beams the first virgin he found that he didn't disqualify first. "Excellent! Prepare for active sonar search."

"But we have them!" Corte' said, "The first warning they have will be our firing!"

"We have to mark them for the others," Delamadrid said, "This attack must be coordinated. Sombre fired too soon the first time, Corte', and then I made a mistake by rushing in. I do not intend to make another such error. The others must be able to close and attack soon, before their batteries go flat. Sonar!"

"Ready, Captain!"

"Torpedo room, you must exceed yourself on reload time. Corte' we will check the laser's solution with sonar. You will fire as soon as you have confirmation. Don't wait for my order."

"Yes Captain!"

"Sonar, initiate active search!"

* * *

"HOOOOleeeshiii—Skipper, Yankee search! We got a Yankee search from Bravo Two at one-six-two relative!"

"I hear it," J.T. said quietly. The current irony of that bit of military slang was not lost on him. "Engineering. Atchison, wake the squirrels up. Helm, ahead one third."

"Ahead one third aye."

"Has he got us?"

"Not sure, sir." Johnson watched his indicators move and tried to remember everything there was to know about German sonar systems. It didn't seem like much. "We're at the edge of his range, I think."

PING. It was weak.

"He got us, Captain," Tullibee said, "He'll narrow the search now."

PING. That one sounded stronger.

"See?"

"Announcement," J.T. told the artificial intelligence, "All hands, this is the Captain. Secure from superquiet. General Quarters, Battle Stations Torpedo. That is all." The last phrase told the AI to cut the all-area broadcast off. He stood up. "Helm, ahead two thirds."

"Ahead two thirds aye." The automatic acknowledgement of orders that was so necessary for safe operations at sea was also very handy when you were communicating with someone you couldn't see.

"Jim, update countermeasures programing—"

"Transients! Danm, that was fast! Torpedo—"

"—and activate the Nixie."

"—correction, torpedoes, two fish wet and running hot!"

"I'm on my way, Ops." J.T. forgot to designate a message-location first as he began to map the situation in his mind. Fortunately, the AI knew to store the phrase until it had a location to broadcast it to. The developers of the system had spent years writing software that could handle the idiosyncrasies of command personnel under stress.

"They're cranking up! All Bravos accelerating."

J.T. was out of Sonar at the run.

PINGPINGPINGPING.

"Multiple Yankee searches! Transient, transient— multiple transients, Bravo, correction, all Bravos are turning to intercept headings...torpedoes, high-speed, one-seven-five!"

"Calm down. Sonar," J.T. said as he skidded to a stop beside the chart table. "By the numbers, range, bearing, speed, whatever you've got on all contacts."

"Sorry, Skipper, I—son of a bitch! Launch transients! Transients and high-speed screws on multiple bearings. Conn, we have multiple incoming, I repeat, multiple incoming torpedoes!"

J.T. smiled.

PAST

"An army without secret agents is exactly like a man
without eyes or ears."

Chia Lin

Gregoriy Aleksiev Alexandrovitch leaned back in his seat, covered his eyes, and put the document he had just read up against the rest of the information that was in his mind.

There was a lot of information in his mind. It had accumulated there during a year, almost two, as deputy at the Brazilian office. It had accumulated rapidly there because the group had been so small that he had done what seemed to be the work of two residents at the time. The office had expanded, though, and so had his role and his rank. For three years he had really been the resident, head of the expanded GRU mission there. Then there had been the transfer to the Academy in Moscow and his work preparing illegals, teaching, consulting with others about matters South American and, as time permitted, working on his "graduate studies." Until recently, focus had been on illegals and preparation for the defense of his written study. He could have cut eight months off the normal time required for a Masters of Military Science degree. He could have. Now those damned Brazilians and their silly world-power games had put him three months behind at least. Three months delayed from returning to a residentura. Three months longer he had been required to stay in Moscow.

It had been a mistake to come back. Gregoriy had been less certain of it then than he was now. He had made a mistake in coming, he had made a mistake in remaining longer than he had planned to, and he had made a mistake by letting them talk him into the graduate program. For only the second time in his life he had allowed himself to succumb to flattery.

Now that he thought about it, the first time had been a disaster too.

Not that Moscow was as bad as it used to be (of course, in some ways it was worse than it used to be, but that was the nature of things). After a bitter struggle at least some of the Yeltsin Reforms were beginning to actually have an effect on things. A majority of the most basic items were in consistently good stock on store shelves, more money was being pumped into the civilian economy, and the military had been trimmed of some (not all) of its excess manpower. Some large-scale privatization was beginning to take place, and improvements were evident in some industries because of that. Letting the Union dissolve, after a suitably dramatic struggle to hold onto it, had been a master stroke of very-long-range planning. Billions of rubles had been freed that would have otherwise gone down the economic black holes of the outer republics. The Russian military, and of course the people (so far, to a lesser extent) had profited greatly by the savings.

There were still many problems, of course. Waste and inefficiency were still widespread. Only basic items were in consistent stock—luxuries, some foreign goods, and certain items of high quality were available only at shops which almost without exception required foreign currency. The ruble was convertible now, but still somewhat unstable and not fully trusted. It generally traded badly against foreign currencies. Its transition to a convertible currency had been almost too much for the State to handle. Gregoriy was glad he had been out of the country during that time. And both unemployment and crime were still high, though both had stabilized in the last year or two and at least one of those categories was apparently about to start going down.

Perhaps the oddest thing about the aftermath of the Changeover was the continued existence of a Communist Party. It didn't have that name, of course.

Communists were still restricted by law from organizing as a political party. But they were still there, still making a very occasional nuisance out of themselves in one way or another, and still not adapting to any of the changes. They talked like the hardliners of old, but without either the ability or the power to do anything that the old rulers used to have.

They are living in the past, confused by the present, and unable to face or even look at any future but their own fantasy of one. They are fools. I am a fool, too, because I was out but I came back, and when I could have gone, I chose to stay longer. Count me the largest and best of all the fools that there are.

He shook his head. It was no good, thinking like this. It was not as bad as all that. This report, the latest information, had put him in the wrong frame of mind. That was certainly the case. Granted, it was still better to be overseas, always. To be a floor cleaner was to be envied, if you were cleaning floors overseas. But it had not been quite so bad here, and he would still be gone soon, even if it were not as soon as he had originally planned.

He picked up the report. *Maybe, perhaps, it could be even sooner than I think now, even.*

It would be so nice to be in the field again.

The South Americans—*no. You know better than to think that way, Gregoriy. The South Americans were no more alike or together than the Arabs. Start again.* The Brazilians would certainly make use of this information. The question is, what use will they make of it? The options ranged from releasing specifics to the press all the way up to sending their Navy after the submarine. They had some reasonably capable surface units, as he recalled, and some good German-designed submarines, two of which had been built locally. There were some other units, too, and something about one of them that he couldn't quite bring to mind—

"Gregoriy Alexandrovitch!"

He looked up, startled. His immediate superior (in this particular area—technically, he served three masters. It was a complicated life.), Ivan Pelitovsky, had his head inside the door.

"Asleep again! Burying yourself in your work! Such dedication! I could have killed you while you worked so hard in your mind! At this rate, you will have to stop calling yourself an assassin!"

It was a running joke among some of the orthodoxly-trained members of Center. A usually light-hearted, no-insult-intended gag. Only a few others, the ones who had come up the same way Gregoriy did, did not at one time or another participate in it. They knew what he had been through, and respected the experience too much to make light of it, even that way.
Neither did the others who had come from Spetsnaz into intelligence work feel intimidated by
Gregoriy's background, so they felt no need to mask uneasiness or defend their egos with jokes of this kind.

Gregoriy held no animosity against those jokesters, especially the ones like Ivan who addressed them directly to him and invited him to take a share of the humor. The only ones he sometimes felt anger about were the whispering ones, the ones who held him in quiet, fearful contempt. But even such anger was rare for him. The ones who felt that way about him were invariably not worth expending any kind of emotion on.

"But, Ivan Pelitovsky, why should I worry about anyone coming upon me suddenly?" Gregoriy answered innocently, "I have only friends here. I have, after all, already destroyed all of my enemies." Perhaps that will turn the joke back upon them. "But you are right anyway. I thank you for making me aware of my lack of alertness." The environment at Center was making him dull. "Now, please don't tell my Systema master about this. The old man would kick my ass three directions at once if he knew. And please come in."

"I am not disturbing you?" Ivan could be overly polite at times. But at least he never assumed that his idea was always more important than whatever you might be: working on, as some others did.

"No, no, of course not." Gregoriy waved the idea away Ivan liked to play the old friend with subordinates. Gregoriy had seen a couple of them trip over the act. He had no intention of repeating their errors "I was just thinking about this damnable Brazilian thing you've handed to me." A wonderful country, or at least it had been before the Leadership had taken control. He hoped it still was, but he knew in his heart that it wasn't. Things were always different, always changing. Perhaps if the old hardliners had understood this, there would still be a

Soviet Union. Though he still thought that they were better off without some of the outer republics.

"It is precisely that about which I want to talk to you." Ivan sat down. "You have read the report?"

"Yes. It's worth every ruble. The deputy who authorized the buy should be highly commended." The deputy resident had authorized a premium payment to the Washington-based agent who had furnished this information. If Gregoriy had been there, he would have paid even more for it.

"He has been." It was a little sad that this kind of information had not fallen into their hands ten or twelve years ago. The Navy would have sold themselves into prostitution for the chance to rape an Ohio. "What we are wondering now is, one, what will the Brazilians do with this, and two, what should we do with this?" But ten or twelve years ago nothing like this would have been happening in that hemisphere, so the information would not have existed to begin with. A pity. Still, we might be able to get something from the Americans for this. "Can you think of any rocks that this lever of ours might move aside?"

"That is a large question."

"Only so as to match our appetites."

Indeed. Sometimes it seemed that the GRU would not be satisfied until it knew Everything, Period. That was probably true of any intelligence service. More often, however, the GRU found that its eyes were bigger than its stomach. That, too, was probably true of any intelligence service.

"Very well." Gregoriy stood up. He was not as large a man as Ivan, but it would be obvious to any observer who would best the other in most physical contests. Gregoriy had not neglected his training and conditioning. What was not obvious to an observer was the difference in the minds of the two men. Not that Ivan was stupid—no one reached his level within the organization by being stupid. It was simply that, in many areas, Gregoriy was the superior performer on that level as well. It was not something he dwelt on, however. It was simply an occasional factor in his calculations, a tool, to be used like a knife or an agent or the used Macintosh he had in his quarters.

"I must move around a little," Gregoriy said, locking the report in his personal safe, 'Will it be all right to discuss this in the cafeteria?"

Ivan's eyes automatically swept the room. A useless habit, he knew, one born of the operational paranoia that pervaded the place. Any monitoring devices that were here would not be visible to him, not to mention that the offices had been swept only recently. The cafeteria could be both better and worse in that respect. The background traffic would drown out conversations on some bugs, but the constant movement through the place also made it impossible to insure proper electronic sanitation. If the discussion were to be truly secure then it was better to stay in the windowless office and us a white- noise generator for insurance.

On the other hand, what Gregoriy had to say might not be particularly sensitive. He didn't seem to think it would be, apparently. Do I?

"I would be happy to do so," Ivan answered. If the discussion became sensitive they could always return to a safer place. "Some coffee would do me good right now."

They used the open cafeteria. Like the CIA headquarters outside of Washington, and probably like the GRU's counterpart in military intelligence at the Pentagon, Center also had a closed dining area where deep-cover agents and illegals dined when they had to be in the building, which was rarely. More often it was used for conferences that wouldn't fit into another room. The most recent head of GRU had put the dining hall to such use more often in the last two years than his predecessors had in the last ten. It was a sign that changes were beginning to take root in Russia where they had too first—in the minds of the people. The clearest sign of that in the isolated, closed off world that Gregoriy existed in was the recent relaxation of restrictions concerning Jewish ancestry of Academy candidates. The unwritten admittance rules, like the bigotry that had driven them, were easing, so that Jewish blood was being allowed as soon as the second or third generation instead of in the fifth as it had been before. For Russians, it was a revolution in the making.

Ivan opted for a strong Turkish-like blend that Gregoriy suspected had been brewed twice for added effect. He drank it black, so black that it resembled oil more than coffee, in small cups. Gregoriy had tried it once, learning from the experience why the cups were so small. Anything with that kind of a kick could only be taken safely in small doses. He made his usual choice, a primarily Columbian blend to which he added milk or cream as the mood struck him. It seemed an appropriate thing to drink when he contemplated or discussed the affairs of South and Central America.

"Now, Gregoiry Alexandrovitch," Ivan said when they were seated, "I know that you have only just finished the report. We will want more detailed consideration of it later, of course. But for now, what are your immediate opinions concerning the matter?"

"First, that it is a very interesting affair. The Americans have a difficult problem, and we both have our first solid test of Tacit, I think."

Gregoriy referred to a very secret agreement between Russia and the United States. It was only three years old and so sensitive that only two copies existed, one in the most secure of the Kremlin's vaults and another buried somewhere around Washington. It was a mark of GRU's trust in Gregoriy, and of their need for his experience, that he knew of the agreement. Tacit allowed for certain measures to be taken by either nation in order to restrict or destroy any new nuclear weapon capability in their hemispheres. The agreement allowed for token protest by the other side, but not for real censure. Under the terms of the agreement, if the United States actually took action against Brazil, then Russia would perhaps issue a statement of protest, but it would abstain from participation in something like a United Nations vote of censure.

It was never expected that Tacit would hold the nuclear proliferation line for very long.
Only extreme measures and perhaps unconscionable actions would do that. In two or three more years, though, enough of the Strategic Defense Initiative and ORBIT SHIELD would be running to at least keep any regional conflicts within their regions. Further enhancement of the systems, combined with greater efforts of diplomacy, would then hopefully remove the perceived need for such weaponry development.

"Yes," Ivan said, automatically glancing around at the mention of the restricted-access document, "we will see how serious their president is about holding the line now."

"I think that, if the Brazilians set off their demonstrator, he will be forced to act, agreement or not," Gregoriy said, "One thing I am less sure of: do the Brazilians believe in the technical capability of the American system? My reports so far haven't shown me enough to judge. Do you have any other word about this?" Multiple networks were the stock-in-trade of GRU operations. Groups of agents and illegals were duplicated at every opportunity and kept completely separate from each other. Heads of GRU residencies, individual military districts and fleets, all directorates of GRU all had their own networks, each one independent of the other. All of these groups could crosscheck each other without anyone knowing what anyone else was doing. All of them fed information to Center. GRU was a large spider with a very extensive web that constantly vibrated with trapped information.

"As far as anyone can tell," Ivan answered, "they believe that the Americans are confident that it will be effective." He shrugged. "It's a simple enough idea, and their guidance systems are still the best in the world."

The nuclear devices were being produced, assembled, and stored at a single hardened site in the vicinity of Capelinha in Minas Gerais state. There were several mines underneath the mountains there, one of which had been converted for that purpose. Brazil's air defense system was good enough to make a strike by anything short of stealth aircraft a chancy business that would probably result in a net political loss for America, especially if captured aircrews were to turn up in Brazilian hands. Even if one of the handful of B-2s available were used, the structure would easily withstand heavy conventional strikes. Engineers had learned from the Iraqi debacle. You couldn't guide a bomb down an air shaft any more. Even the big GBU-28, the five-thousand-pound penetrator that had been used in the final days of Desert Storm, wouldn't get far enough down to have any effect. A nuclear strike was of course out of the question.

"There is no chance that Brazil is bluffing, I suppose," Ivan went on, "Their test-explosion announcement was made some time ago, after all."

The apparent solution the United States had to this problem was simple enough in principle. It was based on the knowledge that any object, even a small one, could do tremendous damage as long as it were moving fast enough on impact. Trident missiles on at least two Ohio-class submarines had been modified. The multiple warheads on each of the twenty-four missiles carried by each platform had been replaced by a single very heavy one that was composed of some superhard substance of very high density that was extremely heat- resistant, since no heat shield was included in the system. An additional rocket motor was also installed, and the guidance system had been replaced. As far as GRU could determine, the resultant delivery vehicle, called "D-X" by the Americans, lost somewhere around half the range of the original Trident. The gain was in accuracy, and it was good—the Circular Error Probable, the radius of a circle inside of which half the warheads fired would

Hit, had been reduced by more than half. The missile was over twice as accurate as it had been before.

"Unfortunately not," Gregoriy said, "The security around the project is extraordinary, but we have verified the site and its purpose. I am satisfied that atomic weapons are being built there. I think that they have delayed this long because they wanted to find out exactly what the Americans would do about it beyond talk. That adds a time element to this, but I don't know how much of one.

It was necessary that the warheads be very accurate indeed. There was no explosive, nuclear or conventional, inside of them. Their destructive effect was based almost completely on the kinetic energy that was generated by their flight profile. The warheads were first lofted high, much higher than normal for any ballistic weapon of this type. They then would nose over almost to the vertical and dive into the target, firing the extra rocket motor to gain even greater impact velocity. The superhard, high-density projectiles would certainly not be moving less than ten kilometers per second when they hit, if that slowly. No explosive was required under those conditions. The concept of kinetic-energy kill was not a new one. Thousands of heavily armored main battle tanks had been destroyed in the last two decades after being hit by kinetic- energy penetrators that were nothing more than very large, very fast arrows. And even this application of it had been foreshadowed by science-fiction writers.

"They must be very sure of the guidance system," Gregoriy said, "How can they insure the required accuracy?"

"We don't know, specifically, yet," Ivan answered, "We think it is some variation of the one their Pershing II carried. That is the best current estimation."

That missile, eliminated by the Intermediate Range Missile Treaty in the late '80s, also carried an earth-penetrator warhead, but one containing an atomic bomb. It had been designed to burrow down next to underground command centers and storage facilities before exploding. Its warhead was supposed to have been extremely accurate due to a system that matched a radar image of the target with one stored in the guidance system's memory.

Gregoriy shook his head. "It can't be. I'm not a scientist, but I don't believe that system could be operated at the speeds this weapon will come in at, not to mention the stress of its re-entry." Tactical missiles like the Pershing II suffered comparatively little re-entry stress. Most of them never even exited the atmosphere during their short flights. "But that's not important to this. It's enough that the Americans believe in it, and that the South Americans believe that the Americans believe in it."

"I note that you say South Americans instead of just Brazilians," Ivan said, "Is this important?"

"I believe so," Gregoriy said, "It has always seemed wise to me to examine the region around the specific state. While the states there are not as interlocked, shall we say, as in the Middle East, there are still effects of one upon the other that must always be considered. Always." He took a sip of coffee. "Excuse me, Ivan. I'm beginning to lecture. I've been in front of classrooms too much lately."

"I don't mind, Gregoriy. I know it is a way of ordering your thoughts. But how should we consider the other states in the region, tactically and strategically, with regard to this situation?"

"Tactically, and specific to this situation, not at all. Argentina is the only neighbor who might support them, though only verbally, treaty or no treaty. That American/British operation that everyone denies ever happened frightened them and made the others in the region nervous. Everyone will wait and see if Brazil can successfully challenge the

Yankee, so tactically they and their drug-lord 'partners' will go this one by themselves.

Strategically, in the longer term—that could be another matter. The Leadership, as they call themselves, makes no secret of their intention to move Brazil into first place in the region.

There are also rumors of some type of eventual Third World coalition against the power states." There were no superpowers in Gregoriy's mind any more. That title had been lost to anyone beginning in '90 with the dissolution of the old Soviet Union, and continuing in late '93 when the European Common Market finally started to deal adequately with the problems of trade and economic unification. America had lost the title in Gregoriy's mind then, especially considering the rise of Japanese economic influence. Russia and America still had the weapons, yes, and some technological edges, America more than Russia, but Russia was better at stealing other's secrets and so was gaining. Both were also finally recovering from their various economic woes, or at least were beginning to. But both nations still had steps to walk up before Gregoriy would reassign either one the rank of superpower again.

"I think," Gregoriy continued, "that if Brazil successfully prevents the United States from acting or forces them to take more radical action, then, nuclear weapons or not, other states will fall into line behind them either from respect or simple fear."

"Then you believe that there will be some attempt to neutralize the American submarines?"

"Almost certainly. If they succeed, the political gain would be tremendous. If they fail, little is lost, and some sympathy might be gained from it." Maybe. No one wanted yet another nuclear club member.

"How do you think they will go about this attempt? How likely are they to succeed?"

"Those are questions I cannot answer quickly. I need time, and the answers to certain questions. How important is this matter, Ivan?"

Ivan considered it. The director thought it was important enough to emphasize that

Ivan assign his best people to it. Certain additional resources could be made available, he had said, if the situation seemed to require it. And they wanted a speedy report. There looked to be a chance here, as Ivan read the situation, to increase GRU penetration of South America, or to gain something on the Americans, or both.

But much of that depended on what Major-acting-Colonel Alexandrovitch had to say.

Ivan's best field man had already become his best analyst, and Ivan thought him capable of going farther still, if he wished. Ivan could easily do worse than to sponsor and support him in his career.

"I believe it to be important enough to divert same resources for you," he answered, "I can begin by having our residencies give priority to your inquiries. I can also guarantee you direct communications access."

Copies of those communications would of course go to Ivan's desk each day, but this did not need to be said. "If necessary, I will put my own group on it." He meant the group of agents that he, personally, directed. Every head of a Directorate, and most of the heads of Directions such as Ivan, controlled a group of agents and illegals that was completely independent of the regular organizations of the undercover residencies. The First

Deputy and the director of GRU also had personal agent groups which were used for special projects and to double-check, or check up on, the other agent groups GRU controlled. It was one of the ways that GRU kept its house in order.

"I will also speak with the Director," Ivan continued, "to see if he wishes to assign further resources to this. Do you wish assistance from Fifth Directorate, or perhaps Cosmic Intelligence?" Fifth Directorate controlled the separate intelligence directorates that each military district and fleet maintained in parallel with the normal GRU residencies. Despite large military reductions cause by the disintegration of both the Warsaw Pact and the Soviet Union,

Fifth Directorate controlled more agents than the rest of GRU combined. Cosmic Intelligence was in charge of satellite reconnaissance operations.

This is more important than I thought. "Let me see what information our own groups can get for us first," he answered carefully, "I don't think anything else will be needed yet." He had learned early that seeking too much information could be a trap. The key to successful analysis was knowing what questions to ask and knowing what the smallest useful answer was. "If we ask for a lot, they may expect more than we can provide." He was careful to bring Ivan in. If something went wrong somehow, he would want an ally. "One thing, however—this source must be followed closely. We must know where he is taking the information, who it goes to and where it stops at. Can this be done? Is it too late?" He could not remember the time that was stamped on the report.

Ivan smiled. "This was anticipated. That agent should be arriving in Rio de Janeiro—" he checked a wall clock and subtracted the time-zone differential, "—about now. The best we have available are waiting for him. I have authorized a complete track." The man would be kept under surveillance by several teams. Anyone he met would be thoroughly checked. Every trace he made would be followed in detail. "Now how soon can you have a report ready?"

A complete track. How many projects were derailed for this? "That depends on how soon I can get my questions answered. I think that most of what I need can be acquired quickly." Give yourself room. "If I can be released from other duties, five days at most." He could probably do it in two or three, but one of the old "Star Trek" movies he had seen once had given him the ability to appear to be a "miracle worker." That fictional tidbit had been of great assistance to him in his career.

"Provide my aide the questions for the networks. I'll expect a detailed briefing in four days." I'll push him a little. It will be a demonstration of our efficiency. "Perhaps by that time we'll know where our South American bird is making its nest as well." Knowing where the information went to would give them a clue as to what would be done with it.

"That might be very useful." Gregoriy made sure to look disappointed about the time limit.

"Fine. Consider yourself relieved of other duties as of now. I will make the arrangements." Ivan leaned forward to emphasize a final point. "Be good with this one, Gregoriy. I think you could go a long way with this, if the cards can be played correctly."

If it gets me away from here, Ivan, it will have taken me more than far enough.

* * *

Three days were required, spent mostly in inquiries to the Eighth and Eleventh Directorates, which studied military technologies and kept track of nuclear forces and nuclear development. Some further time was spent in conversation with a half-dozen different scientists and technologists, and in riffling through various files in Archives. Only a few questions had to be transmitted to the Brazilian residencies, which was just as well, because the most capable group—Gregoriy's former command—was tied up with close-checking the Washington agent's contacts and movements. The agent's code name, Gregoriy discovered, was Odd Man Out, giving him reason to wonder to if the computer-generated titles were as randomized as everyone believed they were. This one had not yet, it was thought, transferred the data he was carrying.

Early morning of the fourth day found Gregoriy preparing for a presentation that would be made not only to Ivan but to the head of Second Directorate, the man who directed all agent activity in North and South America. He prepared for this one the same way he prepared for any other important presentation. He played games on his Macintosh. He had purchased the personal computer during the second year of his Brazilian residency, from the man who was his official (and perhaps unofficial —they could never determine it) counterpart at the American embassy. Anthony was still there, in fact, though in a higher position now. That might prove useful later on. Gregoriy hoped that he was still in good health. Strained relations had led to some reduction in dependent and nonessential official personnel. There had been some minor incidents, but nothing serious so far that anyone knew of. Gregoriy's monitors reported that some preparations were being made for trouble at the newer embassy in Rio, which had been located and built more with security in mind than the older building had been. But in general there was no sign of real concern among the Americans there. He hoped that their lack of worry was valid. Some manner of repeat of the affair in Africa would not be at all desirable.

Getting the Macintosh had not been as simple a matter as handing over cash and taking it home. Anthony had been required to make sure that even a used personal computer did not constituted technology restricted from export, and Gregoriy had been required to maneuver around longstanding GRU biases. The only contact his superiors wanted with most foreigners was for the purpose of recruiting agents. Even though the Cold War was ancient history, and despite many numerous understandings and treaties, the habits and traditions of old died hard. There had also been some KGB interference, some attempt to discredit him over it. Stupid pigs. Some of the overseas officers still had trouble adjusting to the KGB's great loss of power in the early nineties. The Chekists still had to be watched, though. Although the rivalry was not as literally bloody as it had been in the past, it was still occasionally intense.

An opportunity to do damage to a rival organization was not generally passed over.

Gregoriy had managed despite them, however, and had acquired the computer and several interesting programs as well. His current favorite, still not fully mastered, was called

Falcon. He'd had trouble with that game for a long time. He could not get beyond the Colonel's level of the game, try as he might. He kept crashing the damn airplane! And it was not quite as accurate as he would like—the Russian fighters in the game were not as capable as in reality. The simulated SAMs, however, balanced that out somewhat; they could and did shoot him down much more often than he liked. He thought that perhaps the capabilities of the two weapons systems should have been reversed. But it was an older version of the game, and perhaps the designers had not had accurate performance data when they were writing the software.

Another landing attempt, another crash. Gregoriy sighed, switched off, and started getting ready for work. When he was back in the West, he would look for something more up-to-date, perhaps a Macintosh IV or one of those Compaqs or something. And better games, certainly. Someone, somewhere, must have produced an F-22 simulator by now. Now <u>there</u> was a plane fit for a Russian pilot...

* * *

It seems that you have once again fulfilled your reputation as a miracle worker, Colonel Alexandrovitch," the Director said.

"Major, sir. I am a Major." Gregoriy did not want to be pretentious or appear to be fawning by accepting the Director's mistake. Also, he seemed to be in a good mood, though

Gregoriy had not seen him often enough to be sure of that judgement. If he were faking it, then it was Gregoriy's duty to act as if he were being taken in by the projection of joviality and good-will. It was a time-honored tradition among members of bureaucracies everywhere.

"Didn't Ivan tell you?" The Director looked at Ivan, the only other officer in the room.

"Why haven't you informed the Colonel of his promotion?" It was a mock-anger. The Director seemed to be a generally relaxed sort, one of several that had appeared at Center in the last couple of years. It was a sign of what appeared to be a shift in organizational personality, perhaps the truest indication that changes were at last taking root in the government as well as the country. Gregoriy wondered if American military intelligence was also becoming more "relaxed" like this. Probably not. He looked down at the one-of-three copy of his report that was on the table in front of the Director.

"There was no time, sir," Ivan said, "Colonel Alexandrovitch only came in with enough time to proof the copies and bring them here. I have not otherwise seen him for three days."

Ivan looked at Gregoriy. "The authorization came in yesterday, Gregoriy. As of then, your rank is Colonel, with commensurate privilege and responsibility. Congratulations."

"Thank you," Gregoriy said, "and thank you, sir," to the Director. He suppressed a sigh.

They had only made official what had been a working reality. Gregoriy had already been doing a colonel's job and receiving a colonel's pay for it. GRU paid you for the position you worked in, not the rank you carried. Doing the job was the important thing to them. Gregoriy knewof senior lieutenants who were running small residencies and drawing the pay equivalent of a colonel. The rank of the position, not the rank on the uniform, determined what you made here.

So now this. Would it trap him here? Would the weight of the insignia pin him down at Center? He wanted out, to go back into the field. Now. How would this hurt or help that? He would have to see.

"Now, concerning the report," the Director said, "I will read the details later, of course. Provide me, please, with a summary of your findings and conclusions."

"Yes sir. It is evident that Brazil has developed or has access to an agent network of high quality based in Washington. It has provided them with small amounts of very useful information for some time now."

"Do we know anything about the network, other than that it exists?"

"We have secured what appears to be a high-priority messenger that serves this network," Ivan answered, "He has passed on to us the information which concerns us now. He has taken this information personally to Rio de Janeiro to pass it on. We are following him and his contacts carefully there." He looked at Gregoriy. "The latest word is that a transfer has been completed. That's all so far."

"I think it important that we know exactly where the information goes to," Gregoriy explained to the Director, "It will tell us something about where the real power is there."

"Of course. Ivan has briefed me about the information he carries. You believe that the American response is threatened?"

"I believe that the Brazilians may now have the technical capability to threaten the Americans. They have built a Canadian-style tribrid, using, we think, one of those two old but still very capable Dutch submarines. They still have their British-made towed arrays, by the way, which are very capable systems. There is some word of an advancement in fuel-cell technology from there, something apparently beyond what the Germans are running in their Type Two-Twelves. We also have the facts of their extended refit of one submarine under extraordinary conditions of secrecy, as well as the acquisition of that German-built laser seeker, the one they have in operational testing now. One, perhaps two prototypes are in Brazilian hands."

"How is it that they have these prototypes and we do not?" the Director asked.

"We may have, sir, but Ninth Directorate naturally isn't saying," Gregoriy said, "If I had to guess, I would say that we're waiting for further development of the system before we make an acquisition." Why pay for development when you could be patient and buy or steal an operational system? "There are also some limitations to the system as it exists now. The person I talked to in Ninth joked about waiting for the Japanese to come out with a better copy first."

"In other words," Ivan said, "no one will be replacing their sonars for a while. Correct?"

"As far as I can tell, yes. I didn't get many details about this system. It was most significant to me that they had acquired it." He addressed the Director again. "They got it the same way we do, sir, through back channels." They had stolen it or bought it from someone who had stolen it, in other words. There was a small but lucrative underground market that dealt with advanced military technology of this kind. It was open to anyone with enough money to bid, which in practice excluded all but the richest organizations and countries.

"Their resources are extensive," the Director said, "the Canadian reactor system, the old Dutch submarines, this."

"It is very strong indirect confirmation of the government's link to the cartels," Ivan said.

"I think also, sir, that it is evidence of desperation and of a deeper conspiracy."

"Really?" Ivan asked.

"That is interesting," the Director said, "How do you come to this conclusion?"

"My information leads me to believe that the Brazilian government is rushing prototype technology, things that would normally be under further development, into action against the Americans. This kind of push says to me that something is on the line here."

"Certainly. Their nuclear weapons capability."

"Yes sir, but I mean beyond that. This Leadership of theirs has an expressed ambition to put South and Central America under Brazilian guidance. To do that, they must prove themselves worthy to command. Staring down the Yankee is a good way to do that. If they cannot neutralize the Americans, they will lose prestige, and the chance for regional leadership."

"I see," Ivan said, "But where is the conspiracy in this?"

"I think with the cartels in Amazonia. Consider, please: they are in with the government already. They have supplied the bulk of the funds for the new developments that are being applied now. They are allowing the government access to and use of the cocaine distribution networks under their control. Granted, this kind of agent network is of generally poor quality, but it's still potentially bigger than anything in history. Hundreds of millions have been spent on these efforts."

"What of the Libyan cash offerings?"

"Substantial, of course, but irrelevant compared to cartel support," Gregoriy answered,
"They want an Arab bomb, and restoration of influence they lost a long time ago. Their support will fade if the Americans destroy the bomb production and storage facilities."

"So we are back to the cartels," the Director said, "who have, it seems, practically bought the government."

"Precisely," Gregoriy said, "just as we do with certain people we wish to ensnare, so they have done with the Leadership."

"There is something I'm missing here," the Director said, "something in their aims that you have concluded."

"That their money has given them considerable influence I have no doubt. I believe that they are using this influence to play upon already-existing imperialistic ambitions. I believe that the cartel leadership is indirectly forcing the confrontation with the Americans."

"They want to be the government," Ivan said.

Gregoriy nodded. "That is my conclusion, yes. And they have hit on this as the fastest way to do it."

"If the Brazilians fail against America, the government will in the least suffer disruption and loss of face," the Director said, "It might even be toppled by it. The cartels will move into the power vacuum."

"And if the government succeeds, the ties of dependence become strengthened," Ivan said, "It will take a bit longer, but they will eventually have control anyway."

They had it. Gregoriy had made his point. "What better way to protect the industry?" he asked, "This way, they have better insurance against swings of attitude. Only massive internal upheaval or external invasion would shake them loose."

The three men silently considered the idea for a while.

"There is another thing," the Director said to break the silence, "Columbia's economy is still, shall we say, badly disorganized, as are the economies of the neighboring states. The United States can't help them as much as it would like because of a slow growth period or a mild recession or whatever they're calling their latest economic instability."

"That one looks to have stabilized, though," Ivan said, "They could start increasing aid in as little as two or three years, probably sooner."

"Exactly my point," the Director said, "There is a window of opportunity here."

"I see it," Gregoriy said, "If Brazil can be taken over and stabilized quickly enough, the cartels would control one of the strongest military machines on the continent."

"And Argentina is, supposedly, neutralized by treaty," Ivan said.

"They could have their old lands back and the Amazon besides," the Director said, "and vengeance upon those who drove than out."

"The Americans would make war upon than first," Gregoriy said. His mind began to circle around new possibilities. He had not considered this.

"Perhaps, perhaps not," the Director said, "Though there have been improvements, they are still on the edge financially, not to mention the political questions they would face with such an action. There are many ghosts in that region for them, shadows of past interventions. Even their old Contra questions might be reawakened if this came up. I think we must consider this carefully. Gentlemen, I want initial observations and recommendations for action based on our discussion here on my desk by this time tomorrow. We will review and discuss that, and then I will pass the results up the line for final decision and implementation." He leaned toward them. "If we play our cards right, my friends, we can strengthen our presence and influence in the region considerably. We might have America owing us a large favor and, of course, we will benefit the State—perhaps ourselves as well. An excellent job, Colonel," he said to Gregoriy as he stood up to end the meeting, "You've done well for us so far. Now let's see if you can do even better."

* * *

Gregoriy struggled with it all day. It followed him home that evening to his apartment in the auxiliary building near Center. It refused to let him sleep for what felt like a long time. The crux of it haunted him: if they somehow helped the Americans, the cartels took advantage. If they did not, the cartels took advantage. A win was a loss, a loss was a win. Stable governments were desirable. Drug dealers with a real army, perhaps even nuclear weapons, could not be countenanced. What must be done? Russia must gain something. At least it must prevent loss. How far could a stretch go? Nuclear weapons...there must be no more warheads. Tacit must be enforced. But a win was a loss...

At three a.m. he came awake with part of the answer. For an hour after that he lay in bed, staring at a dark ceiling, watching his mind race. At four a.m. he got up, staggered over to the Mac, and started a game. He played for two hours without pause, over and over, not mindlessly, but not concentrating either. At three minutes after six a.m., he successfully landed the airplane. He had successfully made it past the Colonel's level.

Gregoriy sat back, looked at the monitor, and smiled. He had part of it. This was an omen, a sign of rightness about his thinking. Perhaps even a message from the God that his sister had lately begun to look around for. He would go ahead with it.

At fourteen minutes after seven a.m. Gregoriy walked into Ivan's office and sat down in front of Ivan's desk.

"Tell me," he asked Ivan, "does the Director consider himself to be a gambling man?"

PRESENT

"It's very messy in the real world."

—Simone de Beauvoir

"Bad move, Elmer," J.T. whispered. *But only if I can take advantage of it.* He raised his voice. "Sonar, I want torpedo tracks on the display, autotracking at your discretion." The autotrack function allowed the computers to update designated contacts without operator intervention, freeing the sonarmen to monitor the most difficult targets. "I'm going to want to know what the Bravos—uh-hunh—" The chart display was showing four tracks from as many different directions. "—are doing." The nearest torpedo was out of the block from just six thousand yards away. *Hole-in-the-water strikes again.* "Stand by countermeasures and check on Nixie."

Nixies were best known for their use as torpedo decoys by surface ships. Their deployment with submarines was less well known about. The newer ones, smaller, smarter, and more capable, were used the same way beneath the surface, being streamed behind the potential target of a torpedo where it could make more noise than you did. Almost all torpedoes began their short but violent lives as passive homers, driving in on the noise produced by the target. Only in the aptly-named terminal stages did some of than use miniature active sonars to verify and pinpoint the target's location. But the range of that active system wets short, and newer Nixies had the means to decoy even active systems.

Sometimes. Maybe.

"Sonar, if anybody starts to lose anything let me know." At around twenty knots most submarines began to lose significant passive sonar capability as target noises were drowned out by engine noise and the sound of water rushing around the hydrophone arrays. Speed was needed now, but not to outrun the torpedoes, which were far faster than they could ever hope to get. What they needed speed for now was to stretch the time-to-interception so that they had a chance to act against the threats. That had to be balanced, however, against the loss of signal. Speed was suicide if they couldn't hear anything that was coming.

"Helm, come to two-zero-zero, get us twenty knots if we're not there already."

"Two-zero-zero, twenty knots aye sir." *Is he as calm as he sounds?*

"Diving officer, bring us up to five hundred feet. Let's get some maneuvering room."

"Coming up to five hundred feet, aye. Planes, give me ten degrees up angle, level at five hundred. Watch your gauge."

"Ten degrees up angle, level at five hundred." The planesman pulled the yoke back toward his stomach. "Reading ten degrees up angle, sir." They would rise like they had dived, without changing ballast, "flying" on their hydroplanes like an airplane did on its wings.

J.T. pressed two points on the touch-sensitive chart control panel. One initiated a program that calculated intercepts. It was specifically designed for torpedoes, so it worked faster and more accurately than other passive plot predictor systems. Torpedoes were louder, and very predictable in that they always came toward you. Current-course tracks and estimated intercept times appeared alongside each torpedo marker on the display. The closest one was something over five minutes away if nothing changed.

The other control point J.T. pressed brought in a computer program that was designed to analyze the tracks of the incoming rounds and advise him on what course and speed to take to forestall or avoid eventual violent encounters with things that were trying to kill his submarine. It was another of the UPDATE improvements, one that he had not needed the first time because the course of action had been very easy to decide upon. With a more complicated problem awaiting his solution this time, however, he wanted any advice and input he could get.

He didn't get any.

The program had not been designed to cover so many simultaneous tracks. The software writers had never considered the possibility that anyone would fire more than two modem homing torpedoes at a single target at one time. Though they were smarter than they used to be, the torpedoes still preferred to home in on each other instead of the quieter victim if they were running autonomously. This was practically guaranteed to happen if one of them switched on its active sonar. That was blood to any other self-homing shark that was in range. Even if you could guarantee that everything would stay on the wire (which you couldn't do), there was still a danger of something straying off course if not of outright fratricide. For that reason, modem submarines fired modem homing torpedoes only one, occasionally two, at a time (the most modem boat in the world, Seawolf, could fire up to four simultaneously). There were no true spreads allowed in modem underwater warfare.

So the program, presented with more contacts to process than it knew to be normal, concluded that at least part of the information it was receiving was spurious. Since it had no way to tell what part of the information was spurious and what was valid, it rejected all of the information and locked up, refusing to respond to J.T.'s inquiry. J.T. was on his own.

"Great. Sonar, is Nixie getting in your way?"

"No sir. The little darlin's singing right pretty for us. Do you have all the torpedo markers on the board?"

"Yes. I need tracks from all Bravos now. Put the boats up for me."

"Sir-we-are-at-two-zero-zero-speed-fifteen-climbing."

"Acknowledged, level at twenty knots, Helm. Sonar, inform me the instant you get significant loss of signal."

"No problems so far, Skipper."

"Fine." A standard Mark Forty-Eight could run at fifty-five knots for thirteen nautical miles. There were between four and seven such devices conning at Alabama from four different directions and four different ranges. They could not be outdistanced or outrun. They could, however, be evaded, outmaneuvered, and outsmarted. If he made the right decisions at the right time. If the countermeasures worked as they were designed to when he ordered them to. If the torpedoes had not been modified out of predictability. If.

"Communications, this is the Captain. Get a buoy off, set for immediate broadcast, message reads: USS Alabama to any American or allied naval units receiving. We are under attack, repeat under attack, by submarine units of unknown origin." That was almost certainly a lie, but the diplomats would undoubtedly appreciate his discretion. Knowing who it was that was after them was irrelevant for the moment, anyway. "We require immediate assistance. End message. Tag with current location and have it repeat till it runs down. Understood?"

"Understood, sir." The voice sounded a little shaky, but that was probably the fault of the intercom.

"Launch it as soon as its ready."

"Sir we are at twenty knots."

"Five hundred feet and level. Captain."

"Acknowledged." Two minutes had passed. The closest torpedo had covered over one-third of the distance to them in that time.

J.T. looked to where Simmons was looking over Bearkiller's shoulder. "Have we kept any firing solutions?" The chart display was cluttered with track lines and numbers and symbols. All the Bravos were closing at high speed, following their torpedoes in for closer second shots if that became necessary. *At least we can figure out who has what kind of drive.* Surviving with that information was, of course, another matter.

"Best we've got is on Bravo One," Bearkiller answered.

"Fire one to that bearing. Cut it lose as soon as you know it's running good."

A second later there was a shudder that would have been unnoticeable to anyone who wasn't used to living on submarines as their own torpedo left its launch tube. The reduction in tension in the control center when that happened was noticeable. They had finally done something other than to react to what someone else was doing. Whether it was the wise thing to do or not was irrelevant. It was something they had done, an action that they had taken.

Highly trained or not, these men had a tendency to prefer that kind of action

"Running true," Simmons reported, "Cut it!"

The weapons officer pressed the button that ejected the wires and cleared the tube for a reload.

Three minutes, about, had gone by.

"Drop a noisemaker, Jim. Maybe we can distract something with it." J.T. kept his eyes on the display.

"Conn, Communications. The buoy is on the way up."

"Acknowledged. Dump the log while you're at it." Voice logs could be dumped into either normal broadcast units or the disaster buoy at will. "Any reaction to the noisemaker,

Sonar?"

"Not that we can tell, Captain. Everyone is still turning to bearing."

That wasn't surprising. The torpedoes' brains were at least quick enough to judge between a relatively stationary noise source and one that as running at twenty knots.

"Skipper, check the chart track for Bravo Two. I've got a speed calculation of thirty, that is three-zero, knots."

"Son of a bitch," Simmons said, because what Sonar had just reported was impossible.

The impossibility of the act didn't appear to affect Bravo Two's calculated approach speed, however.

"That's very interesting," J.T. said.

He had a habit of describing big problems that way.

* * *

It was very simple. Triunfante would run in behind the torpedoes, using the laser to track the target, slowing down shortly before they were due to strike. This missile submarine was too busy defending itself to take effective counteraction against them. And if by some chance it did survive, Delamadrid would be practically at knife range, ready to launch another strike. They would be able to follow them no matter where they went or how fast they ran.

The risk was that the American might manage to launch torpedoes of its own as it twisted away from its killers. At high speed they could not hear a torpedo coming, and the laser was useless against something that small and dark. It was a small risk, and one that Delamadrid accepted because he wanted to end it. Now. Perhaps the very long confinement was finally affecting him like it had some of his crewmen. How did the Americans manage such long patrols as they did? How did they not go even a little crazy after being weeks underwater?

The navies that followed where Brazil was leading would have a lot to learn when the time came.

It was stupid for everyone to have fired at once. Had we all forgotten our lessons?

Another mistake. But an understandable one. But the American might survive simply because of their not thinking and because of the lack of control and real time communications capability. There had to be a better way, a way to coordinate actions between units. Something like the short-range version of the American's strategic laser communications system that they were said to be working on, or an adaptation of the underwater ladar system that Delamadrid was using against them now. He didn't really blame the others for reacting and firing as they had. Everyone was tense. They were all too vulnerable to the strain of a long patrol and the stress of fighting an undeclared war. How many men, even military men, could casually accept the risk that they were taking?

But it was necessary. Brazil, and Latin America behind her, had to be accorded respect, a place in the first rank of nations. No one could be allowed to pin them back into the so-called

Third World. No one.

Delamadrid still found himself thankful that he would not be a direct witness to the end, however. He didn't really want to watch the men he was killing die.

* * *

"How sure are you of that speed, Tullibee?" J.T. asked, trying to decide whether or not Bravo Two was a thirty-knot monkey wrench in his machinery.

"It's the best we can do on it. Captain. The sumbitch be haulin' ass, I'm telling you."

Four minutes. In less than two, the first torpedo would be trying to make serious contact with them. Why didn't they fire two?

"Noisemaker, Jim. And as soon as you get a solution on Two, fire one. Helm, left rudder, come to one-eight-zero. Active and remote-active jammers on standby." Wait, wait, not yet.

"Noisemaker's off. Active countermeasures to standby. Standing by to fire," Bearkiller reported.

"Left to one-eight-zero aye." The helmsman put his wheel over. "Sir," he echoed to the diving officer, "I am coming to one-eight-zero."

"Suits me," the diving officer said softly.

"Torpedo room reports reload on tube four," Simmons said.

"Active pinging! Torpedo has gone active!" An all-too-brief pause. "Torpedo has acquisition!"

No one was surprised. Ohio-class submarines were the second-largest submersible vehicles in the world. There was a lot of surface area for an active sonar to bounce off of.

"Helm, left to one-two-zero. Weapons, release curtains and Tee-Ayes now." J.T. kept careful control of his voice. "Engage remote-feed jamming. Sonar, Conn, reel the tail in. Quickly!"

"But Cap—damn! The Nixie! Aye sir!" If the Nixie took the torpedo, they would get at least part of the towed array blown away with it if it were not retracted.

'Solution-firing-three!" An ADCAP headed for Bravo Two.

In Sonar, Tullibee confirmed that it was the tail and not the Nixie being reeled in. Then he joined Johnson and Kinsey in taking off their headphones and switching to speakers. There were automatic cut-outs in the sonar systems, but no one was willing to bet their eardrums on their speed or efficiency.

A few feet behind the sail, rotary magazines of Alabama1s new expendable countermeasures launch system turned to selected positions and fed canisters into decoy launch tubes that were recessed into the external hull. The Navy had, in the first part of the decade, reluctantly come to the conclusion that its own submarines were no exception to the increased danger to any platform that was a result in everyone's success at, ironically, making their boats quieter. This increased quietness had spawned several reactive developments such as an improvements in passive sonar capability, the more regular use of active sonar during antisubmarine operations, and, most threatening, the accelerated development of non-acoustic sensing technologies.

Given the increasingly hostile sensor environment, the Navy had decided that they could no longer assume that U.S. submarines would automatically be able to sneak up to or away from anyone they wanted. Cancellation of the Sea Lance program magnified the problem by depriving the Navy of a non-nuclear standoff weapon. The presidential order that removed all nuclear weapons from Navy ships and submarines in '92 left submarines with no antisubmarine alternative but to close in and fire torpedoes, with all the attendant risks involved. With a growing possibility that there would be exchanges instead of ambushes, countermeasure systems beyond "simple" noisemakers and pillenwerfers (the "bubble curtain" that was first used by German U-boats in World War II) were needed. So the Navy had replaced the five-inch room with preloaded rotary racks between the outer and inner hulls and then filled them with a family of new-concept expendable decoys which the weapons officer could eject in any order or pattern that was desired.

The bubble curtain canisters were a new idea in an improved package. The canisters could now generate more bubbles for a longer period than earlier models, which improved the chances that an active sonar would be blocked off from its original target. The first curtains had been generated by expelling chemically-generated gas from torpedo tubes, but blocking a tube for that purpose meant that you couldn't fire torpedoes out of it, which didn't make submariners very happy. That method had now been replaced by a combination of expendable canisters, for defense at a distance, and by purpose-built bubble generators in the hull that would throw up a wall of air as a last resort against an incoming torpedo.

The T/As, Transponder/Amplifiers, were simple enough in concept, but had been very difficult to properly engineer. Each one carried a short-term power supply, a sonar-signal receiver, a processor, and a signal generator/amplifier. When the package heard an incoming active sonar signal, the processor quickly noted frequency and amplitude and other characteristics and manufactured a pattern that it handed to the generator/amplifier for rebroadcast. The signal that each canister sent out was patterned after the echo of the incoming signal off a large hull. Any torpedo that was pinging as it came in would be presented with an additional target to choose from for every T/A that was ejected that worked properly.

For the benefit of any weapon that was still seeking passively by the time it got in that close, each canister also contained a noisemaker chip that sampled the current signature of its submarine just before it was launched and then repeated that noise for as long as power lasted. The purpose-built noisemakers were much better at that, but it was better than nothing, and the engineers had been proud about having included it.

The effect on the closest incoming torpedo had been, this time, accurately predicted by simulations and firing trials. The homing "brain" was presented with too much input, too many targets against a background of flexible active jamming, and its active sonar was being blocked. It had lost its control wire soon after being fired so it could not ask the parent submarine's fire-control processors for help in sorting the mess out. The torpedo reverted to all-passive homing. This helped some, but there were still too many "targets" against a strong noise background.

The torpedo's intercept director had been told what to do about this, however. Brazilian designers and programmers had commanded it to assume that the strongest noise source was the target's attempt at active jamming, which they assumed would be coming from the target itself. It was the nearest thing to a home-on-jam capability that could be given to a system at this level of sophistication. So the torpedo recognized the loss of a clear target signal and followed the instructions that told it to head for the strongest signal source, clear or not. It was the best attempt at counter-countermeasures that could be built into the weapon.

Move, and counter, and a counter to that. What the torpedo and its designers didn't know was that the last two generations of American-built towed torpedo decoys were equipped with jammer-broadcasters. The active jamming that the torpedo was now driving in on was coming from the Nixie, not the submarine.

* * *

Molniya had been placed in a delicate position from the very beginning.
First there had been the original transit, which had to be circuitous to throw off the Americans and their SOSUS sensor farms and hunter units. Arunov was not sure that it wouldn't have been easier to run straight from the

Greenland-Iceland-United Kingdom gap directly to the destination area. But he also had to agree with higher command. He would almost certainly have picked up an American or British shadow had he done that. Probably more than one, once it was known that he was escorting one of Russia's most advanced missile submarines.

Of course, they would not know that the Typhoon (The NATO name, but fitting nonetheless. Had it been a deliberate choice?) had been extensively modified to carry men instead of missiles. It might not have mattered if they had, given Strannik's and Molniya's course near the eastern coasts of the United States. But what could they have done? Sink them? Have a Coast Guard vessel pull them over for possible marine traffic violations?

Still, it was good to be done with it. Strannik had successfully dropped its special operations groups off and departed for home on its own, leaving Molniya to turn to its second mission, an initial survey of the firing-point area that the American missile submarine would have to be at in order to fire its special missiles. There was also the matter of further validation of the new shrouded propulsor and steerable towed array/Remotely Piloted Vehicle combination that was now housed in the tail-fin pod. Molniya was the first submarine to have these improvements, and Arunov was justifiably pleased with the new capabilities it gave him. The West could ooooh and aaaah about the Sharks, the Akulas, and the prototype of the new Barracuda-class attack units all it liked. Arunov knew which class was the most capable, and he knew which member of that class was the best of the best. Now was the chance to prove it. He looked forward to the challenge.

Molniya had done its survey, made its measurements, and been replaced by another submarine in its turn. The Navy was practically an arm of the GRU for this operation, and GRU had decreed that the Americans must be monitored. Under the circumstances the Navy could only afford to send the best it had to do the watching. That meant Sierra and Akula—none of the others were modem enough for this particular mission. Besides, every other unit was required for the deception operations in the north, so that each designated watcher could slip down toward the South Atlantic and takes its turn in the zone.

In a way it was beneficial, this exercise in long-endurance patrolling. The Navy was gaining invaluable experience from these voyages, and it was an excellent test of new procedures and regulations governing submerged operations that had been put into effect recently. Thus far, Arunov had no complaints. Efficiency had gone up measurably. More importantly, there was a better feel about things now. The crew, if not actually happier, was at least more content about their current lot in life than had been true in the past. Arunov was willing to take that if he couldn't get happiness.

But now they were on station for the second time, and there was this...disquieting...report. They had managed, finally, to isolate the American and (by luck as much as skill) follow him. This had been difficult because of the direct-path range of the missile submarine's sonar, which was at least four thousand meters more than Molniya's best unit. It even reached beyond the first convergence zone, so Arunov couldn't even park his submarine that close. Fortunately, the little robot with its own miniature towed array could be. It could easily hover inside the outer edge of the CZ while its parent hovered twelve hundred meters away, outside the area that bent sounds. It was still inside the direct-path range— American systems were damnably good—but it was far enough to the edge of that capability that Arunov didn't fear detection as long as his crew did their jobs properly.

It was frustrating nonetheless. To do the job he might have to do, Arunov needed to be closer, within thirty-five kilometers at least. It was fortunate under these circumstances that he had something the Americans did not, a standoff weapon that would allow attacks at twice the distance he hovered at now. With cancellation of their Sea Lance program, American submarines—their attack units, that is—were deprived of any standoff weapons at all, since the old SUBROC missiles had carried only nuclear depth charges which had long since been removed from all American naval units of any kind. The American, in other words, had no standoff weapons in their submarines.

Stupid.

Of course, having them and knowing if they should be put to use were two very different things. That was the reason that Arunov was crowded into the sonar center with Ulanovitch, a GRU colonel who had been added to the crew for this mission. A clone of Ulanovitch had been present during every patrol since the beginning of the operation. The written orders said that he was there to 'observe and assist in any way possible.' What that really meant, of course, was another matter. But at the moment Arunov didn't mind having an authority to differ to, especially this time because Ulanovitch had previous experience as a submariner before he had gone to GRU. He was therefore more familiar with the technical capabilities of the submarine and of the men that were on it with him. This was far more than the other 'observers' probably had. Ulanovitch knew at least enough to know when to stay out of the way.

Both of them were listening now, trying along with the sonar operators to make sense of what was going on about sixty thousand meters away.

"The first torpedo is almost to contact," the operator said, "the others—can you hear them, sir?"

"Yes, and the submarine speeding up behind them," Arunov answered. In his mind he was drawing a chart of the battle area. "There's not a conventional unit in the world that can do that. Colonel?"

"It's the one I was briefed about, Captain. There is more power there than we thought.
Someone has made a real breakthrough in the technology—what? Do you hear that?"

"Yes." The American had started his active jamming. "Terminal defenses. Damn! What power!"

"There is no doubt, then," Ulanovitch said.

"No. He may not survive the next few minutes, in fact," Arunov said, "We must take action now if we can do anything at all." He straightened up a little, caning to a kind of attention. "Colonel, my orders say that it is time to request the go-code from you now."

Each day for as long as they had been on station a three-letter code group had been transmitted to Ulanovitch by the Extremely Low Frequency radio system that Russia used for communications with submerged submarines. The letter combination, which took nearly a half-hour to send, corresponded to a code word on a one-time pad that Ulanovitch kept locked in a safe in the radio room. Two days ago that code had changed. Ulanovitch didn't know what that would mean to Arunov, but he knew that he was about to find out.

"Epsilon, Captain," he said, "The word is Epsilon."

Arunov's eyes widened. "Release authorization," he breathed, and then he was angry,

"Fools! They may have waited too long!"

"An explosion, sir!" the operator reported, "A torpedo has detonated!"

Arunov heard the distant detonation in the earphone he had up to his left ear. He put the headset down and headed for the attack center with Ulanovitch close behind, the sound of that far-away burst replaying itself in his mind. His orders were now very clear. Only the exact nature of his actions remained a mystery.

Would he now be attempting a rescue, or would he be taking vengeance on the American's destroyers?

* * *

The Forty-Eight's hit on the Nixie wasn't as resounding or dramatic as J.T. thought it would be. There was only a hint of vibration and a sound that was somewhere between a whomp and a thud. That wasn't unreasonable, though— the Nixie, after all, was—had been trailing over a thousand yards astern. J.T. decided that he should stop reading submarine-combat novels.

"Secure countermeasures. Put the MOSS out, Jim, and get it behind us before the water settles down." Water in the area of the explosion was very unsettled, and would severely degrade the attacker's sonars for a little while. J.T.'s plan depended on that short amount of shielding. "Sonar, keep the tail in. We won't need it for the short term."

"Aye, Captain." They sounded doubtful, not without reason. Without her towed array, Alabama lost sixty critical degrees of sonar coverage. But they would lose it anyway every time they turned, until the array straightened out behind them again. That could take up to five minutes, and J.T. was planning more than one turn in the next five minutes. A two-thousand-foot-long string of hydrophones was not something you did hard maneuvering with. The hull and bow sonars would tell them, would have to tell them, what they needed to know for the next few minutes.

The torpedo track from Bravo One was gone, as was the track of their own nautical-mile-a-minute ADCAP that was homing on that submarine. No problem there. J.T. knew exactly what those rounds were doing. The important ones now were coming from Bravo Two at about two-nine-zero relative, and from Bravo Three, heading almost bow-on at them at a combined closure rate of close to forty-five knots.

"Any idea how MOSS is doing, Jim?" There was no way to keep the control wires intact if the decoy as going to slip behind them.

"I think it's settled in, but I won't know for sure until we turn." He was tapping sonar input to listen for the intelligent decoy as it slipped outside the baffles, the blind rear arc they now had, as they turned. If it was there, adjusting to their course change, he would be confident that it was and would follow them anywhere. If it was there, in fact, he had decided to adopt it as his only son.

Almost seven minutes had now gone by.

* * *

"Sir, we are level at one-six-zero meters," the diving officer reported. They had followed the American's depth change, running along a blue-green string of coherent light at thirty knots, without losing the target. Amazing.

"We've lost the contact, Captain," the sonar operator said.

"Slow to fifteen knots!" Delamadrid snapped, "They've turned away from us." The laser gave the best performance when the large, multibladed propeller of the target was turned toward them. It was, relatively speaking, the "brightest" and most reflective part of the submarines that still used them. The latest American, British, and Russian attack submarines used either shrouded propulsors or water jets, eliminating even that future vulnerability, though the original intent had been to reduce the already very low noise production of these platforms. "We'll reacquire them with sonar." Without the rear aspect available, the laser's range was cut fivefold or more.

Triunfante took less than a minute to slow down. Delamadrid gritted his teeth and fought back a driving impatience for a full minute after that, to give his sonar operators (they would have to find another name for them now) time to gain some idea of what was happening. *The laser is better.* He had been converted. *A blue-green laser system, more fully developed, would give them detection and ranging at any speed. Submarine warfare would be revolutionized. A whole generation of attack submarines could be rendered obsolete at one stroke. We will show the wav...*

"I have something, sir," the operator said, "beyond the...torpedoes, many torpedoes..."

"Fools!" he hissed. He felt less charitable toward the other captains now than he had just minutes before.

"—and...yes, the American. He survived the first strike, sir."

"I expected that," Corte' said, "Their decoys are very capable."

"But they're not invincible!" Delamadrid pulled himself down by force of will. "Lieutenant, give me an intercept bearing."

"Yes sir. Wait...something..."

Delamadrid held himself in patience. It was not the lieutenant's fault, after all.

"Torpedo!"

Corte' automatically looked to his Captain. Delamadrid's face was white.

"High-speed screw, incoming, almost zero relative!" The technician could hear Death coming at them. Fast.

Corte' snapped out of shock first.

"Hard-a-port! Helm, make your bearing zero-nine-zero, full head emergency! Now!"

* * *

The sonar operator on Almirante was not as alert or as lucky as Triunfante*s. Distracted by having to track the American missile submarine through their own high-speed clutter, he didn't shout a warning of the approaching torpedo until it was less than a minute away, about the same time that it started pinging for them with its active sonar.

Almirante's captain did the best he could, perhaps the only thing possible. With the torpedo so close a radical turn away was useless, as were any decoys that would drop behind them as soon as they were launched. So he grasped at inspiration, got four extra knots out of his electric motors, and made a ten-degree course change at what he judged to be the last possible moment.

Even an ADCAP required a finite amount of time to acquire, process, and act on the information it received through its homing head. But it was fast and smart enough to realize that it was missing its target. As Almirante slid by at a combined speed of over eighty knots, the intercept-control unit decided not to circle around in hopes of reacquiring the target. Instead, it shifted to a new salvage-fusing mode that used the passive-homing system as a proximity fuse to detonate the warhead the instant that target noise began to fall off.

That instant occurred a few feet aft of the submarine, when propeller cavitation noise crossed the line of the torpedo's seeker cone. Five hundred and eighty pounds of high explosive went off less than fifty feet away from Almirante's single multibladed propeller. The explosion kicked the submarine's tail sideways and down, throwing men and loose objects in all directions. The propeller and major portions of the top and port-side tailplanes were bent and shredded. Flooding occurred instantly where the propeller shaft entered the pressure hull as rotational and vibrational stresses wriggled and bent the shaft against its seals.

What kept Almirante from getting a large part of its stem blown off was a lack of communication between the designers of the ADCAP warhead. Russian submarines were still being produced that incorporated older Soviet design concepts that were meant to dissipate the energy of torpedo hits before the vital pressure hull could be breached. Because many old Soviet and a few current Russian-designed boats were in the hands of potential

U.S. adversaries, American torpedoes had continued to be modified to increase the probability of a single-strike kill against a Russian-designed hull. The major component of that modification was the addition of a shaped-charge warhead that focused most of its explosive power into a forward-driving "lance" of energy. The only new concept about such warheads was their use on torpedoes—the design had been a part of land warfare for decades. The modification had been made on lightweight torpedoes first. Putting shaped charges into the heavyweight ADCAPs was a more recent modification.

The salvage-fusing system in the intercept director, however, was a newer addition to the warhead fusing system, put in almost as an afterthought. But the designers of the electronics had not yet discussed the consequences of the change with the designers of the warhead when this particular torpedo had been built. The idea of getting some effect from even a near miss was only now being reconciled with the presence of a warhead that sent most of its destructive energy in one direction. So most of the explosive force from the detonation just off Almirante's stern was sent into empty water.

What was left was more than enough to threaten the submarine's life. Water was spraying into the two aftmost compartments, the submarine lost propulsion, and there were casualties (though none were fatal). Even before the captain picked himself up they had lost directional and trim control. There was no way they could continue combat. He was ordering full ballast blows before he was fully on his feet.

The roar of compressed air heralded Almirante's exit from combat. Pumps were switched on as she rose. The leak was not fatal, as long as they kept running. Almirante would probably not permanently re-enter the deep places. The major problem now would be simply getting home.

It was up to the others to carry through now.

* * *

No one on board Alabama heard when Bravo One's mission ended. The missile boat was running almost directly away from that one, and with the towed array retracted, there was no way they could hear what was happening behind them.

But in a way, J.T. didn't care about what had happened to Bravo One. He was too intent on what was happening to them. He had brought his submarine to a heading of one-three-zero, a small adjustment that would bring three sets of tracks into proximity in about another ninety seconds.

"Helm, stand by for course change."

"Aye sir."

Bravo Three was the problem. It had fired two torpedoes during their spasm like almost everyone else, but from farther away. There were three sets heading for them now, from One, Two, and Three. Two's set of one would arrive about thirty seconds ahead of the others. That was still within J.T.'s mental time, but not by much. J.T. wanted badly to avoid to a third encounter with torpedoes. One had been survived. The second was still open to question, but there were better odds for that than for a three in a row. He did not want to risk a third such problem.

Ten minutes had passed.

"Helm, go to two-one-zero." It either works now, or we are dead in sixty seconds. "Jim, see if you can pick up the MOSS, stand by countermeasures. Sonar, we'll lose track on one set of incoming and gain one starboard as we turn. Tag it fast." The computer provided an estimated intercept course even without sonar, but it wouldn't be safe to rely on an estimate now. "Crew address." The last command was to the computer, so it would switch channels. "Everybody, this is the Captain. The next course change might be violent. Make sure you're braced for it. That is all." Those three words told the computer to cut off the crew address channel. "Helm—Mr. Petersen." He waited for a response.

"Yes sir?" Petersen didn't take his eyes off his indicators. He wouldn't do that without direct orders or under certain other emergency conditions.

"Listen carefully. The next change I order for will be to a zero degree heading and zero velocity, all stop. Okay so far?" There's plenty of time to break it down. There's plenty of time.

"Yes sir." There was a question in the voice. J.T. had no problem with that.

"You need to bring us there as quickly as possible. I need the tightest possible turn while you kill velocity. You throw out the manual for this one, Mister. If you can get her to pivot around her longitudinal axis, you do it.

You may exceed safety limits by my authority and according to my direct order." It was in the log now. If something went wrong and they were alive for him to do it J.T. would take responsibility for it. That was his job. "Do you understand?"

"Sir, at the next course change I will come to heading zero-zero-zero and a complete halt in the shortest possible space and time, even if such a maneuver exceeds recommended maneuver safety limits. I turn us around and stop us as instantly as possible, in other words, sir, by many means up to and including divine intervention if I can get it."

"Exactly." *Plenty of time to get it right.* "Now start thinking about it, and stand by."

"Aye sir." *What the hell is he UP to? Exceed safety limits-damn. How do I do that? Okay, this is the biggest dirt-track racer in the universe...*

Alabama turned ninety degrees. J.T. steadied himself against a gentle inertial tug and kept his eyes on the chart display. One set of torpedo tracks was replaced by a dashed line as the table's computer made its predictions.

"I've got it!" Bearkiller said, "It's adjusting! Line astern!" The MOSS system was sophisticated, but not enough so that he had not wondered if it would do what it was told this time. He would now adopt it. The wife would understand—if he were alive to explain everything to her later.

Thirty seconds to initial impact now.

"Pinging! Somebody's pinging!"

The new set of tracks on their starboard side appeared on the display. The torpedo tracks from Bravo Three changed course a little. Away from them.

"Countermeasures now, no jamming. Helm, triple-zero and all stop! Brace and pray, gentlemen!"

Deception or death, destruction or survival.

<u>Now</u>.

* * *

Cacador's captain took the news of his dangerously-low battery reserves with a sense of relief that he took care to hide from certain of the more fanatic nationalists on the crew. It was not that he was not patriotic. It was that he could see no benefit to his country from all of this. Sinking the American, killing men, threatening to kill more—for what? America would not allow them atomic weapons. They would not. What did the Leadership think? There was madness here. Had not the Argentine thing, the thing that was whispered about but never spoken aloud, warned them? Had not Iraq warned them?

He had done his duty. He had made an honest attempt. He was also glad to go home. Let the others have their illusion of glory. Delamadrid would learn, if he survived. He was welcome to it.

He issued the necessary orders, and Cacador turned for home and started upward toward snorkel depth.

* * *

"Bring the remote into trail," Arunov ordered as soon as he entered the attack center,
"Helm, come to one-zero-zero and give me turns for thirty knots. Sonar, am I correct in assuming that the tail will keep up?" It would be very counterproductive to get there fast but lose their best sonar in the process. The drive motors on the robot were supposed to lessen the strain of speed and be able to actively adjust to hard maneuvers that might otherwise snap the array off.

"Correct, Captain. We will retain some sense even at speed. I estimate a range drop of fifty to seventy percent."

Not as good as the American's best, but still very good. The engineers had done their work well.

"Very good. Marsilov, what is our tube-load status?"

"Four Eighties in the standard tubes, two Six-Fives and two Sixteens in the oversize tubes," Marsilov answered instantly.

The ET-80B was the standard twenty-one-inch (533 millimeter) torpedo, able to home independently or be wire-guided. It was the less-capable Russian version of the Mark Forty-Eight. The Type Sixty-Five was a newer torpedo fired from the twenty-six-inch (650 millimeter) torpedo tubes that Molniya had four of. The Sixty-Five was relatively slow as torpedoes ran, but it had a range of over fifty miles and a unique homing system— it followed the wakes created by the target's propeller (if it had one), using a powerful active sonar only in the final stages of the attack. The original model had only been effective against surface ships. There had been modifications since then. There was a good possibility that those improvements would be tested today.

"Good." Arunov had second thoughts. "Helm, cancel previous order. Ahead one-third, heading one-zero-zero." That would give them about twenty knots. They would keep their full sonar capability that way.

"Acknowledged, Captain."

"What kind of solution do we have on the Brazilians?"

"We have a pair of bearing-only possibilities," Marsilov said, "We are sure that neither is the American, but that's all we've got on them at this time."

"Good enough, I think. Prepare a Sixteen. We'll fire at the first direct contact, I think, and let the torpedo conduct an autonomous search."

The SS-N-16 (NATO designation: Surface-to-Surface-Naval-series Sixteen) was a torpedo-carrying missile with a range of up to fifty miles. It would rise to the surface, ignite its rocket motor, arc over to the target area, and release a lightweight torpedo that would (hopefully) then find and at least disable its submerged target. The nearest American equivalent no longer existed. SUBROC had carried a nuclear depth charge on its rocket, and so had been removed with all other seaborne nuclear weapons (strategic ballistic missiles excepted) by Presidential order in 1992. Russia also had a nuclear version, the SS-N-15, but they had also been removed from the submarines. Tactical nuclear weapons had lost a lot of their popularity in the last decade of the twentieth century.

For a moment Marsilov looked as if he were unsure of his captain's sanity. Arunov could understand this. He was sure that the somewhat insane joy that had sprung up inside of him suddenly was evident in his eyes or on his face. Suddenly, there was a happiness about actually engaging in real combat and firing real weapons at live, resisting opponents. He knew that he might wonder about it later, but for now there was work to do.

"Is this for real?" Marsilov asked.

Arunov smiled. "You read the orders. The action code has come directly from our GRU shepherd himself. The wolf is removing his sheep disguise now. I just hope it hasn't been done too late."

"One-zero-zero degrees and ahead one third, Captain," the helmsman reported.

Molniya started its run-in and prepared to throw thunderbolts.

* * *

To a torpedo that was homing passively, an active sonar going off was more attractive than catnip was to Felix Domesticus. Bravo Two's torpedoes went active first as passive input crossed certain preprogrammed thresholds. As soon as that happened both other sets of torpedoes discarded whatever tracks they had on Alabama and went for their own kind, even though the big missile submarine was stirring up large volumes of water as it performed the underwater equivalent of a car swapping ends.

It wasn't so much like a skid as it was a slow-motion tail slide—a matter of convincing the stem to move momentarily faster than the bow until the boat had performed a submerged one-eighty. It wasn't a totally impossible concept. Most modem submarines had no trouble turning so quickly and tightly that tail slides were not at all unheard of. Some control systems had rudder/turn limiters built in to prevent just such an occurrence, in fact. That kind of response helped, but it didn't lessen the need for the helmsman to have a great deal of creativity, not only to imagine the maneuver to begin with, but also to come up with the series of finely coordinated and apparently reckless control inputs that relied more on feel and intuition than on instrument feedback to time correctly. A marked absence of conservatism in outlook was also an asset.

It was fortunate that J.T. was being served at that moment by someone young enough to be adventuresome, intelligent enough to figure out what he had to do, and an avid follower of dirt-track car racing. In a series of actions that began with a brief counter-steering movement (and a prayer that the actuators and structure would take the stress) and a "blip" on the throttle, he worked the tail into a single starboard-side oscillation, then threw the wheel hard over to port, throttled completely back to zero revolutions, and activated sets of electrically-powered thrusters that were normally used only for ultra-slow movement or fine adjustments when docking. The result was not so much a skid or tail slide, but it was a far tighter turn than Alabama's designers and manual-writers had ever intended should be done. The stem actually did overtake the bow briefly, in fact, so skidding cars and flat-spinning airplanes were not such inaccurate analogies to what the submarine did, even if she didn't do it nearly as fast as those smaller vehicles could.

The maneuver was not without risk, of course. Eighteen-thousand-plus tons of submerged submarine moving at twenty knots generated considerable momentum, and the laws of physics could not be even temporarily suspended for their benefit. The inertia of the missile boat could not be broken at precisely the same time as the inertia of everything inside of it, namely men and unsecured equipment. There was also the matter of Alabama turning momentarily broadside to her direction of movement. Pressure on the sail and control surfaces made her want to lean away from the direction she was going. Her mass and that same inertial tendency to remain in one state of motion made her want to stay upright and even tip back the other way instead. Woman that she was, she looked first at one alternative, and then at the other, and finally decided that she wouldn't change her mind after all. She remained upright, rocking just a little while the helmsman made fine adjustments to the heading and stabilized things with short bursts from the thrusters.

He had successfully driven his submarine through the moral equivalent of a crash-back, a sudden-stop maneuver that was as likely to kill engines as it was speed, and he had combined that with a turn normally manageable only by racing hydroplanes and, maybe, Spruance-class destroyers.

Not only that, but as far as anyone could tell, nothing had broken off, nothing had come apart, and the submarine wasn't sinking.

"...Thine is the kingdom-the-power-and-the-glory-Amen." J.T. finished, watching the chart display do a fine imitation of a fractal geometry illustration as the sonars were overwhelmed by the massively stirred-up ocean around them. He was gripping the edge of the table so hard his fingers hurt.

Alabama's unlikely maneuver combined with the countermeasures canisters that had been ejected to create a tremendous disturbance in the "minds" of the incoming torpedoes.

The MOSS had also darted away, shifting to an automatic evading-submarine maneuver routine as soon as the first high-frequency pings had touched it, drawing two torpedoes after its amplified echo. The remaining incoming torpedoes, two sets of two each, looked at the wall of noise caused by turbulence, bubble canisters, and noisemakers on the one hand and at the easier-to-understand information provided by the mobile decoy and their terminal-homing fellows behind it on the other hand, and voted for what was easier to understand. The altered course and drove for the MOSS at high speed.

The MOSS had accelerated to its highest speed, equivalent to full emergency power of the submarine it was imitating, and turned up and back, mimicking an effort to get behind the nearest set of torpedoes and out of their cone of acquisition. The effort gained it another twenty seconds of life, after which one of the Forty-Eights defied all probability and actually made contact with the torpedo-sized decoy.

Not only that, but the contact was hard enough to trigger its detonator.

* * *

"Captain," the sonarman said, "there's something you need to listen to."

Arunov and Marsilov looked at each other and picked up headphones to plug in to the nearest remote feed.

Chaos.

"Is this in the zone or direct-path?" Arunov asked. They had just entered the nearest convergence zone on their way to the battle.

"A combination, I believe, sir. The explosions are of course direct." Loud noises could carry for amazing distances in water.

"Damn," Arunov said, "and damn again. They waited too long! This did not have to happen. Marsilov, hold the launch. We'll wait until we have a clearer picture of what's happening. We'll have to re-evaluate once we're at direct-path range."

* * *

A Mark Forty-Eight ADCAP is faster and smarter than the Mark Forty-Eight it is derived from. The one following Triunfante was no exception to the designer's intentions, ignoring every decoy they dropped and boring straight in at twice their speed.

"There is still a chance," Delamadrid said, "We must wait for the last moment and turn into it. Helmsman! On my command, make your sharpest turn to two-four-zero. Wait for my word!"

"Turn to two-four-zero on cormmand, aye Captain," the helmsman repeated. He was sweating, but thank God he wasn't trembling. He didn't want to die today.

"When we make the turn, Corte', drop more decoys," Delamadrid said, "The turbulence and noise will distract it until we're past the cone of detection." He had gambled, again. He had made another mistake. He had lost, and his country had lost with him. *No!* There had to be a way. *They are not invincible! They are not!* There had to be a way.

He fought the combination of dispair and frustration down, desperate to remain alert for the moment of action. One hand holding an earphone on, one hand gradually tightening around the edge of a control panel, he waited.

PINGPINGPINGPING...

"Active homing!"

"Stand by!" It was a roar of defiance. One mile. He knew the numbers as well as anyone. Closing rate...two minutes...one thousand four, one thousand five, one thousand six...

At about forty seconds:

"NOW! Hard over, Helm!"

Triunfante darted around and back like a fish startled by the sudden appearance of a predator, leaving troubled water and prerecorded submarines in its wake. The predator in turn noted the change of bearing and characteristics of the echoes it was closing on and the addition of new noise sources, ran everything through its Lot Four Mod Two-A fire control processors, and decided that it had not been fooled. The ADCAP adjusted course and drove at Triunfante's starboard side from almost a ninety-degree angle.

Halfway beyond thirteen minutes after it had entered actual combat for the first time in its history, Triunfante took a five hundred and eighty-eight pound, directed-energy warhead on its starboard side, just forward of the attack center.

PAST

"One who wishes to unravel the confused and entangled
does not grasp the entire skein... Strike at a salient or
unprotected place."
Sun Pin, a descendant of Sun Tzu

"I...will...be...damned," Captain Aurthur John Simenson said for the hundredth time in just that hour, "I...will...just...be...damned."

He was looking at, and recording, the single most extraordinary sight he had ever seen maybe period, much less through a submarine periscope. So extraordinary was the sight he was seeing and recording that it had kept him locked to his main periscope for almost an hour, oblivious to everything except any warning that might come from his radar detectors and, in the last few minutes, a growing ache and stiffness in his legs.

"You getting this, Irwin?"

"I see it," his executive officer said, "but I do not believe it."

Everyone who wasn't absolutely required to do something else in the control center was staring at the low-light-TV image of a beached Russian Typhoon-class nuclear ballistic missile submarine. Or rather, what was formerly a nuclear ballistic missile submarine. Like Simenson's current command, this one had obviously been converted to a special operations unit delivery platform.

This explained why the world's largest submersible vehicle, as heavy as some World War
II aircraft carriers and just as visually imposing, had come to be beached, its massive bow about three hundred yards from where water met sand. The sail was currently in full view and its decks were awash at about the same level as the tide.

"They're not gonna believe this," Irwin said, "They are not going to believe this."

At the base of the conning tower and on the extensive foredeck, hatches were open.
From what should have been a missile compartment, men and equipment poured out, purposeful ants coming out of a mechanical nest.

"I'll...be...damned..."

Sunfish had discovered the Russian by the purest of coincidences, detecting him in passing as she was going out of the very same cove after using it to deliver her own SEALs.
Sunfish was officially registered as a Department of Defense research vessel. She actually did do research, continually looking for better ways to deliver special operations units to their objectives and to retrieve them

without detection after they had performed their missions. Her own original mission had been to deliver Poseidon missile warheads to targets in Eastern Europe and what used to be the Soviet Union as part of NATO's strategic nuclear reserve. As part of START Two, the former Lafayette-class submarine had been retired. Her missile tubes had either been filled with ballast or been converted to house and launch Swimmer Delivery Vehicles and their associated swimmers, and she had undergone an extensive refit that had equipped her for a new role in submarine life. Then she had gone undercover, though with a name that used to belong to a Sturgeon-class nuclear attack submarine. Simenson sometimes wondered if that hadn't been a Freudian slip. Like her unbelievable Russian counterpart on the beach after her, she delivered men now instead of missiles. It was sometimes a little hard for her captain to decide which load could be more ultimately destructive.

"This is so...weird," someone said.

There was a sizeable contingent offloading, by the looks of it. Simenson could understand why they had beached the whale instead of using SDVs as Sunfish had.

And they were apparently in a hurry. What's the game, here?

"Anybody remember what the satellite coverage is here?" Simenson asked. He lifted a foot and flexed it back and forth. He would have to sit down soon, whether he wanted to or not.

Reconnaissance satellite delivery had improved somewhat, but only somewhat, since the lift crisis in the late eighties. The space station was operating, but it was over a year behind schedule. It was still called Freedom, but there was no substance to the name. It was strait-jacketed by its ties to an aging shuttle group (four shuttles do not a fleet make) that still only worked about half the time NASA wanted it to. The new Heavy Lift Vehicle had finally done a heavy lift, the first operational launch having been hijacked by DOD so it could replace a KH-12 with the bigger, better, more sophisticated, thus more expensive KH-14A. That was something, but HLV was still a long way from steady operations. The second HLV launch, in fact, had been used to put a very large emergency storage facility up where the Freedom crew could get to it in case the shuttles quit again before the National Space Plane was up and running. That way, it was hoped, America's premier manned space effort wouldn't have to be abandoned before it had a chance to justify its many-multi-billion-dollar existence. Smaller satellites were still going up from Vandenberg, of course, but they weren't "eyesats" for the most part, and until either NAS, HLV, or a possible Shuttle Two (depending on X-30 flight tests results, an emergency buy of European Space Agency hardware was being contemplated) was running consistently, the photo interpreters and the people that overworked them would still be unhappy about gaps in the coverage.

"We may have one around, but even if it's here the angle's not gonna be right for them to pick this one up," someone answered, "Anything we got handy's going to be looking somewhere else, anyway." Any orbital eyes would be focused elsewhere, watching for any Brazilian response to what America was doing about their bombs.

"Okay," Simenson said, finally taking himself away from the periscope, "Take over here, Irwin. My guess is they'll do whatever they're doing until the tide cones back in. Keep close watch on ESM—" The Typhoon was not using radar, and Simenson didn't think their surface-search set would pick up the 'scope if they were, but there was no use taking chances. "—and tape everything. When they're through for the day, we'll decide whether to send it up the beam immediately or slide out past their watchdog first." There was a Russian attack boat patrolling in deeper water at the edge of direct-path range. Sunfish had slipped in between it and the Typhoon as dangerously close as she could to observe the operation—there were at best twelve fathoms between keel and bottom now. It was no place for a nuclear submarine to be.

"I'd love to see the looks on whoever's face when they see this stuff," the executive officer said as he took up the periscope watch, "I wonder what they'll do?"

"Not only that," the senior chief said as he watched the periscope's TV monitor, "I wonder how they're planning to refloat that sumbitch when they're ready to take it home?"

* * *

Vanadim was pleased. Strannik was performing wonderfully in his first operation mission. The enhanced structure of the bow had worked according to specifications, allowing him to run his submarine almost onto the beach like some 26,000-ton landing craft. A good thing, too. It would have taken him over two weeks to offload the men and supplies necessary for this mission using mini-submarines and boats from offshore. As it was they were ahead of schedule. Now the only question was whether the enhanced buoyancy systems and special motors and anchor-drag units would work like they had in tests to put the submarine back in deep water where it belonged. The modifications were useful, yes, and necessary now, but Vanadim would still prefer to stand off and use more traditional insertion methods.

Colonel Suvorov climbed up to join the captain and the deck watch on the conning tower. Suvorov was Spetsnaz, commander of the ground forces element of this mission. It was said that he was extremely tough even for Spetsnaz, the more so because he survived in that dangerous group of men and women with a name that had been used by a GRU man who had supposedly defected some time before the end of the Cold War. This defector had written many books full of lies and exaggerations about the Soviet military and intelligence arms, using the pen-name of Suvorov. Undoubtedly, the Colonel of the same name had been given more than a little trouble about the coincidence. He had, in fact, killed because of it, according to rumor.

"An excellent night, Colonel," Vanadim said, and meant it. Hot, yes, but also clear, with breezes off the ocean as compensation for the heat. Vanadim had never been south of the equator before. The stars in the southern sky fascinated him.

"I agree, Captain, I do agree," Suvorov said conversationally, and then lowered his voice. "My scouts have confirmed it. Someone was here before us."

Vanadim looked around automatically. "Who could it have been? Smugglers?" Brazil's economic turmoil had created a thriving black market. But this cove was not in reasonable proximity to anything important, and was thought to be too far away from the Mexican and American coastal loading points to be used for smuggling or drug running. It had been chosen as their landing point for that very reason.

Suvorov shook his head. "They did well at covering their tracks, but we did find one boot print a couple of hundred meters inland. I believe they are American, Captain, probably their own Special Forces, SEALs or Green Berets."

Vanadim was alarmed. *Green Berets? Here?* But Suvorov didn't look very excited about it. But then, he was Spetsnaz. He would look forward to such a contest. Vanadim carefully took his concern out of his voice and expression.

"Was this expected, Colonel? Does it affect our mission?" Or threaten his submarine? Vanadim knew that Western submarines similar to his existed. Had one of them been used recently? Was it still here? They had better sonars, and more than enough torpedoes to cause fatal damage to Strannik, massive and double-hulled as he was. Was it, perhaps, observing them now from offshore? *Don't panic.*

"No, not expected," Suvorov answered, "but it does make some sense." He rested chin on fist, leaning against the top of the sail, and looked out over the dark forest. "It is somehow in support of their bombardment mission, I think. Observation or targeting, probably both. Perhaps even a back-up of some kind, in case the strike mission does not completely destroy the target." He stood up, assuming a loose parade-rest posture. "It is the purest of coincidences that we chose the same point for insertion. I wouldn't expect another accident like this in a hundred years."

"How long have they been gone from here?" It was obvious that Suvorov didn't believe that any of the Americans had remained behind.

"We can't tell. My trackers aren't accustomed to these conditions." It required specific knowledge of the soil and environment of an area before a tracker could give more than the most general estimates of print wear over time. Tracks in Eastern Europe or Siberia did not weather at all like tracks made in South America. "It is a least several hours, however. I'm pushing patrols out further just to make sure."

Vanadim relaxed a little more. If they had been put here that long ago, then it was likely that their parent submarine, if that's what they had used, was long gone away also. And, of course, Molniya was still on watch off the coast. They were more than likely safe, then, as long as the camouflage covers were properly maintained over the parts of Strannik that were still exposed at high water.

* * *

"They're setting up caches," Captain John Thompson told Simenson after only fifteen minutes, "It's the most reasonable explanation."

He sat in the officer's mess with his second-in-command and every Navy officer that wasn't on watch, reviewing sane of the tapes that Sunfish had made before the Russian stopped operations for the day and covered herself up with cloth and high water.

"They're mounting an operation somewhere in the interior," the SEAL commander continued, "They don't have our ability to resupply by air at this distance, and they don't want to involve whatever local nets they've got, even on a small scale. Notice how many didn't go back to the sub when they buttoned up?"

There were embarrassed looks from the Navy men. They had all been too awed by what the Russians had done with the submarine to notice how many of them had gone and come back or not.

"Less than half," Thompson said, "They left security and some 'mules' under that tree cover. And if they're not packing loads farther down whatever trail they're planning to push a team through, I'll resign my commission, Captain."

"That means you're willing to put it on the broadcast." It was not a question.

"Sure. When are you going to broadcast?"

"We're condensing the visuals now." Sunfish was very well equipped to do initial information processing—her secondary task was intelligence collecting. "Before we go back in to check on them again we'll lock the satellite and send it up the beam." A powerful laser, focused up a dedicated periscope, would lock on to a relay satellite that would transmit by the DOD orbital network to the National Reconnaissance Office for evaluation and analysis. The laser was less detectable than even microwave radio, unjammable, and it carried exponentially more information than any radio could. It would still take over a minute to transfer all of the images. Digital picture transmission gobbled gigabits faster than the Cookie Monster went through oatmeal-chocolate-chip.

"Have you got any idea, even a guess, about what they're doing specifically, Captain?" one of the other officers asked.

Thompson shook his head. "No idea. I think it relates to the stuff they're doing up north—"

"Distraction," Simenson said, "Get us looking that way while they slipped they're people in here."

"Looks like it," Thompson said, "I've got no idea what the link is. I thought you guys were the brains here." It was a running joke. Thompson had a Master's degree in Political Science—which he occasionally referred to as a contradiction in terms. He had somehow obtained it in between penetration missions around the Murmansk base that were still being run until just a few years ago. He believed in intelligent soldiers so strongly that almost every SEAL under his command already had or was actively working on a college degree of some kind. Even within the special operations community, which couldn't afford to have anything resembling a dumb grunt, Thompson's men were exceptionally intelligent and well-educated.

"There might be a way to find out, though," Thompson said when the odd chuckle had died away, "I want to add a request to that report, Captain, if you think we can put somebody on the beach behind them when they pull out." Simenson had veto power over any landing operation. It was, after all, his submarine.

"You want to put a tail on them."

"Yes. Jimmy, go get Preacher and Rock-On for me, will you?" As his second went to run the errand, Thompson said, "There's more than enough spares to form a tracker team. The two he's bringing, two more, light loads, emphasis on rations so they won't have to forage. A satellite transmitter for reports. If they need it, we can have Batman drop to them on the way out after they run for Scarlet."

"Might be better to do separate flights," someone said.

"I'm not sure," Thompson responded, "This one's off the top of my head right now."

"I like it," Simenson said, "But Scarlet Cobra has priority. If there's a problem, we may have to cut them loose."

"Understood," Thompson said, "and they'll know that before they say go or not. They'll be able to manage if they have to, Captain. I can back them with a couple of men fresh out of jungle-survival school, and Preacher—come in, Sergeant. Have a seat. We've got something to show you."

The two men who entered and sat down illustrated both the rule and the exception about Special

Forces personnel. Rock-On was the rule—average height, medium build, not overly muscled but very strong with what he had. There was a wiry toughness to him. He moved easily and efficiently, kept a smile or grin within reach at all times, and was always pushing his hair to the limits of regulation length. His nickname came from his tendency to treat the classical music he was most fond of like other's treated the popular rock of the day.

Preacher was the exception to Rock-On's rule. He was very big and very muscular, taller and wider and generally larger than anyone should be who spends very much time on submarines. He had, at one time, considered taking the college-to-NFL-football path to prosperity. A few schools had taken serious looks at him, in fact. Not going that way had been through decision and not circumstance. He was extremely hard, also. He lifted weights with sufficient intensity to tax the facilities at most of the bases he stayed at, and had placed respectably in regional level competitions in both powerlifting and bodybuilding when he was inclined to compete. He filled his battledress out in an intimidating way that made most people overlook a more than adequate level of speed and endurance that balanced his room-dominating physique.

Preacher's nickname derived itself from his seminary background. He was apt to tell questioners that he had been sent from seminary to SEALs as punishment for his sins, but the truth was more ordinary than that. A year into his theological education, he had simply become doubtful about where he should be and what he should be doing. The wondering had led him from seminary to the Navy and from there he had finally made his way into a SEAL team, where he had been now for almost close to five years. And while he did believe that God had put him there, he didn't believe that it was for punishment. He also didn't know exactly why he was where he was, either, though he felt certain that God would eventually tell him. Somehow. He was content to wait for that revelation as long as it came before he had to choose between getting out and going back to school or staying in and becoming an officer. He didn't want to choose between the lesser of those two evils on his own.

"I hope it's a good movie, Captain," Rock-On said, "You interrupted Preacher's workout."

"Hell, Rock-On," Thompson's second replied, "anything interrupts Preacher's workout, eating and sleeping included."

"Not to worry, Sergeant," Thompson said in case the regular navy started to get unsettled, "Look at this for a little while, and then we may have a job for you."

"No problem, Cap—holy shi—sorry, sirs," Rock-On said as he registered what was on the monitor. He became silent and watched.

"Preacher's been through Scout/Sniper training at Quantico," Thompson told Simenson while his men watched TV, "He's the best in the group with a shoulder arm, and he can go so quiet it's scary."

Simenson looked at the designated noncom with doubt in his mind. Scout/Sniper? The man is huge. The other one, maybe, but... Then he noticed how they were both sitting as they watched the recording of the Typhoon on the beach. Neither man was moving. At all. You almost couldn't tell that they were breathing. It wasn't a conscious stillness, maintained only by force of will, either. It was normal, automatic, natural...frightening.

Simenson looked at Thompson. Thompson was smiling.

"I've seen them do that for an hour at a time," Thompson said, "Rock-On usually breaks first. He's the hyper one of the pair."

"I believe you. Son of a bitch I believe you. You'll put them on trail?"

"With the other two," Thompson said, "just to know where everybody's going. No interference, just observation."

"I'm with you," Simenson said, "I'll add my recommendation."

"Thank you. Sergeant?" Thompson noted the way that both of them turned only their heads to look at him. Jimmy must have set them up on the way here. Good idea. They were making the normal Navy people nervous without than knowing why they were nervous.

"It's the first team. Isn't it, Captain?" Rock-On asked.

"We think so, Sergeant. You interested in a little field trip?"

"*Spetsnaz,*" Preacher said, giving the word the proper Russian pronunciation. He'd been beating his head against the wall of that language for two years now. He was thinking about torturing himself with Japanese next. "When do we lock-out, Captain?"

Thompson smiled. It was inconceivable that they would not volunteer. "We've got to get permission and settle the details. This one's off the cuff so far. I'd say forty-eight hours, maybe a little less."

"Make sure they know the downside," Simenson said. It wasn't supposed to amaze him anymore the way that these men volunteered so quickly and casually for this kind of thing. But it did.

Two heads turned toward him. For a moment he felt as if the pairs of eyes in those heads were classifying him, as one would classify a leaf or an insect pinned to a card. He knew it had to be a deliberate display. He knew that it was calculated to impress him. He knew that it was working.

Rock-On smiled. "Ah, hell, Captain, there's always a downside. But it could have been worse. We could've been tapped for Scarlet Cobra." He looked back at the monitor. "That would have meant we'd of missed the fun back here, now wouldn't it?"

* * *

Ivan entered Gregoriy's office unannounced
(though the door was open), dropped a
packet on to Gregoriy's desk, and sat down. The desk was
clean. Gregoriy had made sure to keep it that way for
several days now.

"They started twelve hours ago local time," Ivan
said, "We have cast the dice." The mission group could
not now be recalled. They could be extracted at their
own decision, but that emergency call or the one
indicating success would be the only communication they
would make.

"It has begun," Gregoriy agreed ritually, "What is
the estimate?"

"A week at best, two at worst. Ten days is the
favorite number." Ivan looked at the packet. "The backup
groups are already in place. Your arrangements are
updated?"

A mixed group of Spetsnaz was now in Rio de
Janiero, spreading themselves out in groups of two to
four. Supported by the Brazilian residencies, they would
be available with vehicles and light weapons to assist the
mission group at certain stages of the operation. That not
required, they doubled as direct support for Gregoriy

during the second and third stages, and were responsible for operational security as well.

"I can leave within the hour." Only Gregoriy's clothing remained here. Everything else he needed had already been shipped to Rio.

Ivan nodded at the packet. "Tickets, documents, money. You know the rest. You're sure you want me to keep the Macintosh?"

"Most certainly," Gregoriy said, "I intend to get something more powerful this time.
I'm thinking about an IBM-compatible unit. You're welcome to it. You'll like the game section, I think." He stood up.

Ivan did too. "Very well. Thank you, then." They shook hands. "Good luck, Gregoriy."

"She had certainly better be or I'll break both her legs," Gregoriy said, "Success to us all, Ivan. And goodbye."

* * *

They were not worried about getting to the target within any specific time frame. The information they were after would probably be there no matter how long it took them to get there.

Probably. There was enough doubt that team carried Western weapons and equipment, wore Western military uniforms, and carried identification that marked them as either European or Canadian. If what they were after was not there, any possible survivors would think they were a rival faction or terrorists or maybe even an American special-forces unit. If what they were after was there, then they would remain in the area long enough to make sure that there were no survivors. That was the plan, at least.

There were sixteen. All were Russian, though none had any features that anyone could identify as Russian. Spetsnaz had an extraordinary diversity of ethnic and racial backgrounds to choose from. And choose they did, with general disregard for anything other than the requirements of the service and the mission. Background of any kind was unimportant to Spetsnaz except where it fitted the task that the soldier had to carry out. These were all soldiers. All Spetsnaz.

Even the women. There were two of them in the group, taken from the special-purpose units that were maintained. They were both fit, conditioned, coordinated, intelligent athletes who competed at sports even while they trained at being soldiers, saboteurs, and assassins.

Morana was one of those special ones. She was called Hunter in her unit. Nearly everyone eventually developed or was given a use-name like that. In her other life she was

Morana Ivana Alexandrova. That was her other life, though. Here she was Hunter, given that name because of certain talents she displayed. The use-name was usually related to something like that. Two of the men in the team she was with were called Cutter and Breaker because of their skills with blades and in Sambo—a Russian grappling art that combined aspects of Judo and Western wrestling. The other woman on the team was called Dolphin, because she was a competitive swimmer and a trainer in SCUBA and underwater demolitions. Dolphin had been on cable missions, where minisubs had carried divers to plant taps in underwater telephone cables.

Hunter's sport had been gymnastics. She was a second-level competitor, an alternate for any teammate who fell injured or sick during competition. When not called on to compete, which was most of the time, she was free to move about the cities that her team visited. Scouting. Learning directions, customs, languages, habits, how to move and how to be.

Hunter spoke English and German and was working on French. She practiced languages constantly during her team's trips and on tactical exercises. She never lacked opportunities to do that with native men who were constantly drawn to her beauty. She was beautiful—she retained a gymnast's build, slender and muscular and filled out in all of the very best places. Though that maturity of form had retired her from competition some time ago, she still travelled with the team as a coaching assistant because Spetsnaz had even more use for her now that she was so much more attractive to the men who might one day become her targets.

Hunter was an assassin. A decade ago, when her military training had begun, her primary targets had been European leaders, politicians and businessmen and commanders whom she would have killed at short range with light weapons or poison or just her hands. Her potential target list had expanded since then, as had the means she could employ to kill them. Beneath auburn hair what was tucked away now underneath a camouflage cap, knowledge of long arms and explosives had been filed away with the prior expertise with knife and pistol and toxins. She was one of two snipers assigned to the mission team, in fact. She was pleased with that, and with the rifle she had been given to fulfill the role with.

It was an excellent weapon, a Heckler and Koch sniper rifle that fired a 7.62 millimeter steel-jacked bullet over much longer ranges and with much greater accuracy that the Russian-made weapon she usually employed. No one on the team was carrying anything Russian. The close assault group had been equipped with MF5SDs made by the same company that produced her rifle, and the support group carried M16A2s and SAWs, American-built weapons. Even the demolition team's plastic explosive was US-made Composition Four. No one could be allowed to think that the operation had been staged from so far across the Atlantic Ocean as this one had been.

Hunter marveled at the terrain they travelled through, at the vegetation and the animals, even at the insects. Everything here, even as close to the coastline and development as they were, was so colorful and bright, much more that pictures from above the tree canopies had even hinted at. It was a lush and varied environment, with everything seemingly growing wild all over. It intoxicated the part of her that wasn't occupied with staying on the correct compass heading. The place made her nearly drunk with beauty.

The beauty of the place was a bonus. Hunter would have come on this mission even if it were to be conducted completely within an unlighted cave, not simply because she had been ordered to, though with Spetsnaz the order was enough. She was there for the second part of the mission, the part that would be hers alone. That was the real, primary, most important reason that Hunter was with this group in the forest. She was here for the promise of what would happen after the first phase was complete.

Then would come the part that she was really looking forward to.

* * *

"Yo. Rev'run," Rock-On whispered, "They're moving."

Preacher sighed, a mixed expression of relief and regret, and slid the little Bible, the other source of his nickname, into the pocket beside a jungle-survival guide that was there for review and in case they needed something to start a fire with. Then he slid into position beside his partner and focused the rifle's scope on the Spetsnaz team that was crossing two hundred yards downstream of their position.

He was using an M21 on this mission instead of the modified Winchester 700 that was normally employed by a Marine sniper. The M21 was actually an Army system (though the Marines tried not to think about that), an M-14 with a new barrel, match-tuned trigger and action, and a three-to-nine power telescopic sight that could be removed and remounted repeatedly without losing its zero. He had chosen the system because it was semi-automatic and capable of full-auto fire in an emergency. The added volume might be needed if something went down. There was more than Spetsnaz that could threaten them here, and there was none of the support that Marine sniper teams could usually count on. His four-man was purely it and it alone if things went down—no artillery, no air support, no backup units, no front line or firebase to run to. Just them, their weapons, and the grace of God or other selected deity.

And sixteen Spetsnaz troopers who were armed to the proverbial teeth.

A bad time to be nagged again by the question of what you're going to do with the rest of your life.

He focused the scope on each member of the Russian team as they splashed across ankle-to-knee-deep water by ones and twos. The first two were already across, forming the baseline of a perimeter that each man behind them would expand until the rear guard came over. By the time everyone was in place across the stream, they would be in march formation, flankers out, second in command just back of the point, commander and radioman in the center. Their radioman was carrying a satellite-feed set similar to the one Slider was packing for Preacher's team, though Preacher would bet that his worked differently than theirs did. They were still using tight-beam radio for their communications. It was probably a copy of an

American unit. The GRU had some older models in stock. Still be nice to get a look at it.

He switched to the next man going across. He wanted to get to know these people well, to understand what they were thinking and feeling. It was easier to track someone that you understood.

So—stay in? Move up like the Captain? Go out in a few months—seminary, maybe, college, maybe, business, maybe. There were plenty of doors that would open to an ex-SEAL. Did he want to do that kind of work? Maybe a mix—he'd have to do something outside anyway if he was in school. Call it a different kind of summer job. There was also the possibility of moving within the service. Perhaps he had simply been, long enough where he was, but he didn't need to get completely out of the military. *Could be.*

One carrying an MP5SD, the suppressed member of the Heckler and Koch submachinegun family: Nine millimeter, short-range, relatively quiet. There was one before that one with an M-16A2: Five-point-five-six, probably the SS-109 load that would punch through a standard helmet at four hundred yards. They were taking pains to point north. A picture was forming in Preacher's mind.

He'd done enough here. He could go on and get the bars. He had the "points" and the qualifications, and he knew they wanted him to stay in. Team Six wanted him back. He'd spent a few months with them before, participating in four operations that he still couldn't tell even his current teammates about. He had killed, as a sniper and in the close- assault role. Not a lot, but enough for the occasional dream. There were others he had met, among the several Special Operations Groups in the US, who had killed more and more often. He worried that some of them didn't seem to be bothered by it.

A machine-gunner carrying a Squad Automatic Weapon was going across. You could have taken that and checked it into any armory in the US without anybody blinking. Support,
Security, Close Assault. A raid, probably into a building. The suppressed submachineguns were favored by hostage rescue teams. There was less muzzle flash, they were accurate and easy to move with, and they wouldn't blow your eardrums off when fired indoors. Heavier automatic weapons would seal off the area the assault team was working in and counter stiffer resistance.

Resistance from who?

Bars would start him up, away from field work. *Do I want out of that?* It felt good here, running an op, moving in a threat zone, testing himself against whatever came up. Kept him out of the submarine, too. He didn't hate the boat. It was specially fitted for them, and the accommodations were pretty- nice all things considered. He felt cramped inside of it sometimes, though, and he wondered how Captain Simenson and the Navy guys could stand it, being inside and underwater all the time. *Maybe business*. He could manage French and Russian, French better than Russian by far. That would be good in Europe. Be handy to add Japanese. *What am I saying? Back to school no matter what.* A masters was not a bad idea. Seminary, or regular? There were too many choices. *Life is too complicated. But I knew that already.*

He shifted to look at the next one crossing. Five or six more to go. They were taking their time. He hoped that God wouldn't. Preacher wanted at least a hint about what he should do before his time to decide came up.

Ah—the sniper, to furnish precision fire against hard points, disrupt communications, and open gaps in perimeters so the assault group could drive in more easily. Those were jobs he knew well. He was beginning to sound like a manual. The sniper had an H & K semiautomatic rifle cradled in her arms. Her boonie hat was in one hand, where she had caught it after an overhanging branch had swept it off—

SHE??

Preacher had to do his double take mentally. He couldn't afford to take his attention off the sniper now. Details half-noticed were leaping into memory even as he noticed new things through the rifle sight. The belt, cinched around a narrower-than-male waist—the way the web gear ran a little differently on the body—a few very small differences in uniform fit, barely noticeable through the normal bagginess of fatigues. Without the boonie hat the hair was a dead giveaway. It was dark red or brown, curled on her head so the cap would cover it completely. It would be long when it was let down, thick and soft to the touch...

She was looking at him.

He stopped breathing, blinking, thinking. The shock of seeing something known but only half believed—a woman in a Spetsnaz unit, a female member of a special operations group—had broken his detachment and focused his attention. She was reacting to that, to an eyes-on-you feeling that everyone was sensitive to, some more than others. His momentary focus of attention had triggered some subconscious alarm inside, and she was looking to see who might be staring.

With a rifle in her hands that could put two bullets into a circle the size of Preacher's eye at twice the distance they were separated by now. If she was half as competent as he had to assume she was, she could put a round directly through the telescopic sight on his rifle that would shatter the lenses and the eye behind it without touching the inside of the tube that enclosed it.

The illusion that she was looking at him was caused by the magnification of the sight. He had it set high so he could examine details of their equipment. Now he could see details of her appearance and expression, even through the camouflage paint she had on. He could tell, or reasonably guess, what was going on in her mind. She was studying the area her subconscious was tickled about, looking for something to confirm her feeling— movement, a break in the natural pattern, glint of sunlight on metal —something that would tell her what, if anything, was watching.

The forest seemed to be very quiet now.

They were less than two football fields away, behind underbrush at the water's edge, back in the perpetual shadows of the tree canopy, and further covered by lightweight manufactured versions of the ancient Scottish poacher's camouflaging drape that was called a Ghillie suit. A Ghillie was normally made of strips of cloth of varied length and color, and it was the nearest thing to invisibility for anyone who really knew how to make and use one. Scout/Snipers trained in them from almost the first day at Quantico. The Ghillies that he and Rock-On had on now were improved versions of the homemade model, not only lighter but treated to reduce thermal and radar signatures. They were still hot and heavy and awkward to move in sometimes. They were also about to save lives.

Probably. Maybe. Their teammates were farther back, completely out of sight. They weren't trained for this kind of observation, so Preacher had put them back with the packs. They wouldn't be a factor. The factors now were how good he and Rock-On had laid themselves down, how good the woman with the sniper rifle was, and what she and her teammates would do if she spotted them.

She.

He would not, would <u>not</u> underestimate her. It was first team in the major leagues now. Underestimation was death-on-a-stick. He had no problems talking to God and he was prepared to meet Him if that's the way it was supposed to be, but that didn't mean he wanted a face-to-face conversation just yet.

Preacher was of two minds. Half of him observed a potential threat/point of mission/possible target. It evaluated what she was doing and what she might do and what their own options were. It worked on tactical possibilities.

The other half of him was fascinated and a little in awe. The woman was beautiful. He knew she was, even though there was no way to really see it beneath the layers of equipment and fatigues and face paint. Even the magnified view of the rifle sight couldn't tell him for sure. It didn't have to. He knew she was, knew pretty much what she would look like if he were to see her in the Real World, and beautiful is what she would be.

She started to lift the weapon to her shoulder.

He knew what she was doing. She was about to use the telescopic sight to make a close survey of the area. He would have done the same thing, except that he would have found cover or concealment first. That indicated only a difference in experience, not intelligence or training. Especially training—Spetsnaz training was said to be brutal, almost nightmarish in some respects. If the stories were accurate, what had she been through to get to where she was now?

He could sense that Rock-On was tensing slightly, getting ready to move or, if it came to that, return fire. Assuming the worst, she would see them during a slow sweep at high magnification. Some of the Quantico graduates would be able to. Would she shoot? It depended on the general orders her team was operating under during the mission, the ones that covered chance contact during insertion. Their own covering orders were defensive, with discretionary authority. That meant that the Captain trusted them to know when to shoot first and when not to.

He wouldn't shoot first.

But would he shoot back?

If not, why?

Her head turned in his sight. He thought that her weapon had stopped just below shoulder level. She looked toward the trees and back, quickly. Her mouth was moving. Concentration changed to annoyance on her face.

Someone questioning her, he guessed. *What are you doing? Why have you stopped? Maybe some complaints—You're holding us up. There's nothing there, come on, we haven't got all day.* It would be something like that, from someone who didn't appreciate what a good sniper could do.

She hesitated, looked back toward the speaker, then across the stream where the rest of her team was waiting to cross. *Be cool, mellow out, get a California feeling, will you?* Decision mixed with annoyance, overtaking caution and curiosity. She lowered the rifle and entered the tree line, raising her hat back to her head as she went out of sight.

Rock-On let out a long, slow breath. "Aye Carumba, said Bart," he whispered, taking a line from an early-nineties TV series that had gained a measure of notoriety. "That was a little close."

"No kidding," Preacher sighed back as he focused on the next one in line. *Thank you God, for saving somebody's life today.*

There was another woman, easier to spot after seeing the other one. A grenadier. She carried an M203, an M16A2 with a single-shot forty millimeter grenade launcher mounted under the forestock. Pocket artillery. Some of them were carrying what looked like LAW tubes as well. The US had stopped using those throwaway antiarmor rockets quite a while ago, but there were still a lot of them running around elsewhere. Preacher wondered how old the rockets were, and whether they had been refurbished. The grenadier was bigger than the sniper. Probably not as attractive, either.

They gave the Russians plenty of time to get out of sight and sound and then spent a careful thirty minutes backing out to where the other pair waited. There was no need for speed. The Russians weren't covering their tracks, and a group that big left a trail that a child could follow.

"Well, that was interesting," Rock-On said as they were packing the Ghillie suits up for movement.

"Quite so, quite so," Preacher said in his best bad British accent. His mind was still on the sniper.

"So what's next, fearless leader?"

"Short-run," Preacher said as he tightened pack straps, "we do what we've been doing. Long-run, we work out when it gets here."

"Ya gotta love somebody that plans ahead like you do."

Preacher didn't really hear the conment. He was focusing again on the even longer run, the one beyond this operation that would determine his larger future. He was no longer thinking, though, about the same things he had been thinking about at the OP. And there was less uncertainty to the thought now than there had been just an hour ago.

In fact, he was now beginning to get a pretty good idea about what was going to do.
Perhaps God had, after all, sent him a sign. He would see.

He rocked forward and up to a standing position. The pack still felt heavy after four days.

"Let's move, people."

PRESENT

Now, war is a matter of deception.

Sun Sheng

The communications watch officer ran past the aide and directly into the admiral's office.

"Buoy-from-Alabama-sir-she's-under-attack-now!"

"Damn." Gruwell almost never raised his voice. He snatched the printout from the man's hand. "Who picked this up?"

"An ELINT satellite, on the override. NSA passed it through to us as soon as they knew what it was." There were specific channels available on some of the satellite eavesdroppers for emergency communications such as this, and established procedures for passing the messages through. How fast that really happened, however, was dependent upon how well the equipment functioned and on how well those channels were monitored.

"Have we any record of a response?" There was nothing he could remember that would be close enough.

"I'm not aware of any response yet, sir."

'Damn." *Should have held them for the escort*. But the President had been insistent almost to the point of making it a direct order, and everyone else was up north watching the

Russians surge. When Louisville lost her reactor pump, no one else had been available. It would have done neither Gruwell nor the men on the missile boat any good if he had insisted that the President go fuck himself instead.

Gruwell keyed the intercom. "James. Reference, Southern Exposure."

"I remember some of it, sir. Should I access the record?"

"Only if you can't tell me whether defensive loads for Alabama and Georgia were changed as ordered."

"Yes sir, we recieved confirmation for Alabama, and Georgia is getting reloaded now.
She'll be ready at turnaround. Anything else, sir?"

"Yes. Get me the President. No, cancel that, start with the Secretary. We'll start with him. He should be informed that it concerns HAMMERSTRIKE. It is a priority." He released the key. "Well. It was meant to complement the presence of an escort. Maybe it's not so bad after all, though." He sat back and rubbed his chin. "Thank you, Carmander. You've done what you can for now. We all have. What we do now is wait. And pray, if you're inclined to it. We should know shortly if they survived or not."

* * *

Sometimes he would watch them while they were sleeping.

When he was just back from a patrol, before his biological clock had fully reset itself, he would wake up. Or when he was kept late on base, late enough for the girls to be in bed and Diana asleep on the recliner with the cat curled comfortably in her lap, he would watch them. He would lay quietly in bed and study that woman's face, or sit without moving in the children's room while they rested and dreamed.

It was reassuring to do that: To see his wife's face without the small tensions of the day written in it, to see the children smile, or to watch their expressions change while they dreamed. He felt a different kind of peace then, comforted and calmed in a different way than he was through prayer or worship or from sitting with Diana and reading over her shoulder. It made responsibility for a hundred men and over two hundred nuclear warheads more bearable.

J.T. wanted that comfort now, but what he had was a self-illuminating, computer-driven, flat-table display that was doing a good imitation of an illustration of fractal geometry. It was interpreting, or trying to interpret, the input from Alabama's bow and hull sonars, which were in turn trying to make sense out of boiling water. The torpedo that had hit the MOSS had set off two others that were homing in. A little less than eighteen hundred pounds of high explosive detonating was combining with whatever decoys that were still running to create a chaos ahead of them that neither active nor passive sonar would be cutting through for a little while.

"Jim, deploy the other MOSS. Put it straight ahead, just a knot or two, and keep it one the wire." He wanted it out before the water calmed enough for anyone to hear the launch.

"Sonar, can you make any sense out of this?"

"Not yet, Skipper," Johnson answered, "You got it really stirred up out there."

"All right. Is everybody okay?" The—call it a turn—had been wilder than he thought it would be. That was good. "Check around about casualties, Ed."

"Got one right here," Bearkiller said. He pointed at Simmons, who had his right arm close to his stomach. It wasn't a normal place for it.

"Just a bruise," Simmons said too quickly, "It hit something during the turn. It's all right."

J.T. didn't believe that.

"It's broken or near to it," Bearkiller said, "I saw it hit. It's swelling."

"It'll work," Simmons said.

"Tell me the truth," J.T. said.

"I'm hurt but I'm alive. I'll get it looked at later."

"Okay," J.T. said, "but get a splint or a wrap on it now." He needed his officers whether they had all their arms or not. "Mr. Petersen—"

"Sir!" The helmsman hadn't quite gotten over the adrenalin surge.

"Sharp maneuvering, mister, very sharp. You'll get a commendation at the least, probably a promotion. I'll see to it as soon as we get back." He would not express the slightest doubt about their chances of getting back. He would not. "Sonar, can you interpret anything for me yet?" The visuals were not telling J.T. what he needed to know.

"Out-standing," Petersen said mainly to himself, "A higher pay grade will do me so well." He looked over at his current watch-mate. "Wait'll..." He looked carefully at the planesman's face. "Oh, man...Lieutenant, Jody's in trouble."

The diving officer had just finished prying the last finger off of the crossbar that was behind the helm position specifically for officers to lean on while they did their back-seat driving. He deserved to be tense—he was one of three people with instrumentation data that told them exactly what the boat had just done. He took his eyes off a review of that instrumentation now and put them on the planesman.

His name was Jody Taraway, and he was currently in trouble. He had gone through everything fine to the point where the first torpedo had hit on the Nixie. At that moment something inside of him had taken the commands and overheard pieces of reports and orders to other departments and put them all together and made them intensely personal. When the noise of the torpedo's explosion had reached them, distant and muffled by bulkheads and background noise, it became something more than an especially intense drill. He had at that moment felt the sudden fear that someone does who wakes up to find an intruder in their bedroom. Worse, there was greater certainty to this threat. A bedroom burglar didn't always attack like torpedoes did. He wouldn't come directly at you no matter where you went, wouldn't necessarily turn around and attack you again if the first one didn't succeed, wouldn't try to get to you in spite of any countermeasures you took, wouldn't keep coming at you until he was exhausted or hit his target.

Torpedoes would. Torpedoes <u>did</u>.

It was as if the fear and apprehension and anticipation that the officers were resisting had come to rest inside his mind, all at once. He knew, intellectually, that it wasn't so. Everyone was scared, some more, some less than he was. The officers were probably more frightened than anyone else, since they had more information about what was happening than most crewmen did. The difference was that they were living with the fear and taking action anyway. Jody, on the other hand, suddenly felt as if he had become an emotional magnet that drew fear away from everyone else in the compartment and into his own mind, there to grow and feed upon itself and on him.

He'd been able to resist it, to hold it back while things were happening. He'd managed it well, holding the boat level during that insane tail-slide that Petersen had somehow managed. There had been no angle or depth change. He was proud of that. But now the boat was still, and the sound and feel of torpedoes that could have been exploding on him, that might yet be exploding on him, were filling his mind until there was simply no room for any other thought or feeling.

Today was his twenty-first birthday.

"Whoooohh, Jody," the lieutenant asked softly, "how you doin' down there?"

Taraway's answer came slowly, each word making its way carefully out of somewhere far back in his mind. "Not good. I got to go." The tremors had not reached his hands yet.

Peterson reached over and flipped the switch that transferred complete three-axis control to his station. "I have full control, sir," he said formally, and then to Jody, "Couldn't have done it without you, man."

A smile flickered onto and off of Taraway's face. He let go the yoke and undid his seat restraint, moving slowly, careful of every action he was taking.

"Yo, Chief," the lieutenant called, "take over here a minute, will you?"

"Hold, Sonar," J.T. said, refocusing attention on the planesman as he stood carefully up, "Ed, get a replacement up here." The man seemed to be testing himself with each movement, consciously monitoring the motions to be sure that he was doing things the correct way.

Chief Bateman moved over from the plotting table (which, like the chart table, wasn't really a table any more) and sat down as soon as Taraway was clear of the seat. He would be both planesman and diving officer for a little while.

"He's on the way," Simmons said, "Casualty report—"

J.T. held up a hand. Taraway—yes, that's it—I'm losing track so easily now—had stopped and was looking at him. The lieutenant was hovering close behind the man.

"I'm-very-sorry...sir' Taraway said, "Very...sorry."

"It's all right, son," J.T. answered, because it seemed that Taraway was expecting one, "You did just fine." He hadn't broken when it could have gotten them all killed. It was enough. "Get some rest now."

"Yes...sir," Taraway said, turning away, "Thank you...sir." He let the lieutenant guide him out of Ops.

J.T. waited until he was out of the compartment. "Out of almost a hundred human components in this weapon system," he said then, "I think that a failure rate of one percent under this kind of stress is quite acceptable. Pass the word, gentlemen—I don't want anybody to bother him about this. Anybody. I will personally deal with anyone who does." The man's time in submarines was over, of course, but J.T. would do what he could for him. He was, after all, the Captain. It was his job to. "Okay, start again, Sonar."

"I relieve you, Chief."

"I stand relieved." Bateman let Taraway's replacement take his place and went around behind the bar to hold a place for the lieutenant until he got back. "We're stationary. Hold her in trim."

"Aye, Chief." The new man checked the trim indicators. "Some turn you made there, wild man," he said to Petersen, "They're either clapping or cussing all the way aft. So what happened to Jody?"

Petersen was less conscious of the Captain's wishes than he was of the fact that anyone could have gone the way that Jody had. "A little accident. He hurt himself," he said casually, "in the turn. It's no real problem."

* * *

His first sensation following the thump and shudder of the torpedo's impact was that he needed to breathe and to open his eyes. His first thought was that he was having these sensations. This was a shock to him. He was, after all, supposed to be dying, blown apart by the torpedo's warhead or flattened and crushed by the pressure of water rushing in to a shattered hull or, surviving all that, simply drowning as water forced itself into his lungs as his ship took its last dive into the Atlantic.

He opened his eyes. He breathed in. Something was different. But everything was the same as well. Triunfante was still forming around him, making thirty knots on whatever the last heading was. What was it? Corte' was looking at him, a stare of amazement, or rediscovery, or both, or something else, on his face. He couldn't remember the heading.

A dud. A defective round. They were still alive. The homing system had worked, the propulsion had worked. The detonator—the detonating system had not.

They were still alive.

"All stop!" The words burst out of him like a wild animal released from a cage. He looked at Corte'. "A defective torpedo."

Corte' nodded, swallowed. "Luck."

Delamadrid knew what his first officer would leave unsaid. Maybe we shouldn't push it. They did not have that option. God, or Fate, or simple Chance, had given them another opportunity. Duty, not as generous as the others, forced them to take it.

"The next one will certainly work," Delamadrid said. He had isolated a difference in the air. Something besides the fact of their continued existence. An...odor.

Corte' nodded. "We must be certain not to give them another opportunity." He also knew what Duty commanded of them.

Delamadrid looked at his diving officer. He looked embarrased now. Yes.

Had he cried out at the moment of impact? Had anyone? Delamadrid couldn't remember. He thought someone had.

Delamadrid waited until he had caught the lieutenant's eye. He tilted his head, a slight movement, toward the officer's quarters. "Go. There is enough time."

"Yes, Captain." He had lost control at the moment of impact. "Thank you Captain." He was out of the attack center at a run.

"Sonar!" The sound of his own voice startled him. They had stopped now. "What do you have?" To Corte' he said, "I think that the lieutenant's particular, ah, action, need not be entered in the log." He smiled.

Corte' smiled back. "I understand, Captain. Indeed, I thought I might have to leave with him for just a moment."

"Make sure that we are not damaged. Repeat, Sonar?"

"Bad news, sir. We've lost the tail."

"DAMN!"

The towed array was a copy of the British-made Type Twenty Twenty-Six that had come with the second-hand Dutch submarines, the difference being that

Triunfante's tail was a clip-on. It was attached as the submarine left port by a specialized support vessel and was constantly streamed. There was no way to reel it in and out at will. And no towed array was built to withstand the stress of emergency turns at thirty-knot speeds. Their longest-ranging, most sensitive sonar had been lost, leaving them blind from the rear and with their sonar range reduced by a third.

"There is still turbulence from torpedo detonations at three-forty relative—"

Explosions? Delamadrid's memory was still spotty. Their heading was now two-forty...three-forty relative was...

The American!

They had him.

Maybe.

"Sonar, can you get anything out of that area yet? I must have information!" Was he destroyed? Was the submarine sinking, a few men trapped in the remaining watertight compartments waiting to be crushed by water pressure? All dead instantly, everything in fragments dispersing as they fall to the ocean floor? Or damaged, struggling to surface, preparing to abandon ship or call for help while it tries to crawl home? What? What?

"It's clearing up, Captain, but it will still be a while before anything is clear. There is other information." With the towed array gone, Triunfante could allocate more computer capability to processing the input from bow and hull arrays. This increased their practical sensitivity and allowed for faster interpretation of the input. "I'm fairly certain that Almirante is damaged in some way. She has definitely blown ballast, and there are machinery noises, pumps and grinding sounds. This came in before the tail was lost. I would have reported it then, but there were other priorities at the time."

"Understood."

"There was a torpedo fired at them also," Corte' said, "They didn't get off as cleanly as we did."

"At least they survived," Delamadrid said, "Somehow, they managed a near-miss. A direct hit would have put scrap metal on the bottom. God of War, Corte'! I think it could be our destiny to win this!"

"Perhaps we should not depend on this, however."

Delamadrid laughed. There was a bit of an edge in the laughter. "Well said! There is no confirmation yet, and we have lost one. This American cow has teeth. What else, Sonar?"

"I believe that Cacador is surfacing also, Captain. They did blow ballast. There is not any sign of damage or breakdown that I can discern, however."

"Batteries." Corte' said.

Delamadrid nodded. Of the four boats actually in the hunt, only Sombre and Triunfante were equipped with non-conventional drive systems. Even the tons of high-capacity batteries on modem diesel-electrics would only last for an hour or last of high-speed maneuvering. Even the big old Dutch-made units they had obtained could only sustain such action for about ninety minutes. Advances in battery technology had been offset by the addition of more and newer sensors and processors and other kinds of power-hungry electronics, so that the net gain was zero. The equation remained the same—three to five knots for about a week, about twenty knots for about sixty minutes, or some combination of speeds until you had to surface or snorkel. Cacador was as effectively out of the fight as if she had been torpedoed.

"They will undoubtedly go to assist Almirante."
Delamadrid said, "It is down to two now. This does not
surprise me."

Sombre had gone quiet again. As long as they
stayed below six knots, the Canadian-built minireactor
could supply power and a few amps to freshen her
batteries with. There was undoubtedly enough for at
least one more fast dash. Her weakness was crew and
weapon-load. To increase their search endurance and
ease the burden on the masking system, a third of the
crew had been left behind and torpedo reload space had
been filled with consumables. What was loaded in the
tubes was all they had, minus one that was taken up by
their laser-search system. Their job had been to find the
American and mark his position for the others, using
torpedoes only if a sneak-attack opportunity presented
itself or to make the American react and make noise for
the regular units to hone on. Having fired two torpedoes,
Sombre now had five left. It would be enough. It would
have to.

Triunfante had a full crew and a full load of
torpedoes. Its own laser system took up one tube, of
course, but that was almost irrelevant because only two

torpedoes at a time could be fired without risking some form of mutual interference between rounds. There were seven tubes left and a crew to reload them with. There were also the ceramic "hot" fuel cells, locally developed and better than anything else currently in service, and lightweight electric motors for them to feed with power. Triunfante could run at twenty knots for a month if that was desired, or dash at up to thirty knots for hours, maybe days, at a stretch. Their practical patrol endurance was now tied only to the food supply, the same limitation that the nuclear submarine they were hunting for had. They could do what the nuclear navies could do, and they could do it cheaper.

Revolution.

But Revolution was not going to stop the American from firing his missiles. If that happened, Revolution would not be enough to carry Brazil forward, or perhaps even to keep her stable. If the missiles were fired, Delamadrid wasn't sure if anything would keep the Leadership and its promises of world-power respect and renewed prosperity stable.

"Sonar. Give me the American. He's out there somewhere. I must have him!"

"It's still somewhat confused, Captain," his senior operator said, "but we now have an idea of what has happened."

"Has the American survived?" Ulanovitch asked. It was his primary concern, second only to how he would defend himself if the American had been sunk on his watch.

"I believe so, sir."

As soon as Molniya had entered direct-path range (which had been much improved since the last Western intelligence reports had come out) Arunov had slowed to ten knots and swung the remote into line-a-port. The drone was now keeping station with them five hundred meters out, keeping the towed array- stretched out across their line of approach. This gave Arunov's sonar operators a baseline over fifteen hundred feet long and an ability to calculate range passively even though they were approaching the targets almost bow on, something that couldn't normally be done.

The sonarman pointed to an area on the chart that was about forty-four thousand meters ahead of them. "Many torpedoes fired here. We know that the American increased speed and deployed decoys. One torpedo detonated early, probably on a decoy. We were still able to hear the American at speed afterwards. He fired torpedoes, in fact, here and here."

"We are sure that one of those torpedoes detonated," Arunov said, "We don't know about the other one. We are sure that one Brazilian is damaged."

"First blood," Ulanovigch said, "Good for them! Pity it couldn't be us, Captain."

Arunov smiled. "Agreed. But that will buy them time for us to make our move. And we will do better than a near miss." He nodded to the sonarman. "Continue."

"About five minutes, perhaps six, after the first detonation, a massive disruption occurred here." The sonarman's finger moved to the center of a circle drawn on the chart that covered an area a nautical mile in diameter. "We were able to discern decoy noise, active pings from torpedoes, and then explosions, more than one. A tremendous disturbance."

"Our conclusion," Arunov said, "is that one or more of the torpedoes was diverted by a decoy and that the other went after the active sonar of the first. It is a well known problem where clusters of weapons are fired."

"There were at least four torpedoes in the same area at one time," the sonarman said, "Probably more. Every submarine involved must have fired at least one weapon."

"Did they not know the dangers?" Ulanovitch asked, staring at the confusing mix of lines and circles on the chart, "Damn, what a mess! Why would they have all fired at once?"

"It was an unthinking reaction, I would say," Arunov said, "They are inexperienced, in an area and position they are unaccustomed to, not trained in coordinated tactics, and without the ability to easily communicate with each other. This is almost predictable. Against something as quiet and hard to find as the American is, I'm surprised they managed this much."

"There is one other thing, sir," the sonarman said, "We heard another submarine, besides the damaged one, blowing tanks. We think that he must be in need of a battery charge."

"Ah," Arunov said, "excellent. From four to two. Very good."

"But one of those seems to be invisible," Ulanovitch said, "While the other demonstrates amazing performance capability." We must obtain plans for those fuel cells! A pity that one can't be captured.

"Yes, that one is almost as fast as we are. But it is not faster than a torpedo. As for the other, it can't be totally invisible or else the American would be on the bottom already. It must somehow reveal itself. When it does, we'll kill it to." The challenge of the problem made him cheerful. "The question now is, what of the American? We must confirm his survival and get some idea of what he is doing. Or we must confirm his destruction and carry out the alternative orders." No one was to be allowed to return to Brazil with news of success.

"We think that he still survives. Correct?" Ulanovitch preferred total success and promotion to review boards and a possible discharge.

"Yes." Arunov stroked his chin. "That means we must try to discern his intentions."

"He has survived a major attack," Marsilov said. He had been inspecting the torpedo room. "Surely his aim will be to escape. The loads are set in the required order, Captain."

"Very good," Arunov said, "But we must also remember that his aim is to launch his missiles. He has undoubtedly received orders to do that, or he wouldn't be heading for the launch position. Furthermore, the Brazilians have demonstrated an ability to track him. He cannot assume that he can lose them easily again. He might consider it better to use this confusion to cover an attack, even if only a feigned one that would assist his escape. The alternative is to forsake the primary mission, the missile launch."

"Perhaps they are waiting for help," Ulanovitch said.

"It won't be here in time, I think," Marsilov said, "If they had an attack submarine nearby, it would already have acted. They are on their own."

"I agree," Arunov said, "They are alone, waiting now, assessing the situation. And, if they have detected us, wondering what we are doing here. Helm, slow to five knots. Marsilov, prepare for weapon launch. It is time to announce our intentions."

* * *

"I can't say, Skipper," Johnson said, "I can tell you where he was, but not where he is. Keeping track against that masking system of theirs is an iffy proposition."

"Didn't you have an angle on it?" J.T. asked.

"We thought we did, sort of," Tullibee said, "It's not working for us like we thought it would. We and our processors are going against conditioning, Captain. Nothing is supposed to be safe."

"There's got to be a weakness in the set-up, somewhere," Johnson said, "But it's gonna need a research unit with more brains than we've got to handle the question." He tapped a point on a position-bearing display. "We think he's around here, but that's the center of, say, a four, five thousand yard circle at least. Can't guarantee anything beyond that. Hell, Skipper, I'm not sure we can even guarantee that."

"Okay," J.T. said, "We're all dealing with things we haven't hit before. One boat that acts like a hole in the ocean, another one that hits thirty knots without benefit of a nuclear reactor, and me having to act like I'm in command of a hunter-killer instead of a bomb-thrower."

"What is this underwater world coming to?" Johnson asked.

"A decision point, I hope," J.T. said, "We're going to sit here for a while. There's a piece of bait out in front of us, and I mean to hook something with it. Ed, are we settled in?"

"The boat is now superquiet," Simmons said into J.T.'s earphones, "Three tubes are loaded and ready to shoot." The control wire of the MOSS prevented Number Two torpedo tube from being reloaded. "The worm is wriggling nicely on the hook."

"Good," J.T. said, "I want to Jim to stay with the MOSS, so you direct torpedo launch on my word."

"No problem there," Simmons said, "I'm just waiting for something to shoot at."

"Oh, we've got that," J.T. said, "It's a shadow. We're shooting at a shadow.

* * *

"There is nothing, sir," the technician reported, "Nothing on sonar or with the laser. We are receiving Sombra's beacon, but that's all."

"What is their position?" Delamadrid asked.

"About twenty degrees relative, sir. She has not changed position in the last quarter-hour. I believe she is stationary, sir, holding position as we are."

"And nothing for the American?"

"No sir. That is not surprising. As near as I can remember, her last position was at the edge of our current practical passive range." Practical range, the limit of their ability to have a reasonable chance of acquiring the missile submarine with passive sonar, was about half the hull array's full range capability against less quiet targets. "Sombra is much closer, I think, and may have something we don't."

"We will be patient then. Lieutenant. But we will also close the range a little. Corte', start us ahead, revolutions for three knots. We will play the stalking lion for a while longer.

* * *

Molniya was creeping, giving her sonar operators the best possible chance to pinpoint everything. They could not afford the least doubt about who they were shooting at. There was also the matter of a couple of lost contacts to deal with.

"I find this frustrating," Arunov said, "Every time I prepare to shoot, something happens. First, the melee. Now, everyone seems to have disappeared." He sipped his tea.

"We are faced both with new technologies and with the foremost development of traditional systems, "Ulanovitch said, "The Ohio-class submarines are second only to Seawolf in quietness. The other two, operating as they are on all-electric mode, are almost as good. There is also something on one of them. Something extra." *We must investigate this thoroughly.*

"Yes, and I understand the problem my people are facing," Arunov said, "There is a part of me that is still annoyed by it all." He set the cup down and began to pace around the limited area of the attack center. The men on watch ignored him. They had seen it before. "We think we have something—no we don't—there's one—no, there's not—we can fire—no, there's not enough for a solution now." Generating firing solutions from passive sonar input was still something of an art form at times. New computers and the introduction of "smart" hydrophones with their own preprocessors had cut down the time required for passive solutions, but not the necessity of having a solid contact for a minimum amount of time. "Long range weapons are useless to me under these conditions." Millions of rubles had been spent on a missile he couldn't use. His own plan of attack was stalled by the limitations of his electronic systems. It was irritating.

"Perhaps we have given you youngsters too many toys," Ulanovitch said, "You cannot decide now which one to play with."

Arunov stopped and smiled. "What was it the cat said to the fox? 'I know only one thing, but I know it well.' And he climbed the tree when the dogs came and escaped. Yes?"

"Conn, Sonar. Captain, I think we have isolated the American."

"At last," Arunov said, reaching for a microphone, "It's something, at least. What do you have, Sonar?"

"He seems to be creeping almost due north, sir. Bearing is still uncertain, and there is no range estimate. But I'm sure it's him. Contact is intermittent."

"Very good. Keep at it." Arunov moved to the chart. "North? If our last contacts are accurate, he's trying to sneak between them. That's not going to work!" He slapped the chart table. "I can't fire until I know where they are! I won't know that until they give something away! The Brazilians will fire first again! Can they survive that? How could they be so stupid?"

* * *

"Jim," J.T. said, more quietly than he needed to, "cycle the decoy launchers to Overtures. How many do we have?" He always had a tendency to whisper under superquiet conditions.

"List says four," Bearkiller answered, "We're at about sixty-five percent on decoy load."

Two eighteen-canister rotary launchers—twenty-three-or-four left. "We'll put two out on my signal. Listeners confirm safety interlocks." He pressed a test button on his hand controller. A green light brightened his channel indicator.

Tullibee and Johnson flipped test switches, confirming that their automatic cutoffs were active.

"I have a green light, sir."

"I have a green light, sir."

"We confirm cutoffs all green here," Simmons said.

The cutoffs for the Model One Eight One Two decoys were different from the normal automatic sound level controls the sonar system had due to the nature of the decoy. It was a much newer concept than even the new-concept deception suite that included the decoys, remote-jamming feed systems, intelligent/controllable MOSSes, stand-alone bubble generator systems and advanced sonar jamming and deception units that Alabama had already used to defend itself with. The canisters they were about to launch were an attempt at an offensive defense. They contained microsecond and millisecond "screamer" chips and a specially designed explosive charge. The screamers, theoretically, were tuned to create a burst of noise that would overwhelm the cutoffs of a listener's sonar system and directly attack the ears of the operator, at least momentarily disabling the most important part of the system. That taken care of, theoretically, the explosive charges would then go off, creating a zone of turbulence that would disrupt active sonar and/or confuse the seeker heads of any incoming torpedoes. It was a miniature, planned version of the chaos that any underwater explosion caused in sonar systems.

That was the theory, anyway.

"It's set, then," J.T. said, "Jim, how's MOSS doing?"

"Straight ahead and slow," the weapons officer answered, "All monitors are green. Plenty of string left."

There was up to twenty miles of fiberoptic cable on the spool that connected the decoy to its parent platform.

"Tullibee?"

"Sounds like us, Captain. Slow and quiet."

"I like it. It's time to wait, everybody. I'm betting that we're better at being patient than they are. All stations, stand by."

* * *

Sombra is Portuguese for Shadow. The submarine was one of two that had been built in Dutch shipyards from old U.S. Navy designs. After decommissioning by the Royal Netherlands Navy the two big diesel-electrics had gone through a half-dozen paper transfers and a voyage across the Atlantic under nearly wartime conditions, surfacing only at night if they surfaced at all, arriving in Brazil for refit without the knowledge of any of the "major players" only because the area was not at the time take as seriously by the intelligence community as certain regions of the world. Jane's, publishers of many and varied listings about things of a military nature, had been the first to make the transfer public, if the buyers of their multi-hundred-dollar references could be referred to by that word.

By that time both submarines had been in drydock for quite a while. Both hulls were well over twenty years old and needed extensive re- and retro-fitting in order to make them properly capable again. Sombra had stayed in longest—the Canadian minireactor had been purchased by then, and modifications in the hull spaces and drive trains had to be made for its installation. The Canadians had not been consulted about the work carried out in the covered drydock, though some of the plans for the tribrids they had built were obtained through the services of the drug supplier that worked the Ministry of Defense. They had proven to be very useful. Her sister submarine, rechristened Almirante, had been in the water over a year by the time Sombra was making its first test dives. The experience gained from local construction of Brazil's German-designed Type 209/1400s was invaluable to the project.

Sombra had been operational less than sixty days before she was pulled out again, this time for installation of a prototype noise-masking system. It was a serendipitous breakthrough that was completely Brazilian in origin. A report about a record company's project to develop a way to take extraneous noise out of old recordings had come to the attention of a music buff who was also a highly placed member of the military research and development community. The process, as developed, involved a careful cataloging of noise sources followed by an equally careful placement of sound generators specifically tuned to produce counter-harmonics, sound waves of the same frequency but of opposite amplitude to the noise. On an oscilloscope the result was a flat line as the peak of the noise wave was canceled by the trough of the artificially-generated sound wave. To the ear, the result was an almost perfect silence—there were always minor tuning errors, but most humans couldn't detect them under practical conditions. But even an almost perfect silence was more than even their diesel-electric submarines had been able to produce so far. What they got was more than enough to turn the tables on the, supposedly, more technologically advanced navies.

The system required a dedicated minicomputer and a small purpose-built parallel processor to run it against the varying noise environment that an operating submarine created. Sombra had been chosen for operational testing because it was big enough to fit the equipment needed for the system and because the minireactor provided a constant and consistent power source for its operation. The computers and noise generators took enough power to drop reactor-only cruise speed a knot or two, sometimes, but Sombra's captain was more than happy to make the trade of speed for silence.

Operational trials of the system were nearly complete when Papai's ring was starting to supply information about the nature of the American response to the test detonation. Planning to install the masking system in Almirante and then shrinking it to fit the 209/1400s was suspended, along with the final proof-test of Triunfante's high-output fuel cells. All surface and subsurface units that had any antisubmarine capability had been prepared for an effort to find and kill the American missile sub before it could launch anything.

It was an idea born of panic. Delamadrid had been the first of a group of officers to point out some of the flaws in the initial plan, such as the threat of exposure of the intelligence ring that might follow from the deployment of surface units to hunt the American. Cooler heads had, to the surprise of some, actually prevailed.

The unexpected acquisition of Japanese copies of the German laser-sensor technology and more detailed information from the Washington operatives had spurred the idea of sending the submarines out to kill the American quietly and without trace. Sombra lost a torpedo tube and a third of its crew, its remaining tubes were loaded, the space normally reserved for torpedo reloads was packed with supplies instead, and then it was sent to find and track the American and mark its position for the hunters that followed them. Sombra had been waiting when they came through the launch point the first time to check and update navigation and targeting information for the special missile warheads. The laser had locked on to the big seven-bladed propeller, and Alabama had acquired a Shadow. After that it was simply a matter of waiting for the delay-transmit buoy to bring the rest of the flotilla where they could be waiting when the demonstrator bomb pulled the American in to carry out his fire order.

Now Almirante was gone, damaged and on the surface. Cacador had blown ballast and was also effectively out of action, while Triunfante hovered over eighteen thousand yards away. The American had been detected, crossing their bow, bearing close to zero degrees relative at a heading of nearly zero degrees absolute. Sombra's laser was not confirming the contact, but that was understandable. At that aspect they would have to be at touching distance before a return would come off the darker hull surface. It wasn't necessary any. They had an excellent trace, the target "crossing the T" at about three thousand yards. The captain now had to decide. Sombra had fired single torpedoes up to now to "point" the American out to the others so they could attack, and to conserve rounds. Now they were as close as anyone was going to get, with half their force gone. A better chance was not going to be had. They could launch two torpedoes, the maximum number their fire control system could easily handle, and it could be over in less than three minutes.

It could be over.

Sombra had been out first. Her crew had been under the surface longer than anyone in their naval history, forced to patiently wait and carefully follow the quietest submarine of its kind in the world for day after maddening day, relying on a tenuous beam of light to link them to their target, waiting for the others to arrive and finish it, waiting to know if the computers would keep operating, if the counter-harmonics generators would keep working, wondering if the damned American knew they were there regardless, wondering if their own damned submarines would ever get to them, or if perhaps the operation had been cancelled without them knowing or being able to be told, leaving them more days and days of hiding and waiting and tracking and waiting and following and waiting and waiting and waiting and...

In sequence, Sombra fired two Mark Forty-Eight torpedoes at the target.

* * *

"Transient!" Pause. "Torpedo launch. High speed screws. It's running hot, Captain."

"Ed?"

"PUFFS is feeding." PUFFS was a special-purpose fire-control sonar designed to localize contacts found by their other sonars. The drawback was that PUFFS had to have things located for it first, and, more importantly, it had a very short range, less than half that of Alabama's shortest-ranged search sonar. Seawolf had a much better version of PUFFS with vastly superior range, but Seawolf was an attack submarine and the most modern design in the world. Almost no one would have really, seriously, thought that an Ohio-class submarine would ever be close enough to an attacker to really need PUFFS to begin with, much less anything else. "I'm getting a loose backtrack."

"Second launch! Two torpedoes running." Pause. "They're on the MOSS.

"Get me a bearing."

"Stand by." Pause. "Come on." Pause. "Got him! Got him!"

"Ed?"

"Ready."

"Jim, if they go active let MOSS blossom once and then shut it down. Release the Overtures."

There was no indication that he decoys had left the ejectors. J.T. had to wait for Simmons to tell him that a green light was blinking on the weapon/countermeasure control board.

"Decoys are gone." There was a delay to allow the explosive charges to get clear of their hull.

J.T. cut his sonar-monitor channel out, just in case, "...four, three, two, one, shoot."

There was a barely perceptible shudder.

"One is out. One is running. One is on the way."

PAST

"When the strike of the hawk breaks the body of its prey,

it is because of timing."

Sun Tzu

The cartels were never as unified as some people thought. There was sometimes an impression, perhaps generated by too many two-minute news features, of a many-headed creature, a hydra feeding on the American drug market sending bites of money and chewed-up souls down multiple throats to a single stomach. Some others, perhaps considering themselves more sophisticated, reckoned that it was more like a very rough Mafia-type environment, with territories staked out and sometimes fought over by large organizations.

Most of the people who hold either of the possibilities in their minds have probably never been in an inner-city neighborhood, especially after dark. It is also doubtful that they have ever accompanied an entry team on a drug bust or been with a police unit conducting a gang sweep. They probably wouldn't want to go if they had the chance to. It is far more comfortable to retain the fantasy of an organized-crime-like cartel, a bit more overtly violent perhaps, but still far less messy than the real thing. It's easier not to see the meat grinder in the streets, easier not to watch the heads of the hydra biting each other as much as they do the market while their own fingers turn on hands that attack the arms that they're attached to even as the arms try to rip their own bodies apart to get at a bigger piece of what's coming down the trunk.

Sharks in a feeding frenzy don't bite each other as much as drug organizations at all levels do. Like a cancer patient undergoing treatment, the central organizations were constantly wary of cells growing too fast and eating too much. Such outbreaks required fast "treatment," but like some cancer treatments, killing the infection meant that you also had to kill some healthy tissue. You couldn't kill too much, though. That was dangerous too. There were predators out there, large and small and in-between, waiting to feed on the dead and tear apart the weak even as they hacked off their own rebellious body parts.

The Spetsnaz unit that assaulted a little piece of paradise in an otherwise undeveloped area within the long triangle formed by Carlos Sa dos Aimores, and Nanuque, near where the Pampas meets the Mucuri, knew nothing of these theories and their relationship to reality. Neither would they have cared if they had known about it. It was an American problem, a Central and

South American problem, not a Russian one. Russia had drug traffic, of course.

Everyone did. But it was a different kind of traffic, of a different nature and of a different intensity than the American one. It was also a KGB/Interior Ministry/police problem, not a GRU/Spetsnaz problem. So, in that way, the Spetsnaz team members didn't really care much about the Russian problem either.

The mansion was laid out in an L-shape, a big single-story building in the middle of a sea of manicured green. There was an incomplete stone wall, the height of a tall man, keeping the forest out of the front and side and part of the back yards. The wall incorporated two alarm systems which were easily disabled. There was a swimming pool and two outbuildings—a guest house and a smaller house for the guards—in the huge lot. The guard-house would be reduced by explosives and machinegun fire once any sentries were neutralized. Beginning at zero three hundred local time, four were discovered and removed by suppressed gunfire while the assault and support teams moved into place and the engineers set their charges. Hunter confirmed two kills during that hour. They were not her first.

At about zero four hundred local, when the occupants of the mansion were most deeply asleep and anyone alive and awake was at their lowest biological ebb, the actual assault was launched. Two days of surveillance had indicated that the guest house was empty, so eight men were available to sweep the house. The tactics used had been standardized by special operations groups and hostage-rescue teams over the years. The keys were shock, speed, and surprise: Shock the target, move unexpectedly, and take decisive action faster than the dazed and/or surprised target can react. The entry team had an additional advantage as well, in that there were no hostages to worry about rescuing. Even prisoners were more of a luxury than a necessity, although certain people could facilitate certain parts of the mission if they could be taken alive. The primary objective of the operation, however, was simple documentation— papers, notebooks, tapes, floppy disks, or anything else written, typed, or recorded. Prisoners were desirable only for their ability to produce and explain documents. If prisoners had been the key to the GRU puzzle, the team would have been raiding the home of a cartel head, not a chief accountant.

As it turned out, eight were captured despite the enthusiastic efforts of the entry team. Six in the main house and two others as they crawled out of the wreckage of the guard quarters. One other, trapped under debris, was shot so that his screams would not become a distraction. Three of the prisoners were identified from descriptions given to the team. They were the second assistant to the chief accountant, a male secretary, and a high-level courier of one of the other cartels. The others were rapidly classified: A mistress, a maid, a groundskeeper, and two bodyguards.

The initial stage was completed. The prisoners were put in the guest house and a guard was placed while a detailed examination of the mansion was made. The team was well briefed about how to look and what to look for, and three-quarters of them were specialists in either Spanish or Portuguese. Most of them were cross-trained in computer operations and information analysis as well. Over a dozen Spetsnaz units had been shortened by one or more members for this operation. GRU was very good at finding the necessary tools for its tasks.

The inside of the house was taken carefully apart. Anything that looked like it might be a hiding place was torn open. Safes were blasted— combinations weren't important enough to interrogate anyone about—and three personal computers were tapped. The team worked under paradoxical constraints of limited time and exacting requirements. There was no way to predict how long it would be before the head man returned from a meeting of the cartel head or when someone might come just to visit or deliver supplies. Some of those could be captured or killed, of course, but that would only buy time while increasing the risk to the team. But the information, the documentation they were searching for, was not something that could be easily discovered and wrapped into a small package for quick delivery to a safe house. Every paper and data disk had to be examined, understood, evaluated, and linked to other papers and data disks. Only a cursory examination could be made at the mansion, but even that had to be done as completely and comprehensively as possible. The mesh they sifted everything through had to be as fine as they could manage if there was to be any hope of fully assembling the skeleton that GRU wanted to display.

* * *

"They've established local security following the assault," Preacher said, "and they've been sitting on it. Back."

"Any idea what they're doing?" the Captain asked, "Back."

Interesting concept: Captain Thompson on Sunfish, at periscope depth somewhere in the Atlantic. Preacher kneeling in a small clear spot underneath a hole in the tree cover talking to him with better clarity than a lot of international phone calls were done with. The Navy had howled about shifting LIGHTCQMSAT II over enough to cover them, even though it was a small distance orbitally speaking. But holding the laser communications satellite in an unaccustomed position required almost constant fuel expenditure and took it out of part of the strategic net, which made the strategic communications people unhappy. It had required an Air Force promise of a priority refueling mission and a direct call from the White House to finally start orders up the beam for the orbit change.

"I have no idea, sir. There aren't any more clues now than there were a week ago. Back."

"Guess, Sergeant," Thompson said, "speculate, prophesy if it will work for you. Back."

"Stand by. What'll I tell them, Rock-On?"

"What, I'm clairvoyant now?" Rock-On asked around a mouthful of Meal, Ready-to-Eat, "You're the team leader. You're supposed to know everything." He considered the idea while he finished chewing. "I got no answers, Slick. They could be just waiting for retrieval, right?"

"Can't be that easy," Preacher said, keying the mike, "I'd say they're looking or waiting for something." That wasn't very exact, but it was the best he could do. "They made a beeline for this location and moved right in. I'd guess they know what they're looking for, but whether they've found it or not is up for grabs. You got anything on this location I need to know about? Back."

"So far, we can tell you that it's not military related," Thompson answered, "Inquiries are underway. How are you fixed for hanging in? Back."

"We got another week easy if we stitch Rock-On's mouth shut," Preacher answered. That was one of the better things about MREs. You could carry a lot of them. "We might drop a few pounds, but we'll be healthy."

"Good. Assets have been alerted to your presence. We have a burst with instructions ready for you. Set recorder."

Preacher pressed the buttons to put the recorder/translator on the line. "Set."

"Sending."

The recorder chirped at him three seconds later. They would play the instructions back later.

"We got it. Back."

"That covers contact and recovery. We'll pull you out be in-country channels. Acknowledge."

"Acknowledged." He thought it might be just what he had in mind, in fact. "Anything else, Captain? Back."

"Not for now. Good job so far, stay with it. Sunfish ends."

"No problem sir, we're here for the distance. Houndog ends."

* * *

Decisions had to be made.

Some documents had been acquired. The microcomputers at the target had been linked to consulate mainframes by secured landlines. Some information was being obtained. There were prisoners.

They had not yet been interrogated. The physical security of the field operation was still intact, but it was only a matter of time until there was a compromise. Transport and extra help was on the way, but it would be some time yet before it arrived.

There was also a bigger fish that had not been caught. The meeting with the accountant's bosses had been called on short notice. There was no practical way to adjust the field team's schedule to accommodate his absence. While he was not necessary to what they wanted to accomplish, it would be better to have him than not. On the other hand, they had his lieutenant. Such a person was often better as a source than the boss would be. They often carried more of the details of the day-to-day operations than did their superiors. Still, it was just a lieutenant. Even the man he worked for was himself a lieutenant to the head of the cartel.

Decisions had to be made.

Gregoriy picked up a telephone. "Do we have a location or timetable?"

"Our frontliners believe the conference is ended," the voice at the other end answered, "He might stay another day before driving back. We estimate twenty-four to thirty-six hours before arrival."

"Keep on it. Update me as soon as there is a change." He hung up.

So.

There was no practical way to snatch him at the conference. At least three chiefs were there, and many high-ranking subordinates. Personal contingents of bodyguards and military units on loan from the Leadership made kidnapping a suicidal idea. Easier to simply kill them all, cut off the heads of the coalition. Satisfying, yes, but useful only in the short run. Gregoriy's strategy, if it worked, offered a possibility of a long-term solution to cartel influence in Brazil.

Maybe. Of a sort. It would work against the outside influences, anyway. Perhaps.

He might have nothing that the assistant or the secretary had. He might have exactly what they needed.

Are you a gambling man, Gregoriy?

He lifted another phone, also a continuous line. "Tell them to wait there for the big one. Field commander has discretion on pull-out as before. Priority in that case for items, one, two, three. On contingency, discard the rest. That is all."

* * *

Because there had been relative security for three years and because they were close to home, vigilance was relaxed more than it should have been. The three cars, a Land Rover and two Mercedes, were too close together as they came through the gate, and the arrangement of principal and protective personnel was too obvious.

A rocket-propelled grenade took the last car from the rear, slamming it forward and twisting it sideways so that it blocked the gate. Light armor did nothing to keep the backseaters alive, and a small fire started, kept steady by a trickle of fuel from a faulty self-seal gas tank. Two men staggered out of the wreck. They were shot.

An RPG missed the Land Rover, which then tore up yards of carefully manicured lawn trying to escape machinegun and automatic-rifle fire. The Spetsnaz gunners fired careful, aimed bursts, as they had been trained to do, ignoring the wild return fire from the moving vehicle. The Land Rover overturned finally and lay upside down in the front comer of the yard against the stone wall, all four wheels spinning uselessly in the air. It did not catch fire.

The driver of the center car reacted well, spinning the Mercedes and gunning the turbocharged engine for a run at the blocked gate. The team assigned to that care shot the tires, but they were run-flats, specially made to allow the car to go some distance at speed despite such nuisances as bullet holes. The car was also armored, and equipped with a reinforced bumper that would have butted the wreck of the other car out of the way except for the light truck that had been jammed against it from the other side. The team had intended for the truck to block the gateway by itself, but they were not ungrateful for the extra mass of the wrecked car now.

Before the driver could reverse and try another ram (which would have probably succeeded in spite of the blockage), Hunter made her third kill of the mission, putting an armor-piercing bullet through the armor-glass window and punching a seven-point-six-two millimeter hole in his head. A dead foot on the accelerator kept the engine running and the wheels turning, grinding flat rubber against the concrete driveway. Before the tires could start to bum, an order was shouted and a carefully-aimed rocket grenade sent its charge into the front of the engine compartment, shutting off the engine without threatening the valuable occupants of the vehicle.

There were a few gunshots, someone firing blindly through a gunport in the car, and then silence. Only the crackling of the small fire, fed by the trickle of gas from the wrecked car, could be heard by those who were close enough to it.

A kind of siege was allowed to develop. The fire was extinguished by men careful to keep the wreckage between themselves and any line of fire of the other car. Then the three remaining passengers were allowed to simmer for a while, trapped in a wrecked car with a dead man in the driver's seat.

After an hour a linguist put himself in sight (but out of the direct line of any gun port) to call out a demand for surrender. When the bodyguard in the back seat put a pistol out of his window to shoot the linguist, a sniper from the backup group took away the pistol along with part of the hand that was holding it. Hunter thought it either an extraordinarily good shot or an extraordinarily lucky one.

The screams of more than one man could be heard from inside the car. What was left of the hand was yanked back inside and the window went back up, but not for long. Three snipers carefully began to shoot out the windows with armor-piercing rounds. The men inside kept screaming while this was done. For added psychological effect, several standard bullets were aimed at the passenger compartment itself so that the impact of the bullets on the car's armor could be heard.

When the shooting stopped the translator repeated his demand. This time, results were more satisfying. Weapons were flung out of the windows and doors were flung open. The man in the front seat came out with his hands up. The man whose hand had been shattered did not come out. He had fainted from shock. The accountant, the object of the ambush, didn't step out of the car either. He fell out, on his hands and knees, and then he threw up.

He had been at the top too long. It had softened him.

* * *

"Everybody's alerted," the Captain said, "We'll know at least if they end up someplace we've got covered." That wasn't nearly as much area as they needed. Human intelligence resources were stretched entirely too thin there.

"We've got a working vehicle here, sir," Preacher said, "We can follow them." There were in fact three intact cars, one of them an armored Mercedes like the wrecked vehicle that had been dragged against the wall, out of sight of the approach road.

"I don't think that's a good idea," Thompson said after a moment's hesitation, "You can't afford to get caught in the open. Better you wait for a pickup. There's some Caspers on the way to get you." Caspers were friendly ghosts, spooks—spies—that were on their side. It was most logical and rational for them to wait for an in-country guide and helper. Tracking someone through a tropical forest was one thing, maneuvering in populated areas wearing camouflage fatigues while carrying a lot of military weaponry something else entirely. Preacher wondered briefly why the Captain didn't just have them exfiltrate the same way they'd come in.

He also wondered what he was going to do now. How was he going to find h— them again? If they weren't headed for the nearest consulate, that or a safe house, he was a closet Satanist. They would be buried there and he would never know...

Don't panic. Don't panic. "Say again, Captain?" *There's a way. Has to be a way.*

"What did you find?"

"They tore the place up pretty well, sir. Burned one building. And there's bodies, sir."

"Bodies?"

"Lots of bodies."

* * *

A standard Spetnaz field interrogation is quite brutal but very effective. It is designed with a single overriding purpose—to obtain information as quickly and efficiently as possible. The survival of the prisoner is secondary to the requirement of gaining information. In fact the prisoner is not expected to survive a Spetsnaz interrogation. Living, then, is not normally an option for the subject. The only choice normally given is the manner and length of time taken by their dying. It can come only after a long time and a lot of pain, or it can come very quickly and without any pain at all. The option to withhold information is not even considered.

Information will be obtained-that is an axiom for Spetsnaz interrogators. What the subject trades for information is an absence of pain. It is the only coin, and the only bargain, that is allowed.

The three most important prisoners were not interrogated in the field. They were instead made to watch the interrogation of some of the others, beginning with the standard demonstrations of intent-a spike in the brain of one, the trick with the wedge in a tree trunk and a male's genitals with another, both performed after only the most cursory of questionings.

Two of the remaining men and both women were babbling almost incoherently following these demonstrations. This pleased the field interrogators greatly. The important prisoners now had examples of acceptable and unacceptable behavior to remember and consider during the trip they were about to take. The two women and one of the men were questioned quickly and taken away. There was no useful information there. The other cooperative one was lightly abused, just a few needles and hot coals, to verify his truthfulness and to soften the stubborn one a little. Then he was taken away with the others, away from what was about to happen.

The important ones were bound to chairs and gagged so that they would be alone with their thoughts. Because of the growing concerns about security the interrogators worked faster than normal, so that after only four hours what was left of the man was taken out of the big house and thrown in the guest house with the other bodies. Then the cooperative ones were taken out and shot and their bodies were added to the ones in the guest house.

As the hoods were being placed over their heads the last three prisoners were matter-of-factly asked to take their remaining time deciding how they were going to die. They were reminded that the one who had resisted was just as dead as the others, and that where they were going there would be more time and better tools available with which to break their resistance. They would not be allowed to die until they had satisfied their handlers about what they knew. That was the simple fact of it.

Hooded and gagged, the three were placed in separate vehicles for the trip out. Documents, computer disks, and personal computers with their supporting equipment were loaded on to other vehicles, along with a respectable store of cash and convertable valuables that had been found in the house. The backup team had brought several cars and trucks with them. None of the available vehicles in the garage were needed.

The wrecks of the ambush were moved out of sight of the approach road and the caravan set out for a safe house located a few miles outside of Rio de Janiero. The last man in the last car set off the igniter that started the fire in the guest house.

* * *

"Damn," the CIA man said, "what a mess."

His name (maybe) was Redondo Hickman, and he had arrived with two old trucks, two helpers, and a short-barreled AK with a folding stock. He was dressed in a worn but clean outfit that looked like it had been ordered from a Banana Republics catalog, the Banana Republics didn't sell shoulder holsters, especially ones big enough to fit his revolver.

"Can't be too careful," he answered when Rock-On inquired about the armament, "Where I live, things can still get a little Wild West, and I can't afford to pay everybody and his second cousin to lay off my business. Know what I mean?"

"And here I thought all the cowboys were out of the Company," Rock-On said later.

Hickman called himself a part-timer. His main business was smuggling. What he smuggled he didn't say because nobody thought he would tell the truth if they asked, so they didn't. With the chop in relations with the U.S. and the general anti-American sentiments in some areas the CIA, DEA, DIA, and the rest of the alphabet agencies had been forced to reduce their personnel rosters there. Almost everyone working under non-diplomatic cover had been pulled out already, and even diplomatic staffs were now pared down pretty much to the bone. At the same time that the case officers and agent handlers were going home the demands for information were increasing, however. It struck Hickman as stupid—here was a man gouging out one eye and demanding greater vision from his doctor at the same time. But as long as Hickman was turning a profit from it, he could and did keep his opinions to himself.

And there was money to be made, no doubt about it. Electronic intercepts and satellite photography could only go so far. A set of plans on paper couldn't be intercepted by radio. Construction under a roof couldn't be photographed from space. A man's intentions could not be ascertained by a computer and an analyst thousands of miles away.

So Redondo Hickman, among others, got hired by the CIA (maybe). It was not his main line of work. He was too independent for that. He considered spook work as simply a profitable addition to this other business. Uncle paid well for the equipment and supplies that he took in to field agents, and for the occasional privilege of adding another Caucasian to his staff for a few days at a time. Information and handlers came in, information and handlers went out, and Hickman and other "businessmen" like him got paid. And a good time was had by all (maybe).

"Damn, you're a big one," he said when he shook Preacher's hand, "They told me, but I'm impressed anyway. I think we got the fit for you, though. Anything left in the house there? Damn, what a mess. What happened here, anyway?"

"Tell me some things first," Preacher said, "I may can answer you then." Hickman's helpers were both armed. There was an old pump shotgun with a pistol grip and an automatic, .45 or Beretta, in a flap holster. Both were clean—Hickman seemed to have a thing about that—and looking around alertly. "You'd better stay out of the house. You might leave traces." Preacher said nothing about the fact that they had already gone through it carefully.

"Yeah. Right. Good idea." Hickman turned and said something in Portuguese. One of the helpers went to the truck and picked up a bundle.

"Clothes," Hickman said, "Can't take you guys on a main road—damn, can't take you guys anywhere dressed like that." He eyed Preacher again. "Gonna be a little tight on you, maybe."

"So where do we go from here?" Rock-On asked, coming back from a look down the road.

"My directions say, you guys go home with me and out my pipeline," Hickman answered, "That's north of Vitoria on the coast. I'm told you may have other directions for me, but it's my discretion whether I can do 'em or not."

"That depends on whether you've got anything for us," Preacher said, mentally scrambling through the discretionary power that the Captain's orders gave him. "Any word on the people that did this?"

"No word period it's been done, far as I hear," Hickman answered, "My money says let somebody else talk about it if they want to."

"Money?" Rock-On asked.

"I get paid to be selectively deaf, dumb, and blind, among other things," Hickman said, "I start talkin' it's bad for business. Get it?"

"I hear you," Preacher said, and searched for a way to find out what he needed to know without giving too much away. He lectured himself for losing track of time. The Russians had been here less than four days. Until someone came and saw, word of the attack was going nowhere. "You got any idea whose place this is?"

"Oh sure," Hickman said, "Guy named Arado owns what's left of it. Big man amongst the producers here. Does their bookkeeping, I think." He eyed the big house speculatively. "Wonder if they got all the safes, whoever it was?"

"Producers? What kind of producers?" Rock-On asked.

"Drug producers What, you don't watch the news? You got any idea who hit this place? Damn, what a mess."

Rock-On looked at Preacher. Preacher looked at Rock-On. They had the same question, but not an answer. *Spetsnaz? Coming thousands of miles to do a drug raid?*

"What are you supposed to know about this, Mr. Hickman?" Preacher asked.   "Mostly what I've been told to do: cane here, pick you up, take you home or wherever, and get paid. Damn, you spooks are all alike. And I pass word of any group fitting such-and-such characteristics that shows up on my net. Not very damn likely that'll happen, but I'm supposed to keep the ears open anyway. That's it." He shrugged. "They would have told me more if they hadn't been in a hurry about you guys."

"I just bet," Rock-On muttered.

"I see," Preacher said, "Have you got anything on the group they mentioned?" *How much discretion? How much?*

"Not from anybody I know," Hickman said, "Not that I'm surprised, you know? My set up's in the back country mostly. I don't got too many ears the place they're most likely headed."

"I see. Where do you think they're going, then?" Preacher asked.

Rock-On realized that he was concentrating harder than usual on what his partner was doing. Something about the big man's questions—yes, the questions, and the politeness he asked them with—not that he wasn't usually polite, just—either way, something wasn't quite normal about the line of the conversation. What Rock-On couldn't quite decide was what. But he trusted his instincts, and his instincts were making him pay attention.

"Hell, that's easy," Hickman answered, "I mean, best place to get lost around this region is Rio. Damn, it's the biggest city in the area, it's a tourist trap, and it's got a ton of foreign nationals compared to anyplace else but Brazilia— maybe more than Brazilia, for that matter. Diplomats don't like that place much. It's a perfect place to get lost, to make contacts—great place to spend money. There was probably a lot of that here for them to spend there. Know what I mean? You sure we can't take a look in the house?"

"Not a good idea," Preacher said, "They were here a few days. It's cleaned out already. Take my word for it."

He put off threatening to shoot the man if he went inside. For now.

"Damn. Well, no use crying and all that," Hickman said, "You guys better get changed. We need to be out of here before somebody shows up." He seemed to only just then have realized that there was an exposure threat.

"Fine," Preacher said, "Get you vehicles back down the road that way," he pointed, "and out of sight." He picked up the bundle of clothing. "We'll be with you shortly." He started toward the rear of the property with Rock-On slightly behind him.

Rock-On looked back at Hickman, who had taken off his wide-brimmed hat so that he could scratch his head at them. He lengthened his stride until he was beside his partner.

"Something on your mind, Slick," he observed.

"Uh-huh."

"Care to tell your good friend and close associate about it?"

"Rather not." Preacher whistled for the other half of the team to come out of the woods. "You'd think it was crazy."

"More so than usual?"

Preacher looked back to make sure that Hickman was moving the vehicles instead of moving toward the house. "Uh-huh."

"Interesting concept, Slick. But try me anyway. They say confession's good for the soul, you know."

"I'm not Catholic, I'm Baptist." Preacher was silent for a few seconds. Then he shrugged and said, "I'm going to Rio."

"Uh-huh." Rock-On pondered the revelation for a few steps. "I see. Hold it." He stopped and waited for Preacher to turn around. Seeing the other two at the edge of the brush, he showed them a hand signal so they would pause out of earshot. "You just said, 'I'm going to Rio.' Right?"

"You didn't say 'I think we should go to Rio' or 'I'm going to ask the Captain about going to Rio' or 'It's too bad we're not going to Rio.' You said 'I'm going to Rio.' Right?"

"Uh-huh."

Rock-On pondered the clarification for a little while. "And how do you figure to pull off this minor miracle here?"

A shrug. "Don't know yet."

"Uh-huh. But you're going to Rio."

"I'd say so, yes."

"Orders or not?"

Pause. "Probably."

"Uh-huh." Rock-On studied his partner. "I don't remember any trees falling on you, and you don't appear to be brain-damaged from sleeping outside all this time. Why?"

Memory of red hair in a telescopic sight. "Rather not say."

Rock-On looked right. He looked left. He looked back at his partner. "You're serious."

Preacher nodded.

"Might wreck you, man."

A shrug. "I was getting out pretty soon anyway."

They looked at each other for a little while. Finally, Rock-On shrugged and turned back to the tree line.

"You win, Slick." He started walking. "We'll go to Rio. Been curious about the place anyway."

"You're not going," Preacher said.

"Helll'mnot. You go, I go. Stupid dweeb." Rock-On kept going.

"We'll see." Preacher followed him, considering the second of the two problems he was currently confronted with now. He had to get permission if he could, and if he couldn't get permission he had to get away from Rock-On. Great. Maybe God was telling him something.

"We got a burst on the radio," Fast Eddie said when they were in low earshot, "'Sposed to run it out first thing."

"Okay," Preacher said, and tossed him the bundle of clothing, "Change out and then go keep an eye on the ride home. Make sure he doesn't screw up the crime scene here, okay? We'll show you the film at eleven."

Fast Eddie and Slider went to find out what the fashionable Special Operations Man was wearing in South America while Preacher busied himself with the "radio." LIGHTCQMSAT II had gotten a burst from Sunfish, swept the area with a low powered beacon-finder, aimed one of its communications lasers at the backpack when it answered automatically, and pumped a millisecond-length message into it. The recorder was ready with a version that was slow enough for than to comprehend.

"Houndog from Sunfish," the Captain said, "Change of plan. Word is that raiders will probably end up in or around Rio. Consulate people there want somebody to debrief directly and make identifications. I don't like it, but it's higher than I want to fight. Preacher and Rock-On go in with Hickman. Authorization code Bravo Orange. He knows what it means. Everybody else out with the equipment. Consulate will provide assets. Sidearms only, gentlemen. No acknowledgement required. Check in on arrival. Good luck. Sunfish ends."

The message repeated itself, standard practice with short transmissions. The recorder shut off and erased itself. Preacher rubbed his chin and looked up at Rock-On, who stared at him with an expression that mixed amazement, awe and disbelief.

"Ah. Well," Preacher said slowly, "God _is_ good, isn't He?"

PRESENT

In planning, never a useless move; in strategy, no step
taken in vain.

Chen Hao

Submarine warfare shared a few similarities with combat between aircraft at BVR, Beyond Visual Range. There were some differences, of course. Some maneuvers couldn't be duplicated, though there was a recurring rumor that a boat had (depending on what story version was in vogue at the time) once performed a voluntary roll or loop. Submarines didn't have anything like the kind of support that aircraft did with AWACs and ground control stations and other aircraft, either. The laser communications systems were beginning to change that aspect, but it was still some time before anybody would be able to count on talking things out with another friendly underwater. The most important difference that J.T. faced now, however, was that submarines didn't get the kind of precise and near-instantaneous information from sonar that airplanes got from radar. There was less certainty about what was happening underwater.

That uncertainty was what J.T. was facing now. He was in the position of a big bomber facing off against a group of fighters—in slow motion. And he had less information coming in than that bomber commander would. Sitting in Sonar, where all of the information came in, looking at the same multifunction, multimode displays his sonarmen were watching, in whispering distance of men that were highly trained specifically to interpret the signals generated by the best sonars that could be built by the best technology in the world, J.T. felt...well, not really blind.

He did feel rather nearsighted though.

The fact that torpedoes weren't heading back at them indicated that the Overtures had surprised the opposing sonar operators and masked their own launch transients. Whether they had actually disabled a sonarman was another question.

"Ed, status on the torpedo."

"Running well. I want to start pinging in about thirty seconds."

"Fine. It's your baby."

"Aye-sir-boss."

They had, of course, announced their presence and position to Bravo Two, who was too far away for the Eighteen-Twelves to do much of anything with. That one was fifteen thousand yards away and intact despite the best efforts of an ADCAP. Ah, well. J.T. made a mental note to stop reading books where everything always worked like it was supposed to.

Patience. At fifty-five knots the Brazilian Four-Eights would get to the MOSS at about the same time the sixty-knot ADCAP got close enough to the Brazilian. J.T. didn't think that they would hit the MOSS this time. Odds only allowed for that to happen once.

"Pinging! Bravo fish are pinging," Tullibee said.

"Ed?"

"A few seconds." Pause. "Mark. Torpedo is active."

"Srully?"

"Got it. Skipper." Johnson's job was to read the input from the active sonar on their torpedo. Missile submarines, unlike attack submarines, were not meant to attack anything except strategic targets on land, so they had nothing like the big active sonar sets that the attack boats had. Alabama was equipped with combination mine-hunting/under-ice navigation active sonar, but it was no good unless something was within two thousand yards. Even the hole-in-the-water was farther away than that. So they were using the torpedo's active seeker head as a kind of remote-controlled search unit. It was the only thing they had that had a chance to find and pinpoint a submarine that was able to swallow its own noise and disappear.

"Down five. Circle left." The torpedo would automatically initiate a cloverleaf search pattern if it didn't find a target where it expected one to be, but that would quickly break the wires. They would only be able to listen for the torpedo's shift to rapid pinging or the sound of the active sonar coming off a target hull if that happened, and they wanted more precise information than that would provide. So Simmons was going to try and "fly" the ADCAP through gentler maneuvers for as long as the twin control lines stayed connected to their spools. No one was taking bets on that being very long.

"We've got a blossom," Tullibee reported. The transponder on the MOSS had reacted to an active signal from the torpedoes coming toward it. It had given than an Alabama-sized return. Now it would shut down. "They're turning a little—they're going for it." The torpedoes would go to the area the MOSS was in and begin a search pattern now.

"Jim, turn the MOSS ninety degrees to port, maintain speed. We'll see if that surprises them." The decoy would be heading down the line of the torpedoes, directly (he hoped) at the silent Brazilian.

"Torpedoes are circling," Tullibee said, "They're on automatic, chasing each other. Bravo Two is closing slowly, no other action there."

"They're not sure what's happening," J.T. said. The Overtures had told them one thing, the MOSS something else. They were confused. Maybe. "They're waiting to see if anything else happens."

And so are we.

* * *

"Here," Corte' pointed, "Our torpedoes, searching. Here, another one of theirs. It has to be. Those bursts came from about here." He rubbed an ear in unconscious sympathy for their sonar operator. The strange bursts of noise would have hurt him if they had been closer.

"One is a decoy," Delamadrid said, "This one here, probably." He pointed to where Sombra's torpedoes were circling.

"We can't tell for sure," Corte' said, "There's nothing we can get a lock on."

"Is Sombra threatened?"

"Not so far," Corte' answered, "The torpedo search cone is limited. They've done well not to panic and try to run. As long as the masker works they should do well. They also have a full decoy load still." He wondered if that would help them any more than it had Triunfante.

"Very well. We'll wait for this to sort itself out. Keep moving in."

* * *

"We lost it," Simmons said, "It's auto-searching now. Seven or eight minutes running time left." The control wires had been crossed too often.

"It was better than we expected. Lead the next one a little and let it go.

A few seconds later there was a mild vibration.

"Out. Running."

"Jim, slow the MOSS down, maintain heading. Stay loose, everyone."

They were at the point of maximum risk.

* * *

"What are they doing?" Ulanovitch asked.

"I see it now," Arunov said, "Yes. They must eliminate that shadow of theirs if they are to have a chance to escape. They have no active sonar on their own submarine, and the Brazilian is somehow masked against their passive sets. They have drawn it out with a decoy and are now attempting to find and fix it using their own torpedoes in the active mode, like a remotely piloted vehicle."

"Very risky," Marsilov said, "See here. The other one is moving in. The American reveals himself every time he fires."

"Transient! Torpedo fired," the sonar room reported at that moment.

Arunov waited for the approximate position of the transient to be marked. "The American again. It has to be."

"His first round is still searching," Marsilov said, "It's going to get confusing again if this keeps up."

"Not only that, but he marks himself for the other one," Arunov said, "They will fire soon."

"Another thing," Ulanovitch said, "What if this gambit of theirs doesn't work? How many torpedoes can they afford to expend looking for this masked unit?"

"Not many," Arunov said, "They carry just a dozen rounds to begin with. Sonar! Give me your best solution on Contact Two! Marsilov, ready tube five. We must act now if they are to have a chance!"

* * *

"They'll go active next," J.T. said, "Jim, re-enable the MOSS transponder." Their own torpedo might activate it while it was searching for Bravo Four, but he was willing to take that chance. It might even work in their favor if it did. "Status on Bravo Two."

"Still closing, Captain," Tullibee said.

"He wants to be sure," J.T. said.

"Bring it back forty-five," Johnson said.

"I don't know if I can," Simmons said. He was breathing hard, as if he had been running laps in the Missile Room. Torpedoes were not designed to allow for fine directional control like MOSSes were. They were normally steered by computer. Simmons was having trouble keeping control.

PINGpingPINGpingpingPINGpingpingping...

"Two is active! Bravo Two is active!"

"I got it! I got it!"

"Cut it loose, Ed! Ready three and four!"

"Transient! Launching!"

"Match on three!"

"Shoot and cut! Match four to Two, four to Two!"

"Launching at MOSS! They're going for the decoy!" A slight shudder.

"Transient! Launch transient on Two, Two is launching!"

"Match on four!"

"Shoot! Keep it on the string!"

"Three is running." Another slight shudder. "Four is on the string. Tube one is ready."

"Hold it. We've got to sort this out. Stand by countermeasures."

* * *

"Fire," Arunov said. The answering vibration made him feel slightly euphoric.

* * *

"It's running well, Captain," Corte' said.

"Make sure it's kept to the right target," Delamadrid said.

"Transient! Another launch, Captain!"

"Where at?"

"It's—something else—torpedo incoming! Incoming!"

"Calm yourself." Delamadrid had been thinking about this a lot since their lucky escape. He knew that another such incident was all but unavoidable, but this time he also thought he knew what he could do about it. "They want to throw us off, Corte'." It was a standard tactic, firing a torpedo at someone who had fired at you. That would force them to cut their control wires in order to initiate evasive and countermeasures action, making their torpedo much easier to evade or decoy.

"Of course, Captain." Corte' was not getting the reaction he had expected. Did his captain expect another miracle like the last one?

"We'll indulge them. Let the round go free. We'll have to sacrifice it." It would go off toward the largest disturbance, following the torpedoes that were chasing the decoy. "And launch another, to be guided according to my direction. They aren't the only ones who can use torpedoes in new ways."

* * *

Sombra was barely out of the arc of the first torpedo's search pattern. Wisely, her captain kept everything quiet rather than take any evasive action. The passive systems the American carried could pin than down in an instant if they tried anything like that.

Once the first ping of the second torpedo hit them, however, all bets were off. It was too late to deal with the failure of their own torpedoes to hit, too late to separate the targets that Triunfante's active search had revealed, too late for anything but the most active of defensive measures taken as quickly as possible. The active sonar range of the torpedo was two thousand yards, and it would switch to high speed automatically. That gave them about sixty seconds to do something about it.

The weapon officer's hands had been resting on his countermeasures control panel for the last thirty minutes. Bubble curtains were released and decoys were deployed. Lots of them. There was no logic in being stingy with them, when destruction became the price of cheapness.

The curtain temporarily interrupted the torpedo's sonar, enabling Sombra to engage her batteries and accelerate past the edge of the active seeker cone. On automatic, finding the active seeker blocked, the torpedo switched back to passive mode. The combined noise of the release of the bubble curtain, the decoys, and the motor and cavitation noises of the submarine target mixed together and confused the torpedo momentarily. It turned a little toward the decoys. The mistake, however, was quickly registered and corrected. The torpedo turned back toward the real target, which was accelerating and turning hard to port to get not only behind the search cone of this torpedo, but away from the other one that could now be detected coming in.

The leading ADCAP reacquired Sombra with its active seeker and turned inside. Another bubble curtain was released and, with about fifteen seconds to impact, cyclic jamming was initiated. The rapid sweep of sound waves through a range of frequencies was an attempt to convince the torpedo that the target was somewhere else, somewhere other than where it was. The torpedo would then go after the illusion or perhaps even detonate its proximity warhead too far away to damage the target.

Had the ADCAP still been linked to its parent submarine, it wouldn't have worked. Alabama's fire-control processors would have isolated the jamming source and zeroed the torpedo on to it. The ADCAP did have an internal home- on-jam processor, but there wasn't enough time for the homing head to fully analyze the input. The torpedo had to make a fast decision, and it decided wrong. It passed above Sombra a few feet aft of the conning tower.

The torpedo waited for contact and didn't get it. Realizing that it had missed, the guidance/fusing system ran through the salvage-fusing parameters first, but it didn't find enough there to justify a detonation command. Accordingly, the guidance center started the torpedo back around for another try.

It wasn't necessary. Alabama's third torpedo headed first for the general cacophony caused by the release of bubble curtains and noismakers. Ninety seconds into the run, it sorted out the running target from the background and altered course slightly. When jamming started because of the second torpedo, number three had plenty of time to enable its home-on-jam processor and get proper advice from it. It bored straight in at a nautical mile a minute.

Unaware of what the torpedo was really following, Sombra shifted from cyclic to barrage jamming, a brute-force attempt to overwhelm the torpedo's homing head with sheer multi-frequency noise. And they practically emptied themselves of expendable decoys. The ADCAP ignored the jamming, ignored the decoys, ignored the bubble curtains, ignored the target's attempt to create a lure of turbulent water with a fast turn, and kept closing distance.

Approximately three minutes and thirty seconds after it had been fired, the torpedo made contact almost dead on with the propeller cap. It blew the submarine's stern off.

* * *

"Captain! My God! Captain!"

"Control, Lieutenant!" The impact of the dud torpedo had put them too close to the edge. "What is it?" A panic was the last thing Delamadrid needed while another torpedo was coining toward them.

"They're gone! Sombra is gone!"

"_What_?" A chill, a sudden cold spot in the stomach. He shook it off. He had to. There was the torpedo. He would, he must, deal with the other later. "Not now! The torpedo, damn you! Concentrate on the torpedo!" _First, survive._

"Sir! Yes sir!" What they were trying to do required finer control than normal. "Sorry sir. Target still closing. The solution has not changed." The lieutenant's voice was very much calmer now. "About thirty seconds."

The American and Brazilian torpedoes were closing on each other's targets at a combined speed of almost two nautical miles a minute. Their respective headings were almost exactly opposite, separated by just a few degrees. If nothing were done, they would pass within a very few hundred feet of each other.

"Now, Corte'."

"Active seeker is enabled." Corte' threw the safety cover back and put his fingers on the red switch underneath. "Ready."

"Sonar, you have control."

"Aye sir." Pause. "Stand by." Their computers weren't up to this. "Ready." They had to use human judgement for the final phase. "Now! Now!"

One of the rarely-appreciated benefits of wire-guided torpedoes is the ability to detonate them by command if it became necessary for some reason (and if the wires stayed intact). This was useful for those extremely rare occasions when a live torpedo was fired by accident. On a more day-to-day basis, a kill switch was used to inflate floatation collars on practice torpedoes so that they could be recovered and reused after firing.

Corte's fingers flipped the kill switch at the moment the sonar operator judged the outgoing and incoming rounds to be close together and still ahead of each other. The older model Mark Forty-Eight didn't have a directed-energy warhead like its younger cousin the ADCAP did. The spreading shockwave that Alabama's torpedo flew into was roughly spherical and much larger than was necessary to engulf it.

The original aim of Delamadrid's gamble was to create a large area of extreme turbulence that would break the control wires and throw the incoming torpedo radically off its track. The actual result for Triunfante was far happier. The two-ton projectile was shattered by the explosive wave into three major pieces that inmediately sank, joining a number of other pieces of war machinery that were now heading for the bottom of the South Atlantic.

* * *

"Sonofabitch!"

J.T. couldn't tell which operator had said that.

"Captain-"

"What is it?"

He was back in Ops, having finally decided to give the T/K seat to someone who could use it better. The headphones were still on. He found it easier to concentrate when he could chose his distractions.

"You won't believe this, Captain. I think they just took the torpedo out."

"Say again?"

"Bravo Two apparently destroyed our torpedo. It looks like they intercepted it with one of their own."

J.T. looked at chart display. A "cloud" of disturbed water was spreading out about halfway between them and Bravo Two. "You got any idea how they could do that, Tullibee?"

"I'll give you a guess—"

"I thought you only gave estimates."

"Captain, I've just seen one torpedo imitate a remotely-piloted vehicle and another one imitate an antimissile missle. I'm not estimating anything else until this is over."

J.T. smiled. "Fine. Your best guess then."

"We heard the round go active just before it went off. Hard to tell for sure, but I'd bet that ours veered toward the active source before our fire controller could tell it not to. That might not have mattered, they were running real close to each other anyway. After that, it's a matter of judgement, I guess. They set theirs off and ours goes away."

"Jim? You in on this?"

"Uh-huh." There was a distracted tone to the reply.

"What do you think?"

"Sounds tricky. Sounds possible. Even with the wires on, that kind of active source that close could pull one away for at least a few seconds while the parent processors were digesting the information. It'd be easier if the round were homing autonomously. It could work. Need good judgement on the other side, I'd say."

"I'd say. Can we do the same thing?"

"Oooooo...certainly, maybe, if they can, we, can, maybe. I guess."

"Understood. Think about it, Jim. Think about it real hard."

"Aye, Captain."

"Something else too, Skipper," Johnson said, "Give me control of your display."

J.T. pressed a button. "Okay, do it fast." He went back over the idea. Intercepting torpedoes? There didn't seen to be any reason it wouldn't work. Expending one round for another would be expensive, though. *But not as expensive as dying.* "Helm, ahead full course two-one-zero." He would get some distance and put the tail out while the water was stirred up.

The answering vibration when the throttle advanced would have been felt by anyone who had been on board longer than a few days.

"All stop! Hold it, Srully." J.T. looked up from the display. Simmons was looking over a seaman's shoulder at the Engineering monitors.

"Engineering, Conn. Talk to me, Chief."

"It's in the shaft somewhere, Captain. That's all I've got right now."

"Find it fast, Chief. Conn out. Ed, get back there and get me a report." *Bad.* If they couldn't move at all, they were sitting ducks. *Blow the tanks and abandon ship before they hit us?* If they could move there would be noise. Sonar quality would be reduced and Bravo Two would have a clear target. *The big advantage is gone. How do I fight without it?* "Okay, Srully, give-it-to- me- quick."

"Split's from about four, five minutes back. Look down three-four-zero relative at very long range."

He did. "Transient."

"Yessir. Very faint, far away. Now, a bit later—" The display ran forward, "-something broke the surface, I think."

"You're sure of this?" *Makes no sense.* But Johnson wouldn't have brought it up now if he didn't think it was important. Especially not now.

"The second one could be my imagination, but I don't think so, Skipper. That's it."

"Status on Two?"

"Still creeping forward," Tullibee answered, "Water's still pretty stirred up."

Nobody was giving thought to a sunken submarine and thirty or forty dead men. Nobody had time to.

"What do think about this, Tullibee?" *Four torpedoes left. Four.*

"A wild hair at best. Captain. Something almost crazy enough to be right."

And decoys, and jammers, and bee-cees. And one Nixie. "Let's hear it." They started with, what? Sixteen or twenty? *We can stop most of them.*

But only one had to get through.

"I'd rather wait on it, Captain, because if I'm right about this we'll know in about another forty-five seconds or so."

* * *

"There is no sign, sir. I believe we've done it."

Delamadrid breathed in, and then out, and then he smiled. "You see, Corte'? This round is ours. Soon, the fight will be also."

"Perhaps." Corte' considered pessimism to be a job requirement. "It sears an expensive solution, though I cannot say that I prefer the alternative."

"Expensive, yes, but more so for him than for us. His defensive load is limited, and he has already fired several rounds. We still have ten. He can't decoy them all."

"He could do the same thing we did," Corte* said, "Explode our torpedoes with his own."

"That would be excellent! The more he uses for that, the fewer he will threaten us with. We can fire two for his one, Corte' I'm sure of it. We'll move in and take him. We must succeed. The others must be avenged. America must pay for her impertinence. Sonar, what do you have for me?"

"I must confirm Sombra's destruction, Captain."

"You're sure of it?"

"The beacon was operative to the moment of impact, sir. There is no doubt."

"We will mourn for them later. We must avenge them now. What of the American?"

"I think he is damaged, sir, though I'm not absolutely sure of it. As the disturbance from the explosion was clearing up, I heard what I think are machinery noises, more than before. For just a few seconds, sir, but it's on the correct bearing."

"That chain of explosions nearby might have shaken something loose," Corte' said.

"Luck is with us at last," Delamadrid said.

"One thing more, Captain," the sonarman said.

"Yes?"

"A little while ago I picked up something at very long range. I can't say what it was, but I don't think it's normal."

"How far away? What bearing? Any idea what it might be?" None of the possibilities Delamadrid's mind suggested to him were good ones.

"No range numbers, sir, and it was very brief. Bearing was—stand by." Pause. "Sir, something just— something above us, sir, perhaps at the surface..."

He felt the blood draining from his face.

"High-speed screws! My God, Captain, a torpedo! Torpedo in the water!"

PAST

Of all rewards, none more liberal than those given to

secret agents.

Sun Tzu

With thousands of lives lost already and thousands more on the line, the governments of the United States, Mexico and Central America were finally pressed into making significant changes. The war on drugs had failed—not completely but substantially—from a military point of view. There was, however, evidence that it could be won from a personal and economic standpoint if enough could be done at the people level.

It was not easy. The reconstruction efforts in Eastern Europe and Russia demanded money, the reduction of the military had provided no peace dividend, and the Balanced Budget Amendment caused tremendous strain on the economy even though it phased in the balancing process over ten years. It had never been easy to divide the pie even before it started to shrink. Finding money after that was a problem that was likened more than once with performing a do-it-yourself emergency appendectomy.

There was some good news. America did not have to reconstruct Eastern Europe on its own the same way it did Western Europe and Japan after World War II. The money requirement was substantial, yes, but most of that could be covered by investment that would bring profits in the long term. Relatively little of it was outright gifts or grants. As it turned out, American business advice and expertise were more in demand than the money, once it was firmly understood that there wasn't much money to be had from America. And economic measures, forced by the Balanced Budget Amendment, that had gotten the '94 Congress substantially thrown out of office finally began to turn the tide of the deposit problem. Funds were not easy to find, but they could be found. Once found, the funds were put into two major thrust lines—enhancement of social programs at home, and a multidirectional experiment in comprehensive drug control that started in Columbia.

The main aim of the experiment was to take the people away from the cartels. The three lines of action chosen were education, increased social services, and a modified law-enforcement program. The aim overall was to make it easier and more attractive for people to live without the drug lords. While shrinking the cartels' base of support in this way, the program would also tighten the noose of law enforcement around their necks. The first year was very hard, because the programs were limited in area and resources available, and because the cartels fought back savagely, much as they had in the later part of the '80s. Scores died, injuries were in the hundreds. Everybody suffered. The Columbian government dug in and gripped hard and hung on. The second year was marked by what some termed a miraculous decrease in violence and death. Everyone was delighted, except for the analysts, who were confused.

By the first quarter of the fourth year of the program, the cartels were, for all intents and purposes, gone from Columbia. They had almost disappeared, or at least the largest and best-known of than had. Where once there had been almost continuous violence and an invasive, pernicious influence there was now basically nothing. Nothing. The politicians congratulated themselves and basked in the glory of their supposed accomplishments. The analysts were bewildered.

* * *

Hunter's head was almost spinning from all the information she had received in the last two days. The fat-pig-analyst had pressed facts into her brain as hard as he had tried to press his loathsome body upon hers. The pain of a joint lock and the sight of her sharpest-edged fighting knife were enough to remind him of his primary task, however, and he had proven to be a reasonable instructor in the end. But there was a lot of material to absorb in the time given them. She had to know enough to be able to convince the Americans to take her seriously, and to guide them to the most important parts of the material she would carry with her. In Hunter's view, ninety percent of the briefings were unnecessary to the task. But that was typical of the military, and she was after all a soldier, so she obeyed her orders and took the briefings as they were given.

Now, besides a spinning head filled with hundreds of probably irrelevant pieces of information, she was extremely nervous. This was the last act, the culmination of both her mission and her personal ambition of the moment. Across the intersection and down the street was the beginning of a new and very different life. Stepping off the comer would be the end of everything she knew and was familiar with. She might be able to return to Russia one day, but that would be just to visit. Realistically, that idea was pure fantasy, though. She had just been officially listed as missing in action, and if other word of her got back she would be considered a deserter by Spetsnaz. They would not forgive her that. Ever.

She honestly didn't want to give up her home so completely, either. Why would anyone want to leave their home? For all of the promise of life in the West, it still wasn't perfect. For all the problems Russia still faced, there was still promise. And in the end it was still her home. She had been born and raised there, she had spent her life there, and now she was about to leave part of herself there. It was not a simple task, this thing she was about to do.

Gregoriy could sense part of this from where he stood beside her on the comer. They made an unusual sight: A worried man in a suit standing beside a beautiful redhead who was dressed in a Russian paratrooper's uniform. They were getting curious looks from passers-by on the sidewalk and in cars, but no one stopped for them. Two dozen of Russia's finest were around them making sure of that. It was the final stage. No interruptions would be tolerated.

And to begin that stage, another life would now be changed at his direction. How many had he changed in his career? Had any of them been so important as this one now was to him? Would there come a day when he would take action to change his own life instead of someone else's? Perhaps. But not for now.

"It's time," he said, "My friend Anthony will be in his office now. Be sure you are not diverted from speaking directly to him first."

"I understand," she said.

"It's hard, I know," Gregoriy said, "Consider the good that will come of this."

"I do," she said, "but I also think of what I'm losing." She looked up at him. "Goodbye, Gregoriy. I love you."

He smiled and kissed her forehead. "I love you too. How could I not? And I'm very proud of you, little sister." He hugged her hard. "I hope that you find the God you're looking for."

Hunter squeezed back, and smiled, and held her tears inside. "I will pray for you," she said. It was good to say that, and it would be good to do that, without fear of censure or punishment. Some parts of the military still heavily discouraged any expression of religion.

"Thank you," Gregoriy said as he adjusted the strap of her shoulder bag, "I need all the help I can get."

He meant it. "Now go, quickly. Don't worry, it's not the end. We'll talk again when I visit the embassy. Good luck, Morana."

"Good luck to you, Gregoriy," Hunter said, and took the briefcase from him. Then she stepped out to cross the intersection, away from her brother, away from her unit, away from her service, away from her home and everything she had known before this moment in time.

Before she was five feet across the street, she could feel the chains beginning to fall away.

* * *

What had happened in Columbia was simply the result of market trends. When the increased emphasis on (and funding for) social programs finally began to do what years of Just

Saying No couldn't, demand in the US began to fall off. The numbers were still large, but they showed the beginning of the trend to the cartels that were at the same time firming up production and creating distribution networks for the new markets opening up in Eastern

Europe. The creation of the new networks and expansion of distribution alone was going to require tens of millions.

There was also the costs of relocating production and processing facilities, developing new transshipment points, and the probable opposition from the Asian heroin merchants to consider and prepare for. Money was available, yes, but not infinite supplies, and money couldn't buy extra time to set up the organization they needed for the new markets. So the war in Columbia would have to be cancelled due to unprofitability.

Developments in Brazilian politics led the cartels to put large amounts of money into that area, allowing a weakened democracy to be toppled before it had time to recover from its latest problems. The void created was filled by a shadowy council of ministers, sharing decisions and power. They would come to be called the Leadership. Stability was restored, but a price was paid. There were economic problems from before the change of government, and a crackdown on dissenters that led to international condemnation. The Leadership ignored the protests about the latter and made deals with two devils to deal with the former. Secret (at the time) agreements were made with certain of the Columbian organizations who exchanged hard currency for the exclusive use of certain areas of Amazonia for production and storage as well as for access to ports on the Amazon for loading and shipment of their "product."

The second devil dealt with was environmental damage. The Leadership accelerated development in other regions of the rain forest and repudiated some international agreements in a crash attempt to develop their way into a stable economy. This eventually led to difficulties with both the World Bank and the International Monetary Fund, the repudiation of some debt payments, the cut-off of future loans, and a greater reliance on cartel financing. One devil led them to another, which grew ever larger as it fed on the sins of the Leadership.

* * *

"Now, I do want you to look at that," the lieutenant said.

"That's what the heavies are for," Rock-On said from where they stood just inside the personnel gate.

"Uh-huh." Preacher was suddenly more frightened than he remembered ever being short of during certain stages of a firefight. He knew, in a manner of speaking, who the redhead in the Russian paratrooper's uniform was. He had what he thought was a pretty good idea of what she was doing, or about to do. From that, he concluded that it was no accident that he had showed up with Rock-On at this particular post at this particular time. That frightened him too.

Reaching a dream—even a somewhat nebulous one—can be like that, sometimes.

Preacher and Rock-On had rattled into Rio in the back of Redondo Hickman's pickup. The civilian clothing he had provided looked a lot better on Rock-On than they had on Preacher, which wasn't saying much. It hadn't helped that they had spent days in what remained of the coastal forest regions of Brazil, then an eternity (give or take a few millennia) on what passed for highways to get to the new embassy compound, all without benefit of soap and water that wasn't needed for drinking. The sergeant manning the back gate was a member of the Special Protective Group and a former SEAL candidate, injuries having washed him out of two attempts. He understood and asked no questions other than to verify their identity and authorization. Then he led them immediately to hot showers, food and beds. When they returned to consciousness some hours later, Olive Drabs in the right sizes were in reach, and their weapons—the ones they hadn't kept very close, that is—had been cleaned and oiled. And there was an invitation to an immediate meeting with the assistant ambassador and the head spook.

The CIA's top man there looked like he'd been born nervous. He was still trying to reconstruct what few networks there had been before the pullout began at the same time he was dealing with the increased demands for information that kept coming down the wire. And he was having to deal with "part-timers" like Hickman to boot. Preacher sympathized with him as much as he did with most spooks.

The assistant to the ambassador and the de facto head man, now that the ambassador was recalled "for consultations," a Mr. Blake, looked calmer, though whether he was or not was another question. Tension between the Leadership and the US government was rising steadily. There had been a few staged demonstrations already, and a few shots had been fired at a couple of consulates. After Kuwait and what State like to call "the Incident" in Africa, nothing was being taken for granted. Marines of the Special Protective Group had replaced the normal embassy guard detachment, the vault below the basement had been checked and overstocked, and arrangements with other embassies for refuge and assistance had been verified. It was doubtful that anything extreme would happen even if a complete breakdown in relations were to occur, but they were ready for it anyway. There were to be no further "incidents" if anyone could help it.

After the first round of debriefings and while they waited for the Russians to show up (if they did), Preacher and Rock-On spent most of their time with the Marines. The SPG sniper team had set up a miniature range in the subbasement hallway, with targets scaled to size and air rifles. Preacher exchanged shooting techniques with them there, and passed on what he knew about "interior work"—building entry and clearance—to the perimeter watch and reaction team members. Rock-On spent most of his time with the combat engineers the Marines had brought in, exploring ways to further harden the new embassy compound without making it obvious that it was being hardened.

There wasn't really that much for them to do, though. The SPG was, after all, trained for the job, and the embassy was on much better ground, militarily speaking, than the old one had been. It was partially built into the side of a mountain, in fact, the result of a decision to put the diplomats "in with the ordinary people of the country." There had also been the fact that land in the favelas, the hillside slums that overlooked Rio de Janiero, was much cheaper and easier to clear than anything available near the old embassy location in the business sector of the city. There had been some complaints, of course, mainly from those diplomats who didn't like to associate themselves with ordinary people of any country. But the move had been made anyway, and for the majority of the parties involved it had been beneficial. Some "ordinary people" had been at least temporarily elevated to middle-class status, the area around the embassy had improved dramatically in quality of such services as sewers, roads, and law enforcement, and the US had gotten a place that was much easier to protect now that things were getting bad for the officials that worked in it.

Preacher had been wandering around since before daybreak, going from outpost to outpost with a restless feeling that he wasn't used to having. The pattern of what were probably GRU operatives drifting into place had been pointed out to him by one of the snipers in the crow's nest, a disguised observation and firing platform on top of the main building. Those men and women, moving in by ones and twos to establish a perimeter, had brought

Preacher to the front personnel entrance. It was one of three breaks in the wall of the compound, set so that walk-ins could be properly controlled without the main vehicle gate having to be left open. Rock-On had found him there just after sunrise, and had stood with him watching until the car had pulled up at the downhill intersection and the man in the business suit and the woman in the paratrooper's uniform had stepped out.

"I could learn to love this job," the lieutenant said to no one in particular. He brushed nonexistent dust off of a spotless dress uniform.

Preacher didn't know what to do. The lieutenant was in charge of the watch. Since he was here now, the contact was his baby. The lieutenant was also new to the job, and hadn't impressed either of the SEALs with his attitude about his assignment. *He's an officer. He'll come up with some way to screw it up. Trouble, I'm in trouble...*

Rock-On looked first at his partner, who was standing very still just inside gate in the morning shadows. He noted Preacher's eyes, which were locked on to the cute redhead—make that a very cute redhead—with the shoulder bag and the briefcase. Then he studied Preacher's face, which was apparently in vigorous debate with itself over what emotion to show the world. Rock-On then looked at the watch commander, who was busy getting ready to posture, and then at the gate-guard, who was doing his job keeping an eye on everyone that wandered into his sector. Rock-On then took note to himself that the watch commander was a second lieutenant on his first assignment following SPG training, and that he hadn't been doing a very bang-up job of things so far. He definitely didn't seem to have his mind on his work right now.

The tendency of many officers to wander in to the wrong place at the wrong time is a regrettable aspect of military life. Rock-On quietly positioned himself behind the lieutenant's left shoulder, within easy reach.

* * *

The process of linking with the Leadership and moving facilities to Amazonia had actually begun about two years before the Columbian initiatives were underway. It was initially a simple business decision to open outlets on the Amazon for products to be transshipped to distribution centers for the new overseas markets. There was no intention to take over the government. That relocation was driven mainly by accountants who wanted to begin adjusting to a drop in demand in what was still the major market. No one remembers where the grander plans came from, whether it had been whispered in someone's ear or perhaps come to them in a dream one night. What the money trail on the data disks in Hunter's briefcase showed was not the reasoning and planning behind the move, just the evidence of what had been done. The interrogation of the prisoners had provided some evidence of the whys behind the what, however. Edited transcripts of the questioning were also inside the briefcase.

The first cash transfers went to regional military and government officers, and were intended to guarantee security for cartel operations. What the cartels didn't know was that Brazil was beginning its slide into Leadership control. Their payoffs, in fact, were (less the customary percentage off the top) a major part of the financing for that particular political struggle. When the country-vs.-city struggle began to show success for what would become the Leadership, the cartels began to understand and consider that there were larger possibilities at hand.

The opportunity to enhance operational security was the first one taken. Payoffs were carefully documented by the accountants in order to make the threat of blackmail real. The cartel coalition wanted to have all the facts if the stick had to replace the carrot. Payments for regional security became payments for national security. Army troops secured production and distribution sites. Product was sometimes transported to Amazonian ports on government vehicles and aircraft. The "hiring" of the Leadership by the cartels became more evident and overt.

The drug money link broke into the international news reports eighteen months after the Leadership assumed overt power. It wasn't so much that a government had never been bought by anyone that shocked people and governments so much as that the relationship became so openly acknowledged at some levels. The Leadership handled the revelation relatively well, mounting a media and diplomatic campaign that combined outright denial (which worked best locally and regionally) with counteraccusations and the creative construction of "facts." The cartels dealt with the loss of the blackmail option by increasing the flow of money, which strengthened the threat of withdrawal. The people of Brazil, and to a great extent the people of most other countries, dealt with the revelation by ignoring anything that didn't affect than directly.

The height of the merger came at about the same time that World Bank and International Monetary Fund loans were suspended. A liaison group led by a high-level lieutenant established offices in a corporate building in downtown Brazilia. The cartel had officially joined the government.

* * *

Preacher was thinking about the Old Testament story of Isaac and Rebecca as he watched The Woman approach the gate. It was all he could do. He seemed otherwise to be rooted to the spot he stood at, just inside the gate on the left side a little behind the wall. He felt frozen, unable to move at all. Helpless. He wasn't used to that feeling.

Abraham had sent his most trusted servant to find a wife for his son Isaac. The servant had in turned asked God to point out the woman that God wanted his master's son to marry, the method of said pointing being that the woman chosen would perform a specific set of actions. A woman had appeared and performed the series of actions the servant was watching for, he had taken her home to his master's son Isaac and a good time had been had by all. That's the way Preacher figured it went, anyway.

It looked like something like that would have to happen now, because he couldn't move. Why couldn't he move? He needed to move, but he couldn't. He had to get the lootynut out of the way. But he couldn't move. Why couldn't he move? *Oh, God...*

Hunter was surprised when the lieutenant stepped out from the gate. Not wildly or completely surprised, but enough that she stopped and looked around quickly as if she had been in the forest when a twig snapped. Then she advanced to within a few feet of the lieutenant, where she could see into the small gate, carefully set the briefcase down, and looked around again as she adjusted the strap of her shoulder bag.

There were four men at the gate. All were soldiers. This was unusual. There was the lieutenant standing in front of her on the street itself. He had a polite smile on his face and lust in his eyes. This was annoying. Hunter was aware that she had above-average looks, but the attention she drew from men, especially this one, could be annoying at times. She didn't like this one. His dress uniform wasn't properly cut, for one thing. She could tell he was wearing body armor. This one and the other one in a dress uniform, the one watching the street, were members of the specially-trained unit that the Americans had formed following the African problem. Hunter's unit had studied that operation. She considered it well done, under the circumstances, though coordination between Foreign Legion and Russian relief forces could have been better—

Irrelevant. She brought herself back, looking at the third man present. He was a small man in standard non-camouflaged fatigues. This was rather more unusual. That one smiled and nodded politely when she looked at him, but his eyes were on the lieutenant. Hunter wondered about this as she shifted her attention to the fourth one. He was big, this one, bigger than Vadim, who was the largest man in her unit—her former unit. He wore a plain battle uniform like the small one behind the lieutenant did, though the small man looked much more comfortable wearing his. The expression on the big man's face was hard for

Hunter to identify. There seemed to be mixtures of and changes between apprehension, hope, fear, and perhaps joy, even during the few seconds she really observed him. He was staring at her too, but it didn't make her uncomfortable like staring usually did. She found it to be rather interesting, in fact.

The moment of observation passed. Hunter looked back at the lieutenant.

"Good morning—" he said, and hesitated over her rank insignia, "—ma'am. Is there something I can help you with?"

Did he expect her to be overcome by his beauty? "I am here to speak with Mr. Anthony

Blake," she said in unaccented English, "The matter is urgent." She directed the second sentence toward the big man in the background.

"Did you have an appointment, ma'am?" the lieutenant asked.

"No, I don't." That would have announced her and Gregoriy's presence. It would not have satisfied Gregoriy's sense of humor, either. "But I must see him immediately. It is important that I speak directly with him."

"I'm afraid I'll have to clear it." He didn't look afraid to her. He looked more like he was enjoying his control of the situation. Hunter wondered how this one had survived the selection process. "Who should I say is calling, please?"

"I am Senior Lieutenant Alexandrova, of the Russian Army," Hunter answered in a sharper tone than she meant to speak with. The stress of the sudden transition she was making and her irritation with the inexperienced officer in front of her were making her lose patience. She looked at the big man. "I must see the ambassador. Please." What now? *Oh God, please help me.*

Preacher got his voice back. "Let her through, sir," he said. It was a bit of shock to him to hear himself speak. "I'll guarantee her. Anything happens, you can blame me." The even tone of his words amazed him.

The lieutenant was annoyed. It was his watch, after all, and a first command, and he felt a need to assert himself in it. And the man was just a sergeant, even if he was the biggest man the lieutenant had ever seen and a SEAL besides. But the annoyance was mixed with confusion and a little caution. The two had materialized at the back gate. They had been debriefed by the same man the Russian fox was asking for, and the head CIA man. What kind of pull might they have? The lieutenant decided that he could probably manage to exert some authority and let something go, too. That seemed to be the safest way to do it. And that would get the fox in the compound, where he would definitely manage another approach. A paratrooper? He intended to find out if she was really jump-qualified, yes, he would...

"Very well, Sergeant," he said without looking back. He added a hint of a sneer to the tone so that the outsider noncom would know that he was annoyed. Then he re-modulated his voice and spoke to the woman. "I'll conduct you to the front office, Lieutenant. Perhaps we can get you to Mr. Blake from there. But I must verify the contents of your bags first." He indicated a guard shack inset into the wall. It was slightly smaller than two old-style phone booths put side-by-side. "If you would, please."

There is no way I'm going into any enclosed area with this one. Hunter picked up the briefcase. "I can't allow that," she said, "There are documents here for Ambassador Blake. He alone must see them." She looked again at the big one. "Examine my credentials and rum a scanner over it if you must, but I can't allow you to open the case." Her orders were clear on that point, and she was still a soldier.

The lieutenant frowned. "Ma'am, my orders are very specific on this point. I must—"

Rock-On concluded that the lieutenant was close to getting himself killed. He thought that he would not be unhappy about such an incident. He might even learn something from the Russian woman, if he observed carefully. Rock-On was always happy if he could learn something new.

Preacher's voice escaped from his mouth again. "Lieutenant, my partner and I can run the checks. We've got the training, sir, it's no problem. Let's get Lieutenant Alexandrova inside, sir, and we can do that." It was going to be—technically, at least—insubordination. He could see it coming.

The lieutenant felt he was losing control of the situation, and so he did what some people do when that happens. He became irrationally stubborn. "I have trouble with that, Ser—"

That's it. Rock-On put a hand on the lieutenant's shoulder. "A moment of your time. Lieutenant," he said, and jerked the man out of Hunter's way with one hand.

Hunter looked at the gate-guard, to see what he would do. A sudden sense of tension told her that the big soldier was not only waiting to see what would happen, but he was preparing to act if anything did. This was of great concern to her. There were a dozen Spetsnaz within sprinting distance, and no telling how many Americans ready to back up the gate watch. She had not come here to start a riot.

The guard saluted her and continued to watch the street. He was grinning as she passed him.

Hunter returned his salute and went in past the lieutenant, who was struggling against a joint lock and a hand over his mouth. The small man was talking rapidly and softly into the officer's ear. Hunter went directly up to the big man, who still seemed to be very tense, and did something she had never done before with any man. She put her free hand out to him.

Preacher took the hand, automatically. It felt very good, held in his.
It was like it belonged there. He relaxed and smiled at her.

She smiled, really smiled, back. She couldn't remember the last time she had done that, but now she was, and at a complete stranger no less. But she couldn't help it. It was amazing, the way she felt now. Hunter felt—in place-now, for perhaps the first time in her life. And it was a marvelous place to be.

It was not going to be so hard to leave home as she had thought.

"Privyet," he said.

"<You speak Russian?>" she asked, shifting automatically to her first language.

"<I'm working on it,>" Preacher said to the most beautiful woman in the world, "<How am I doing?>"

Morana laughed. "<You need more practice,>" she said, "<But don't worry. I can help you with that.>"

There were three men, embassy guards, coming down the walkway toward them. Help for the lieutenant, who was free and obviously angry. The small man that had been holding the officer had covered his eyes with one hand and was shaking his head slowly. Officers could have that kind of effect on you.

"<I need your help,>" Morana said to the one who was holding her hand, "<I am Morana Ivana Alexandrova. I must see the ambassador now. It is very important.>"

Preacher smiled. "<That is a beautiful name. Mine is Eric. My friend there is Jonathan, but most of us call him Rock-On. He calls me Preacher. I will take your bags for you.>"

"You're under arrest," the lieutenant said, "You're all under arrest." "Of course," Morana said, switching back to English, and handed the briefcase to him.

"Did you hear me?" the lieutenant said. Rock-On shook his head again.

"That is an interesting nickname," Morana said as Eric took her shoulder bag, "Are you, then, a—how should I say it—a man of God?"

The backup team, a sergeant with a pair of privates in tow, stopped, staying a few feet out of anybody's reach until they could find out what exactly was happening here.

"Sergeant, place these men under arrest!" the lieutenant said.

"Sir?" The gate overwatch had not given the sergeant the impression that there was much of a problem. Everyone was merely following standard procedure. Arresting SEALs in the presence of what appeared to be a Russian officer was not what he had anticipated.

"You could say that," Eric said, softly enough so that only Morana—A wonderful name. Simply wonderful —could hear, "Perhaps I should see about calling down a curse on the lieutenant."

"The wrath of God will not be necessary," Morana said, "My own will be enough for this, I think. Watch." She took her hand out of his and turned toward the guard sergeant, composing herself for the outburst.

"I said—"

"If anyone is going to be arrested here," Morana said, giving every indication that she was on the verge of exploding, "it should be <u>that</u> one!" She thrust a finger at the lieutenant as if it were a knife.

"Ma'am?" the sergeant said.

"Ma'am?" the lieutenant said, looking as if Morana's finger were the barrel of a pistol pointed at him.

"He has blocked legitimate access rights of registered member of the diplomatic contingent of a friendly nation," Morana said, steadily building up the volume as she went, "He has interfered with the process of important diplomatic communications, he has _dared_ to imply that I might be a terrorist or an assassin, and—" She looked at the lieutenant and abruptly softened her voice. "You are a second lieutenant?"

"Ma'am?" He was too busy trying to follow her to be alert. "Yes ma'am, second lieutenant ma'am."

"AND HE HAS FAILED TO ACKNOWLEDGE A SUPERIOR OFFICER!"

Dead silence.

After her chosen number of seconds of shock had passed, Morana assumed a tone of the utmost reasonableness. "However, I am prepared to forgive these relatively small indiscretions, if only for the sake of continued goodwill and cooperation between our governments, and if this gentleman is prepared to forgive these others who were acting—perhaps a bit exuberantly—in my behalf." She fixed the lieutenant with a look that was as sharp as any blade she was carrying. "Well?"

He might not be facing a diplomatic incident, technically speaking, but he was facing a possible major career block and he knew it. The lieutenant drew himself up to perfect attention and saluted. "Yes ma'am. I understand, ma'am. Forget I ever said anything, ma'am."

Behind him, Rock-On offered Morana silent applause.

She smiled benevolently at the child. "Thank you, Lieutenant," she said, "Your cooperation is very much appreciated. Now, I must be about my business. The sergeant will accompany me as my guide." She returned his salute with parade-ground exactness. "You may carry on, Lieutenant." She pivoted toward Preacher. "You may proceed, Sergeant."

"Ma'am." Eric saluted the lieutenant, who made a weak return. "Sir." He made a crisp half-turn and walked with Morana past the reaction team and toward the main embassy building.

"So, what do you want us to do, Lieutenant?" the sergeant leading the backup team asked. *And what the hell am I going to put in the watch report about this?*

"Don't worry about it, Sergeant," the lieutenant said, making a mental note to stay well out of sight for the foreseeable future, "I'm not going to worry about it anymore. So just forget about it. I've got rounds to make." Then he just walked away, going down the clear strip on the inside of the wall.

The sergeant waited until the officer was out of hearing. Then he went over to Rock-On and asked, "You wouldn't be able to tell me what happened—I mean what really happened—here, would you?"

Rock-On was watching Eric and Morana go out of sight around the curve in the walkway. They were holding hands. He smiled.

"It looks to me, friend, like the end of yet another successful special operation," Rock-On said.

* * *

The United States probably would have kept the cartel-government link further in the background had it not been for the revival of the nuclear weapons program that had been canceled by an earlier, democratically elected, president. It was part of a number of developments that seemed to come into being all at once, even though they were all the end result of years of chained-together events.

By the mid-nineties over a dozen other countries either possessed or were capable of building nuclear weapons. This was at the same time that the U.S. and Russia were in the process of dramatic nuclear force reductions that had been agreed to in 1992. The threat of further proliferation was threatening to undermine that effort as arguments were advanced that stockpiles should be kept larger in order to discourage adventurism by the new members of the Nuclear Club. It was a weak argument, but there seemed to be few alternatives to the former enemies keeping the biggest sticks in their respective neighborhoods.

The Tacit agreement, more secret than the antiweapon operations that had been conducted since its inception, was nothing more than desperation. It was a secret and temporary dike erected against what appeared to be the rising waters of nuclear proliferation. The announcement of renewed development by Brazil, combined with known development programs in other potentially problematic places, had not only revived the Strategic Defense

Initiative concept but had added several new wrinkles to that scheme. It also provided the first test of the Tacit agreement. Brazil had missiles and was going to have a bomb. The idea of drug lords paying for nuclear weapons was just as frightening, if not more so, than the thought of someone like Qaddafi of Libya having one. That was before Libya had actually stepped in after years of inactivity to fill in the financing gaps that had been left by suspension of international loans to Brazil. The only people not frightened after that were either totally ignorant of the situation or were bankers who had been previously threatened by defaults.

At the Pentagon, they were scared enough to return several contingency plans from the dead. One of these was rumored to have resulted in an American/British operation on Argentine soil that everyone suspected but no one admitted. Another program, one that had started two or three years after the operations against Iraq, was put on an accelerated track. It involved the use of submarine-launched ballistic missiles with special non-nuclear warheads against deeply buried blinkers. It was a strange thought, using a ballistic missile submarine as a tactical bombardment platform.

It was maybe even crazy enough to work.

* * *

"My word," Anthony Blake said, looking up from his terminal, "this is interesting." He looked at his chief of station. "What do you think?"

The head spook still looked nervous. Eric had decided that it was his normal expression.

"It's possible," he said, "The information looks good." He looked at Morana. "We'll have to check it, of course."

"Of course," she said. "We don't expect you not to. We've tried to provide some sources for you in the material." She looked at Blake. "Colonel Alexandrovitch will assist you. Off the record."

"He can stay as far away from the record as he wants to. For that matter, there isn't even a record anymore. It's all CD's now." Blake sighed. "Something of a pity, that. How is Gregoriy, by the way? I didn't know he was in town."

"You weren't supposed to," Morana said, "He's well and sends his greetings. He will announce himself before I leave here."

"That's great," Blake said, using the small talk as a tool of concentration while he considered the information on the disks that Morana had given them. "It will be good to see him again." There was more than a money trail on those disks. The Russians had information there that had been gathered from nets that were stretched across two continents.

"He wants another computer," Morana said.

Blake looked up. "Pardon me?"

"He wants another computer," Morana said again, "He left the old one in Moscow. He's looking for something newer. More powerful. You understand?" She made a note to look at computer schools as soon as she was settled in America.

"Ah! Yes," Blake said, "of course. For this," He tapped the display screen, "top-of-the-line isn't good enough. Roger?"

"Hell, yes," the CIA man said without looking up from the printouts in his lap, "If half of this is half as good as it looks, I'll buy him one myself." *When word of this*

Washington net gets out, there's gonna be blood in the streets.

Blake studied Morana for a moment. "We've been remiss, Lieutenant—"

"I'm retired now," Morana said, "As of the moment I take this uniform off." Once she got into the civilian clothing that she had brought, she intended to make the uniform and all that it meant become the literal ashes of the past.

"I see. Miss Alexandrova—"

"Call me Morana."

"Very well, Morana. I can't begin to understand what you've given up to bring us this information." Russia's free emigration policies were not free to members of groups such as Spetsnaz. To Russia, Morana, was a defector. Gregoriy had chosen to sacrifice the messenger in order to emphasize the importance of the message. "I do know that it was a lot. I want to thank you personally, and on behalf of the government of the United States. The State Department—"

"And the CIA," the station chief said without looking up. He knew what was coming. The Director would have him shot if the Agency didn't get a piece of it. "Don't forget the CIA."

"—will do as much as we can to assist your adjustment." Blake made a mental note to see what chips he could call in so that State would have first crack at the opportunity that had walked through their gate. Once word about Morana—a Spetsnaz officer and the sister of a high-ranked GRU analyst and field man—got out, agencies would be lining up to help, and be helped out by, her. "Is there anything we can do for you? Aside from letting you rest, of course. We've kept you here a very long time." Six hours, in fact, and she had sat calmly beside the big SEAL through all of it, answering questions, explaining and expanding information for them, and guiding than through the introduction that Gregoriy had prepared. She looked not a bit worse for the long session. It was probably the mildest of stresses compared to her past experience and training.

"If you have no other questions, I'd like to get rid of this uniform first," Morana said, "Then I suppose that I should start filling out forms, should I not?"

"There aren't as many as you might think," Morana," Blake answered, "Perhaps you'd like to relax a while first. We can start that process tomorrow." There were accelerated channels set up just for catches like this. She would have no trouble getting in. "Would there be anything else, perhaps?"

"Could Eric—I mean the sergeant—remain with me? I mean, could he possibly be detached? I would be most grateful if something like that could be arranged." She put her hand out. His hand found it without him looking.

"I'm sure that we can work something out." Blake looked at Eric. "Well, what will it be? Temporary detachment, or would you rather just get totally out of this man's SEALs?"

"I'm just inside of six months on the current enlistment, anyway, sir," Eric answered, "It wouldn't bother me if they could just go ahead and run me out. It would be easier for me to stay with her that way." He had a big grin on his face that most people would describe as silly, though it was doubtful that anyone would describe it that way in his hearing.

"I'll see what can be worked out, Sergeant," Blake said. *Love is a wonderful thing—at least under certain circumstances.* Emigration was open to most Russians, and their intelligence people probably had better things to do than hunt down a defector But Morana Alexandrova was not most Russians or your average defector. It was possible (though not probable—probably) that someone would try to do that when (not if—Blake was realistic about that) word of this got back to Moscow. Even a highly-placed brother might not know about, or be able to prevent, some sort of GRU or Spetsnaz effort at retribution. Their system was even more compartmentalized than the American one, which suffered less from compartments than it did from the mess that any giant bureaucracy can make of something. Having an ex-SEAL with Team Six experience close by might be a very handy thing for Morana. More than that, it was what she wanted. Blake would only be the first official that would be very concerned with keeping Morana as happy and content as they could. "I'll talk to my people and see what we have to do to get that done for you. Roger?"

"Just a couple of questions, miss, and then we'll let you go," the CIA man said, "Is this press campaign going to be launched anytime soon?"

"No. That will be coordinated with you as to time, place, and content," Morana said. GRU was preparing a press campaign that would play upon nationalist sentiments. The people would be shown how Brazil was being sold to outsiders by the Leadership. If done properly, the resulting unrest might be enough to topple the Leadership by itself. Then the UN could step in to help, and things would be back to normal, more or less. *Maybe. It will be the UN or similar international agency, after all. They seem to be very good about messing things up.* "There is the belief that the message will be better received and believed if it comes from sources that are outside your control."

"I fully agree with that. Fine, then. We'll wait for the call."

"And your other question?"

A slight hesitation. "I have to ask. Are you really jump-qualified?"

Morana laughed. "Does it seem so strange?" She looked at Eric. "Don't you have women in your parachute units?"

"Some, yes," Eric answered, "but still not too many. And none in any special ops group that I know of."

"How interesting." She looked at the station chief. "All the members of my unit are parachute-qualified. It was required. I couldn't wear the uniform otherwise."

"I see. Thank you." He looked as if he still weren't quite sure about that. Morana decided that it was probably a normal attitude for spies. "That's it for me, then." He stood up. "I've got a long night ahead with this stuff, if you'll excuse me. Tony, I'll see you later, of course." He left the room.

"Well." Blake blanked the terminal and turned in his chair to face them. "That's it for me too, Morana. You take some time off, now. We'll start your formal processing tomorrow. Do you have any thoughts about what you want to do in America?"

"Well..." Morana smiled at Eric. "I think I want to go to school and start a family. I think that would be nice. What do you think?"

He could recognize an ambush when one was sprung in his face. He fell back on hard training and combat-conditioned reflexes.

"Oh. Aaaa, sure, I guess. Uhm. A couple of kids might be nice."

"Four," she said, "Four children."

"Uhm. Maybe three."

"Six. Large families intrigue me."

"Woman, I am not Catholic. There are several effect contraceptive options that will be available." *I gotta get out. How do I get out?*

"Really." She put on a look of wide-eyed innocence. "Will you help me try some of them out?"

Blake was trying not to laugh out loud. Eric was trying to get out of the conversational kill zone.

"Would it be possible to talk about this later, maybe?"

"Well," Morana said, "I certainly hope you'll do more than talk about it..."

PRESENT

War is hell.

W.T. Sherman

"The round has entered the water, Captain. I have it clearly."

"Very good," Arunov said, "Fire two and three."

* * *

"Where?" Delamadrid checked an impulse to look around as if he could see what was happening. "Where is the torpedo?" What was it? A surface unit?

"Sir, torpedo is bearing three hundred relative. It is...it seems to have begun a search pattern."

"It hasn't acquired us?" They would have heard a surface ship! Or perhaps it was there all along, somehow. The Spruance-class destroyers were extremely quiet. Their Oliver Hazard

Perry-class frigates had electric motors they could use to creep with. And both of them carried helicopters and variable-depth sonar arrays. But why hadn't it acted earlier?

"I don't believe so, sir." The sonarman didn't sound as nervous as his captain did.

"Helm, steer zero-five-zero." That would take them away from the torpedo while keeping the American within their sonar arc. "Sonar, are you sure that it came from the surface?" A helicopter, then, or an airplane. But they would have had to fly low and drop buoys! Or perhaps it was a dipping sonar. But they would have heard a low-flying aircraft or hovering helicopter or the splash of the buoys—not certainly, but probably. Where, then? Where was the launch platform? "Corte', prepare two tubes. We'll swing around quickly and fire, after we've moved away a bit." They had to press the attack hOme. It was the imperative that the American not escape. No matter what.

Who was firing? Who?

* * *

"Somebody over there likes us, Captain," Tullibee said.

"That's a torpedo." There was wonder in J.T.'s voice. "Is it one of ours?"

"You're gonna love this. Skipper," Johnson said, "Computer identifies it as Russian."

"Say what?" Simmons asked.

"That was a missile launch back there," J.T. said.

"Correct, Captain. We've got a guardian angel with tricolor wings."

"Son of a bitch," Simmons said, "Son of a bitch."

"Another launch, Captain," Tullibee said, "Range is undetermined, bearing almost zero relative. He's inside direct-path distance, I can tell you that much."

"He's good," Simmons said.

"He's launching sequentially," J.T. said, "He's trying to keep a round running all the time." It would keep Bravo reacting. The attacker would have initiative as long as he had rounds to fire. "What's Bravo doing?"

"Moving away from the torpedo, but not increasing speed or dropping decoys."

"Sounds too confident to suit me."

"I don't think he has to worry yet, sir. The round is searching. It didn't drop close enough to hit on them."

"We could put one in the water at him," Simmons suggested.

Four left. "Not yet. They might interfere with each other. I'd rather try to get out while he's busy. Engineering, Conn. Talk to me. Chief, we've got a chance to move."

"I don't think it'll hurt us, Captain, but it's going to make noise when we move. It'll take a drydock to nail it down."

Run or hide? Can't do both.

"Suggestions?"

"He may forget we're here if we stay quiet," Simmons said.

"Or maybe they'll nail him before he gets back around to us," Bearkiller said, "Besides, if we move we could attract one of those missile drops by mistake."

"We might get some distance on him, sir," Petersen said from the helm, "but we'd be blind and noisy doing it." They wouldn't get far over ten knots before the sonar became useless.

"Can't outrun a torpedo," Simmons said. Tigerfish was over twenty knots faster than they were healthy and it could sustain that speed for more than enough time to run them down.

"What can we get from the trolling motors?" J.T. asked. The steerable docking thrusters wouldn't be powerful, but they would be silent. "Maybe we can ease away somewhere, slowly."

"Conn, Sonar. Skipper, that first torpedo is dying. I've got another one in the water just north of Bravo, and he's turning to get away from it now. Another launch transient from long range, too."

"Bracketing," Simmons said, "And his timing's almost dead on. Who the hell is he?"

"We can try to find out," J.T. said, "Helm, get us enough to stream the tail at least. Sonar, let the tail out slowly. We don't want tangles. Get me something on our mysterious benefactor as soon as you can. I like to know about people who are saving my life."

* * *

"Another torpedo! Very close, bearing thirty relative."

"Helm, one-eight-zero. Sonar, has it acquired us?" *Maddening! Where? Who? What?* "Corte', do American attack submarines carry this kind of weapon?"

"Not to my knowledge. It must be an airplane or helicopter."

"We are at one-eight-zero, sir."

"Sonar, active search! Give me six pulses!"

"The torpedo will hear!"

"It doesn't matter! We must finish it! We must finish them off!"

"Sonar ready, Captain."

"Initiate!"

* * *

PING-PING-PING-PING-PING-PING.

"They got us," Simmons muttered.

"Transient! Transient! Bravo has fired. Bravo has one—two, count two, torpedoes in the water, Conn."

"Acknowledged. Jim, fire one to intercept."

"I still don't know if we can manage it."

"Let's try. They did it, we can do it better, right? Unless you want to rely on the decoys?"

A pause. Then: "Firing one. One is out, one is running."

Three are left.

"Trail the last Nixie."

* * *

"An active search?" Ulanovitch asked, "But our torpedo—"

"Has started to home. Marsilov, fire four." He waited for the answering vibration of the round leaving its tube.

"But the torpedo has acquired—"

"It can be decoyed. We must make sure. Helm, all ahead emergency for thirty seconds, then reduce to twenty knots."

"They will hear us!" Ulanovitch said, "They will know where we are!" "Exactly," Arunov replied, "Hopefully, they will turn to deal with us first. The American can escape, or perhaps they will even help us take than." He could feel Molniya gathering speed. He drew power from it. "Sonar, what do you have?" They would not gain enough speed to totally mask the sonar or require that he tail be brought to line astern. The surge of acceleration and the noise of the reactor at full power was the signal he was sending, the announcement that he hoped would make the Brazilian pay attention.

Arunov had no way of knowing that the other submarine was "tailless," and so was blind to anything behind them.

"Captain, they have fired torpedoes."

"At us?" There was room enough to outdistance them if necessary. Molniya was thirty thousand meters away.

"No sir."

"Aahh!" Ulanovitch cried out softly. There was only one other possible target.

"The American—it has to be—has released one also, sir."

"Almost thirty seconds, Captain," the helmsman said.

"Bring us back to twenty knots." Arunov looked at Ulanovitch and shrugged. "The Brazilian is determined. There is nothing further that we can do. We must rely on their countermeasures, even as they do."

"Do you think they will work?" Ulanovitch asked.

Another shrug. "We'll see."

"Tube one reloaded," Marsilov reported, "I am reminded that three missiles are left."

"Load them all," Arunov ordered, "put the Six-Five in last." When those were gone they would be left with shorter-ranged ET-80As.

Arunov looked at Ulanovitch. "I find myself wishing that we had risked even one nuclear-armed weapon."

Ulanovitch nodded. "I understand." One of the old SS-N-15s with its nuclear depth charge warhead would have ended the confrontation instantly, probably without harm to the American. "We must do with what we have." If they had not been destroyed already, all the old tactical nuclear warheads were in very secure storage sites in Russia.

"Sonar, what's happening out there?"

"He's jamming, sir. I don't think we're going to get him this time."

* * *

"Will it work?"

"It's got a chance. Computer didn't want to, but I convinced—stand by!" Bearkiller flipped the safety cover off the kill switch. "Three, one—" He pressed it.

Because of the directional warhead on the ADCAP, the weapons officer detonated the round in front of the oncoming torpedoes. The shock wave and turbulence rushed mostly forward, hammering the lead Tigerfish in such a way that the warhead thought it had hit something solid. That caused it to detonate. The force of the second explosion combined with the shock of the ADCAP detonation literally shook the second torpedo to pieces. As more debris fell slowly to join what was already on the bottom, another wall of disrupted water blocked friend and foe off from each other.

* * *

The E45-75A-mod torpedo carried by the SS-N-16 antisubmarine missile has two basic limitations, both resulting from its relatively small size. One was its range, which is only eight thousand yards. Another was the sophistication of its homing system, which is not high. There wasn't room for the processing power that a heavyweight torpedo can carry. So the one that had acquired Triunfante was in the end unable to differentiate between the real submarine and the false images created by the Brazilian's jamming systems. It ran past the real thing, heading first for the stirred up area of the explosions. By the time it realized that it was mistaken, it was out of fuel.

And another one was starting its run from above them.

"Damn!" Delamadrid slapped the periscope casing. "Who are these people? Sonar, is it on to us?"

"I don't think so, sir. It seems to be too far away, about one-forty relative."

"Helm, two-seven-zero. Sonar, check carefully in that area." Without the towed array, periodic returns were necessary to listen behind them, lest they be taken unawares. "What do you think, Corte'?"

"How are we supposed to fight something we can't see? They are dropping torpedoes on us like God throwing lightning from the sky. We've lost our best sonar. We're blind to anything behind us. The situation tells me to recommend withdrawal. I'm sorry, Captain."

"Don't apologize for honesty, Corte'. I agree that the situation is not the best. But our duty forces us to ignore it. Do you think the government will hold if the American is allowed to carry out his mission?"

"Captain, I have something."

"What is it, Lieutenant?"

"The aerial torpedo is searching away from us. But Captain, I hear highspeed screws coming in from long range. A torpedo, sir! That is, another one!"

Delamadrid said nothing. He was listening to what sounded like a dam bursting in his head. The sound of water rushing through his mind overpowered thought for a moment.

"Captain?"

"Can you tell anything else about it?" he asked when the sound of rushing water had subsided somewhat.

"It's not like one of ours, or like an American one. It's far away still, and not going as fast, I think. I'm trying to get more on it."

Delamadrid opened his mouth to snap at the sonar operator, but then he changed his mind. It suddenly seemed useless to snap at anyone. "What about the submarine it came from?" The rushing water in his mind—it wasn't speaking, but there seemed to be a message in the noise.

"A possible, sir, behind the torpedo at very long range."

"Active search. Sonar. Listen for that torpedo and the American. Corte', prepare to fire.
Sonar, initiate search." Something had changed in his voice. There was less fire in it than there had been before. Perhaps the water was putting it out. "Another submarine, Corte'." He didn't seem to care if his first officer was listening. "One of their attack units, probably. There is little time to decide." He could almost make out what the water was saying...

"Contact!"

"Who?"

"The American."

"Fire two torpedoes." Over the shudder of compressed air driving the torpedoes out, he said to himself, "There may yet be time. There must be time. Must be time..."

He thought the water was saying something about duty. Or just the word, alone. Duty. Repeated over and over.

Duty.

Duty.

Duty...

* * *

"You're gonna love this, Skipper. Our guardian angel classifies as a Mod Sierra. And he's let go a regular torpedo, I think."

"Son of a bitch," Simmons said. There was a trace of awe in his voice.

"I wonder how long he's been out there," J.T. said.

PING PING PING...

"Aw, shit!" That came from the diving officer.

"Deep, too," J.T. said, "and we're still in it."

"Transients, we got transients! Bravo has fired."

"Get one out, Jim. You know the drill now."

"One is out. One is running."

Two are left. "Countermeasures to standby. Srully, what about that torpedo the Sierra fired?"

"Not fast—not fast as ours, that is. We're registering another one from the surface, too. That's all I've got right now, Skipper."

J.T. looked around, but Bearkiller and Simmons were busy keeping them alive, maybe. J.T. couldn't think of anything that would help them at that moment, so he let them do the job he had given them to do. For a little while he would be a spectator on his own boat. But he had trained them, and he trusted them, so he had no trouble living with inactivity for the moment. Besides, it wasn't really inactivity. He had quite a bit to do still.

"Bravo status."

"He's turned back to our line. Something funny about that maneuver. Wait! Dropping decoys now. I guess the last one's got him spooked a little."

On the table display, the tracks of the incoming torpedoes and the ADCAP were converging. Bravo Two was taking no evasive action, and didn't appear to need it—the Russian lightweight torpedo was curving off toward one of the decoys the attacker had left behind. Behind and to starboard of Bravo Two, the single Russian torpedo seemed to be crawling across the space between its target and the submarine that had fired it. There was something odd about that, but J.T. couldn't at that moment pin down what it was.

They were closing the distance, trying to cut down Alabama's reaction time. His command was between the proverbial rock and the equally-proverbial hard place. If they moved fast, they made noise. Bravo would be able to follow than passively. And no matter how fast they could move, they couldn't outrun either the hunter or its arrows. But Bravo knew where they were now. And there was still enough time for them to make the kill before the Russian got close enough to guide anything in with any certainty.

Time. He had to gain time. He had to gain time.

It would, after all, be impolite to not be around to thank the Russians for saving their lives.

* * *

"Do you know what they're doing?" Arunov asked, "They are using their own torpedoes against the ones that are fired at them!"

"Like an antimissile missile," Ulanovitch said, "Clever." If the idea took hold, submarine tactics would have to be reconsidered.

"It's expensive, but it keeps them alive," Marsilov said.

"For how long is the question," Arunov said, "Their torpedo load is small, no more than a dozen. They've got to be nearly empty. We have to get closer, force the Brazilian to pay attention to us. What is our weapon status?"

"Two Sixteens, one Six-Five in the major tubes, all minor tubes with standard loads. Eight standard reloads remain."

"We have one running already," Arunov said, "Anything more would be risking interference. We'll have to let events run their course." It looked like it would be a near thing if it were anything at all. "I just hope there will be something left for us to salvage. The government will want some kind of return for its weapon expenditures."

* * *

"—and fire," Bearkiller said, and pressed the kill switch. J.T. watched the black cloud that marked sonar interference on the chart display spread out and envelop the two incoming torpedoes.

"Jim, as soon as it clears I want one for Bravo." Maybe a mistake, but he wasn't inclined to sit around and get shot at, either. "Sonar, what's the status on the Russian?"

"He's closing at a steady rate, Captain. It's probably as fast as he can go without—stand by...high-speed—damn!—torpedo's still coming! We got one still inbound!"

The marker appeared on their side of the turbulence zone, a Tigerfish running at forty knots.

"Launch decoys. Jammers to standby, BeeGees to standby." *Do I pray for direct assistance, or should I just ask Him to make sure that the subcontractors did their jobs?*

Green lights flickered on the weapons control console. On the chart display decoys appeared as tiny x's beside the Alabama marker. The torpedo track curved a little away from the center mark.

That's it, that's it, that's it...

They heard it pass just a few feet to starboard. The hum of the torpedo as it passed was actually barely audible. It was anxiety that made it sound as if it filled and then emptied each compartment as it ran almost directly from bow to stem before it passed out of hearing behind them.

J.T. didn't relax. The Tigerfish had as good an autonomous capability as an ADCAP. It would undoubtedly start curving back as soon as it registered the miss.

* * *

"Helm, go to two-two-zero. Sonar, acquire the incoming torpedo and ready an intercept. It's lucky they fired from so far away—"

"Captain!"

The tone of the voice put a crack in Delamadrid's recently regained sense of control.

"Torpedo incoming two-eight-zero relative! It passed ours!"

"Bastards! That wasn't an interception! Quickly! Prepare one!"

"Captain, there's not enough time—"

"Damn you! There has to be or we're dead! Do it now!"

Corte' fired as soon as the solution was fed to him. Delamadrid wiped sweat from his forehead and waited.

"_Now_! _Now_!"

Corte' pressed the kill switch. They could hear the torpedo's detonation clearly. It was very close. Delamadrid waited to find out whether or not they were all going to die.

"Nothing, Captain. We've done it again."

Delamadrid relaxed, a little. "Corte' get back to the other one now."

"Captain, an aerial torpedo has dropped about two-four-zero relative."

"Damn, damn, damn!" He punctuated the last one by slamming his fist against a panel.
"We're too close! Fire, Corte', fire!"

"There will be only three left then," Corte' said, "Perhaps we should take a chance on deception."

Three? He'd lost count. The sound of rushing water was back inside his mind. *So soon? So many?* What could he do? *It wasn't supposed to be like this!* "We must survive! We must be sure! Fire! Fire!"

The torpedo left the tube. They didn't have to wait long for that one, either.

"We have it, Captain. And another aerial torpedo, approximately two-seven-zero relative." The sonar operator sounded almost complacent about it.

"This is <u>madness</u>!" Corte' said.

Perhaps. Delamadrid said nothing. The water-sound was now very calming to listen to.

Corte' looked around from the fire control position. "Captain?"

"Sonar." Delamadrid looked straight ahead, as if he could see through the forward bulkhead. "Do you have anything on the screens besides the American?" He said nothing about the torpedo that was now searching for them. "Yes Captain, finally. A contact at medium-long range. I can give you a bearing only, though. The last few transients have come from that direction every three or four minutes."

Delamadrid nodded. "Of course," he said quietly, "Corte', set one along that bearing and cut it loose. Shoot the last two at the American." They could only guide two by wire at a time. They would guide them toward the most important target. "He must be empty by now." His duty was to make sure of the most important target. His duty...

"And if he is not? What then?" Corte' asked.

Delamadrid finally looked at him. And smiled. "Then we'll be finished. We'll go home." He knew what to do now. He turned away. "I wish to speak directly to the lieutenant. I will return shortly. Fire the torpedoes and prepare an evasive course away from here. Don't start it until I return." Without another word he left the attack center.

Corte' stared after his captain for a moment. There was something different about his behavior suddenly. It was surprising that the Captain accepted the probable failure of the mission as quietly as he did. But there was nothing really wrong with it. Anyone might be so affected by what had happened, the stress of the mission and the realization of failure, the deaths of men serving under his command. How much more might it affect the commander of the entire mission?

Having reassured himself, Corte' began setting up the final firings. He would fire, and they would escape if they could. But at least the last act of the play was underway. One way or another, there would be an end to it.

Somehow, it was not a very consoling thought.

* * *

"They intercepted the torpedo, sir," the sonar operator reported, "The American almost got them, but they managed to get that one and ours as well."

Arunov considered the situation. They were too close to use their last missile, but still well outside the range of their standard torpedoes. Why couldn't they get ones like the American had? The only weapon available was the last Mod Sixty-Five. There was about eighteen thousand meters separating them. It could go three times that far at high speed. It was the only thing they could do until the range had been closed.

"Fire," he said, "tube four. That's the torpedo, correct?" He waited for Marsilov's answering nod. "It will perhaps occupy them a little. Keep it on the wire as long as possible." The first one had stayed linked for almost twenty miles. That had to be a record. "Colonel, could you give me some idea about why none of five missiles, five of our latest and best weapons, could hit their target?"

Ulanovitch recognized the frustration Arunov was expressing, and was careful with his reply. He spread his hands and said, "I'm sorry, Captain, but I'm not involved with those specific areas. I can offer only theories. Only two of the missiles fired dropped their torpedoes close enough for them to find their target. At such ranges as this, targeting is understandably imprecise. That is not anyone's fault." He waited for Arunov to nod agreement. "Then there is the matter of the honing head, which does not have a lot of processing capability because the torpedo is small and tradeoffs undoubtedly had to be made in the design. This is especially important when the target takes measures to decoy the weapon. The seeker simply isn't smart enough to cope with such things, I'd say. I'm sure that someone is working on it."

"A lot of good 'working on it' does us now," Marsilov muttered.

"Captain," the sonar operator said, "we've got transients from the Brazilian. He has fired torpedoes."

"How many? At what target?" Maybe they were finally close enough to get

his attention.

"A moment, sir, it was a short series, I'm trying to sort it out—ah. Yes. Three torpedoes, sir, one of them coming this way." He didn't sound very bothered by the idea.

"Countermeasures to standby," Arunov said, "Activate the towed decoy." He didn't sound very concerned, either. Molniya was double-hulled, with a standoff distance between a titanium pressure hull and the outer hull that was specifically built to dissipate the energy of an explosion before it reached anything important. Even a directed-energy warhead was unlikely to sink them. A hit would undoubtedly affect their combat potential, however. But this was not a DE warhead, and it had not faced their decoys and jammers yet. It was intelligent, yes, but it was still only a Mod Two. It was not as good as the latest Tigerfish, and less intelligent than the American weapons, thank God. And they had more knowledge of it than they did the Mod Four that the British were using now. It could probably be dealt with.

"Strange," Arunov said, "what he's done. Sonar. You say he fired three?"

"Yes, Captain. Two at the American."

"Damn!" They couldn't go much faster without losing sonar quality. "Why couldn't they have let me intervene before this contact? We could have killed them all by now. How many rounds does that Brazilian carry? Does anyone know?"

"Twelve or sixteen, I think," Marsilov said, "Not many, considering." He was thinking about the number of torpedoes and missiles that had been expended to kill one submarine and damage another. Theories of underwater warfare were being toppled today. "You think he is empty?"

"Or very near to it," Arunov answered, "I think we will know for sure within the next few minutes, if the American can stay alive."

* * *

"Three, two, fire," Bearkiller said, and pressed the kill switch.

J.T. heard the sudden silence as the threshold relays kicked in. He watched the dark cloud representing blocking turbulence spread between them and Bravo on the liquid-crystal display. He waited. They all waited.

"It's clear, Captain. No secondary explosions. Nothing coming through."

J.T. breathed, once. Empty. No more tricks with torpedoes. And the decoy load was below forty percent. They still had integral jammers and bubble curtain generators, which had come into play when the last torpedo had curved back and reacquired them. A wall of air and several noisemakers and T/As had finally exhausted the torpedo's fuel. But that was it, now. They couldn't run, they couldn't hide. They could only wait, and cope as best as they could, and hope that the Russian would do something.

Marvelous day. Simply marvelous.

"What's Bravo doing?"

"Still manning at two-seven-zero absolute."

"And the Russian?"

"Running at the torpedo, still. We've got a tentative speed of twenty knots, range still over twenty thousand. A second noise source has come up, too, probably his Nixie. He's getting ready to welcome his visitor."

"Okay. Keep me informed."

"You might want to know. Skipper, that the other two Bravo boats are running away on the surface. One's making lot's of machinery noise and the other's heading for it at speed."

"They won't be back, I think. Thank you. Ed, how many torpedoes does a two-oh-nine carry?"

"Fourteen or sixteen, I think."

"Fourteen," Bearkiller said.

"Okay, now the hard part. Anybody got any idea how many he's fired so far?"

"A lot," Simmons answered, "He's empty or near to it by now."

"We could try counting back from the recordings, Skipper," Johnson said in one ear.

"That would take too long. We'll have to wait and see if he shoots any more. Something will happen soon, either way. We'll know then."

* * *

"Clear the bridge," Delamadrid said.

Corte' looked up, puzzled, at his captain's face, and then down at the pistol that was in his captain's hand.

"Sir?" The diving officer had not seen the gun.

"Clear the bridge," Delamadrid repeated, "Everyone forward, now."

Corte' straightened up from the chart table and turned toward him. "Whatever it is, Captain, I can't let you do it. Please, Captain."

Delamadrid shot him, twice, in the center of the chest. Corte' shook at the impact of each bullet, stood still and upright for a moment after he was hit, and then sat slowly down against the chart table. He died with a look of great sadness on his face.

"I'm sorry, old friend," Delamadrid said to the dead man. He had to speak louder than usual because his ears were ringing from the gunshots, and because of the sound of the water rushing through his mind. "Everyone out!" he ordered again, gesturing with the pistol. "Move forward! Clear the bridge! You too," he said to the helmsman, pointing the pistol like a finger at him, "Lock the controls and go! Close the hatch behind you!"

When everyone was gone Delamadrid stood without moving, looking after them. He was momentarily confused. The water, and what it said in his mind, was pushing other thoughts out of his consciousness. Drowning him with its message. Sweeping him away...

He shook himself, turned and locked the hatch behind him, crossed the compartment, and locked the forward hatch too. Tucking the pistol into his belt, he sat down at the helm position and belted himself tightly in.

The sonar operator was dead, his head crushed by a heavy wrench after he had answered Delamadrid's questions. The men aft and forward were locked away from each other by heavy bulkheads and watertight doors. They were further isolated because Delamadrid had disabled the intercom. It was no problem doing that—he had been with Triunfante almost from the beginning of her reconstruction and knew exactly what parts to break. Engineering didn't know that two men were dead by their own Captain's hand. They would not question his orders or interfere with his duty.

His duty.

His duty….

He turned on and tested the direct relay he had established between Sonar and the helm position. Then he reconfigured one of the programmable displays so that it would receive input from the sonar unit. When he was satisfied that it would work well enough for what he wanted to do he unlocked the helm controls, ran the throttles all the way forward, and activated Triunfante's active sonar.

The American had over fourteen times his submarine's mass and was four times her length, and he was close. The display had "painted" him by the third ping.

Delamadrid started to turn toward the contact. Through the seat and the aircraft-style control wheel in his hands, he could feel the buildup of speed and power as high-temperature ceramic fuel cells drove lightweight high-output electric motors to turn an efficient five-blade propeller, pushing his submarine, his Navy, his very nation toward the fulfillment of their destiny and toward the attainment of the leadership position and the respect that they had deserved for so long.

It was unfortunate that he would not be there to see it achieved.

But he had his duty.

His duty.

His duty...

* * *

"Come to two-four-zero," Arunov ordered, "Bring the trail decoy to full output and swing the array to port, two-three-five relative. Stand by jamming, stand by decoys. Sonar, report."

"Torpedo closing at high speed. I can hear the decoy...wait..

"Two-four-zero, Captain," the helmsman reported.

"Torpedo changing bearing, changing..."

Arunov felt absolutely confident. It was not the way he had expected to feel, a hundred meters deep and with a heavyweight torpedo coming at his submarine.

"It's bearing on the decoy!" There was a small emitter, basically a fancy speaker system, at the end of the remote's mini-array. It broadcast an amplified version of Molniya's noise signature when it was activated. The torpedo was turning toward the louder, closer noise source. "Yes! Confirm! There and—pass! It's gone by!"

"Shut down the decoy," Arunov ordered, "Helm, one-eight-zero now. Sonar, keep an eye on that torpedo, it may circle back. Bring the array into trail position." That would put the decoy between them and the torpedo if it came back. "Report on the Brazilian."

"Captain." The voice was that of his senior operator, the man who trained all of his new listeners. "The Brazilian has accelerated and turned toward the

American. He is very loud now. His active sonar is on. It's strange, Captain."

Aiyah? "Are you sure about this?"

"Very sure, sir."

"He's closing for a point-blank shot," Ulanovitch said.

Point blank...

"But why now instead of before?" Marsilov asked, "And why this way? It's not quite normal, to maneuver like that—"

Point blank...

"—it's crazy—"

<u>*Point blank*</u>*!*

"He's going to ram!" Arunov said, "He's out of torpedoes and he's going to ram!"

"But that's insane!" Marsilov said.

"I agree," Ulanovitch said, "It is insane. Exactly."

* * *

PINGPINGPINGPING...

"What's he doing?" J.T. asked. He watched Bravo's course indicator settle down at record speed. "Sonar, talk to me."

"He's at full speed," Tullibee said, "Stand by, we've got to filter out the pinging."

PINGPINGPINGPING...

"No launches? No transients?" J.T. asked.

"Negative, negative, Conn, he's just turned and is running fast. I got— Devil's <u>Balls</u>, Captain!"

"I see it."

The table display had laid out a predicted course based on the sonar input. It overran Alabama's position almost head-on.

PINGPINGPINGPING...

"He's out of rounds. He's turning himself into a weapon," Bearkiller said.

"He's either desperate or crazy," Simmons said, "maybe both. How do we evade?"

PINGPINGPINGPING...

Alabama was well over ten times Bravo's weight and four times his length. The boat was not designed to be able to turn on a dime, desperate captain and crazy helmsmen notwithstanding. Besides, they had momentum on their side then. Bravo was faster, Bravo was more agile, Bravo had active sonar—

Stop. Think. What are our strengths? What do we have that he doesn't? Size. Mass. Power. Power. Power.

Power.

"Helm, get us underway. Give me ten knots and point the bow at Bravo."

"Sir?"

"You heard me. Get the bearing from Sonar. Go!"

"Sir! Aye sir!" Alabama vibrated into motion. "Sonar, Helm. What's the direct bearing to Bravo? You heard me! It's what the Captain wants, I don't know..."

"Engineering, Conn, Chief-get-up-here-I-need-you-now! Crew address." J.T. paused for the intercom controller to switch channels and to make sure of what he was about to say. "All hands, this is the Captain. Rig for collision, I repeat, rig for collision. This is no joke, gentlemen. Close all watertight doors, evacuate forward compartments, damage control personnel man emergency stations. If it happens, it will be very soon. Be ready. That is all." He paused for the system to cut itself off. "Ed, give me five seconds on the collision alarm. Chief—" he said as Atchison skidded to an almost-fall beside the chart table, "if we really want to go up fast, I mean fast, blow everything and push it to the firewall, how quick can we pop up?"

PINGPINGPINGPING...

"Everything, sir?"

"Mains, trim tanks, everything we can get air into, big up-angle and full speed. How quick? Fast, Chief, fast, I need an answer!"

"Ten knots, Captain." The submarine vibrated steadily.

"Wouldn't recomnend much more," Atchison said, "I'm still not sure something's not ready to break loose. Captain, if we did what you said at this depth we'd broach in ninety seconds at most, probably way less. She'd come almost clear out of the water, Captain. It'd be worse than Bremerton." He was referring to the attack submarine that made a high-angle surface for cameras once. The pictures were all over the place. The video had made it into at least one motion picture. It was not something that was casually done by a nuclear submarine.

"Okay," J.T. said, "help us set it up. A full emergency blow, as many tanks as you can at one time." He looked down at the chart display. "You've got two or three minutes maybe. As soon as we blow, we'll have to re-flood and level out. Got that?"

"Sir, that's crazy—"

PINGPINGPINGPING...

"Do you want to die, Chief? We've got to pop up, get up fast at least a hundred feet, and level out. If we broach we won't be able to do anything about him coming back again. We've got to get up suddenly so he can't compensate. Got it?"

Atchison didn't offer any more arguments. He went to the ballast-control panel and started flipping switches and turning knobs and pulling levers.

"Planesman!" *Could we possibly stay level? No.* "When I say go, I want as much up-angle as you can give me without stalling her out." If Alabama got hung up for any time at all the Brazilian would take her stem off. "We'll be blowing everything and applying full power. You've got to get us up and then get the stern for God's sake out of the way." He again considered turning instead, and he again rejected the idea. They couldn't do it fast enough without a high risk of doing a snap roll. He could turn faster than they could, anyway. "So it's pull up, climb, level off, all in a hurry." Keep your voice level. "I don't know how much trim control you'll have—"

"None at all," Atchison said, "It'll go down too fast."

"You hear that? Both of you—control surfaces only. We've got to stay in control, gentlemen. Understood?"

"Understood, sir!"

"Sonar, feed Helm the direct bearing to the Russian. We're going to sprint for him as soon as we get level. Is that clear?"

"Clear, Captain!" Petersen said, and dropped his voice, "I didn't sign up for this."

"Me neither," the planesman said as quietly, "And if they think I'm gonna re-up after this..."

"All stations stand by," J.T. said.

He watched his display, and he waited.

* * *

There were sounds, voices that he could hear but not understand. Was it the crew on the intercom? They couldn't speak to each other, but they could to the Bridge. There was a mist, something clouding his vision, but not enough so that he couldn't see the target image growing on the display in front of him. The sonar's computerized interpreter was making an image for him as he drove closer to the target. The outgoing beam was literally painting it for him, creating a recognizable picture of the huge missile submarine on his display. It was getting bigger, growing in size more rapidly than he thought it would. That didn't bother him. He wanted to finish it as quickly as possible so that he could do something about the rushing water that was filling his head. Besides, it was his duty to finish it.

It was his duty.

His duty.

His duty....

* * *

"DamndamndamndamnDAMN!" Arunov slapped the chart table with his open hand. "We could have killed them all before this!" In his anger he forgot the one that had been invisible to them. "Now it's over!"

"They are brave, though, these Brazilians," Ulanovitch muttered.

"Perhaps the American can cope," Marsilov said.

"Perhaps <u>not</u>! He would have fired by now, if he had a round left. Sonar, what about the torpedo chasing us?"

"Turning back, Captain. It will try again."

"Reactivate the towed decoy. Launch distraction canisters. Keep it occupied. What of ours?"

"The wire is still connected. It's beginning to sense a trail, I think." "<u>Good</u>! When the two have met, it can send what's left to the <u>bottom</u>! DAMN!"

* * *

"All hands, this is the Captain," J.T. said, "There will be abrupt depth and angle and bearing changes coming, maybe all at once. Strap down or hang on. That is all. Jim, when you hear me say go give me everything we've got, jammers, decoys, everything. Got it?"

"Understood." Bearkiller checked his status board and put a hand close to the panic button.

PINGPINGPINGPING...

"Chief, are you ready?"

"Master switch is set."

"Helm? Planes?"

"Full power and steer for the Russian when we level out. Captain."

"I'll pull us up two hundred and level out as near as I can, sir."

"Good enough. Countermeasures?"

"Ready." Bearkiller covered the panic button with the palm of his hand.

PINGPINGPINGPING...

"All right. Stand by." J.T. watched the tiny submarine symbol on his chart display. Under normal conditions such a bow-on approach would give them nothing but a bearing, but with the noise that Bravo was making the computers and their operators were having no trouble with range calculations.

PINGPINGPINGPING...

He tried to reach out with his mind and feel exactly how close the other submarine really was.

PINGPINGPINGPING...

Was he really that crazy? Did he really intend to kill everyone just to stop them?

PINGPINGPINGPING...

He had to give his people enough time to angle up, rise, and level the stern out of the way, and not much more. There could be no margin for this, or Bravo would correct for it.

PINGPINGPINGPING...

Diana. The children.

PINGPINGPINGPING...

If he was wrong—never again—if he was wrong...

PINGPINGPINGPING...

Never.

PINGPINGPING...

"NoW! GO NOW! GO NOW!"

It wasn't a conscious decision to say it at that moment. The words were coming out, lunging away from him, before he knew he was saying it.

The symbols on his display were merging.

On the countermeasures control panel, set away by itself and carefully marked, was the Panic Button. It was called that because it was what the weapons officer was supposed to activate when he panicked, which would theoretically happen when an intelligently-planned, computer-assisted, carefully schemed pattern of decoys and janming and deception measures had failed to stop an incoming torpedo. "When all else has failed," the instructor at the weapons school told everyone, "When you've done all you can and it's still coming, and it's certain death if you don't," he said, "then do."

Bearkiller didn't simply press that button, he slapped it down with his open palm as his other hand flipped half-a-dozen switches besides. And then he got the best hold he could, because they were already past twenty degrees of up-angle by the time he was finished, and he didn't really trust the seatbelt.

Atchison triggered the cascade blow he had set up. High-pressure air pushed water out of the largest ballast tanks first and then started to fill space in everything that was left, from secondary ballast to trim tanks. Almost everything in Alabama's high-pressure tanks went into a frenzied effort to turn an eighteen-thousand-ton submarine into a cork.

The helmsman punched the throttles all the way forward as the planesman pulled his yoke all the way back toward his stomach. Alabama trembled, roared, shrieked, raised her nose and very nearly stood on her tail. Cavitation was severe, enhanced by the vibration of the propeller shaft. Water roared out from her ballast tanks, mixing chaotically with air from high-pressure tanks and chemically-created walls of bubbles coming from the hull generators. Decoy canisters were tossed and tumbled by instantaneous currents and vortexes that formed and were disrupted and formed again around the surface of the hull. Even the sonar jammers, set to their most powerful mode, contributed to the disruption of the ocean's substance with the energy they poured into the fluid that surrounded them.

Around Alabama, the water boiled.

* * *

"Captain! Damn! This is amazing!"

Arunov found a set of headphones and plugged them into the nearest audio repeater. He made sure the volume was well down, closed his eyes, and smoothly dialed the volume up.

His eyes snapped open. An expression of amazement took his face over.

"What is it, Captain?" Ulanovitch asked.

"Chaos," Arunov almost whispered, "Sheer chaos."

Submarine officers in all services, especially if they wanted to command, spent some time a sonar school. While there they learned at least the basics of how to see in their minds what they heard with their ears. An important part of that training was the time spent listening to recordings of actual contacts. The students learned to differentiate between the big multi-bladed propeller of a submarine and the contra-rotating blades of a torpedo. They listened to the sound of a reactor pump at high power and to the whine of gas-turbines driving fast-maneuvering surface units. They started with recordings of their own units and progressed to anything that could be obtained about anyone else, enemy or ally or in-between. And they remembered what they heard.

What Arunov heard now was like nothing he had encountered in hundreds of hours spent listening to recordings and to the real thing while on patrols. It was as if someone had taken a tape of each individual thing— mechanical noise, various decoys, sonar jammers, cavitation, bubble curtains and more—and put each onto one track of a multichannel tape, and then played the tape with the volume set as high as it could go. This would probably be picked up for hundreds of miles, perhaps even by the sea floor sensors that the Americans had placed on the coasts. It was as if someone had turned on everything that could be turned on and then turned it all up as high as if it would go.

"What is it, Captain?" Ulanovitch asked again, "Have they collided?"

"No, they haven't," Arunov answered quietly, still inner-directed, and then he was silent, listening until the words repeated themselves in his mind.

No, they haven't!

"Sonar!" His head straightened suddenly. "Can you get anything specific out of this?"

"Impossible, sir. There are too many emitters in that area."

"This is amazing," Marsilov said, holding an earphone over his left ear, "I never thought there was so much—"

"Active search, Sonar! Now!"

"But why?" Ulanovitch asked.

"They're doing something," Arunov said, "I have to know if it worked. Even false returns—the torpedo! Damn! Is it still on the wire?"

"Yes sir," the weapons officer answered, "Indications are that it has a trail, and that it is ignoring deception efforts so far." It could do that because the Type Sixty-Five's main tracking system was unique. Normal decoy and deception methods would have little if any effect on it.

"Coordinate with sonar!" Arunov said, "Keep it clear of the American!"

"You think they survived?" Ulanovitch asked.

"I think they're trying to," Arunov said, "They have to be." He raised the headphone back to his ear. "Don't stop," he commanded the spot that was marked on his plotting board, "Don't stop! Stay alive, damn you! Stay alive!"

* * *

Delamadrid kept his eyes open all the way through. He was proud of that, and of the way he had held his course and driven straight in after the visual display went completely white after filling up with images and designs that made it look like glass was shattering. He had gone straight in regardless, and braced for the impact.

But there had been no impact, no forward thrust against his seat restraints, no crashing and crumpling sounds filling his ears, no sight of the forward bulkhead giving way and filling his vision with a wall of water carrying in pieces of his submarine, no glimpse of the hull of the American caving in under the impact of his submarine against theirs.

Nothing.

Even the sonar was clear now, still pinging continuously but putting no returns on his screen.

He had missed. Somehow he had missed.

It didn't make him angry. A few seconds of pride, of pleasure in himself, was all that the rushing water in his mind had not already washed away from him. He was now so fully locked into his intention that he had become little more than a control processor for a gigantic torpedo.

And just like a control processor would, he commanded and initiated a hard turn to starboard, intent only on reacquisition and pursuit of the target.

He found it again midway through the turn.

* * *

"Secure countermeasures! How does it look, Chief?" He was impressed that he didn't sound more excited.

"My God, Captain, that was unique!" Atchison scanned the diving board and the helm and plane indicators, "it looks okay for now, sir. Take a minute to get the details."

"Take it. Helm, report! Sonar, what's happening out there?"

"Sir, steering course one-eight-zero and ahead full!" The vibration was increasing.

"He's turning, Skipper. Gonna have us back shortly. We're losing sensitivity too."

"I've got red lights on starboard bow plane," the planesman said to Atchison.

"Helm, back off the throttle. We've got to keep our ears. Jim, what's the decoy count?"

PING. It was weak.

"That's the Russian, Captain."

"How's your control response?" Atchison asked.

"Expendables at five, the Nixie, hull jammers and curtains after that."

"I don't like it, but I can live with it," the planesman said.

"What about the torpedo?" Simmons asked.

"Torpedo?" J.T. had to think about it. "The Russian!"

"You'll have to," Atchison said, and then raised his voice, "Captain, I think we've lost the starboard bow plane. It probably ripped off in the climb somewhere."

Great. "Can we go without it? Better say yes, Chief. Sonar, where is the Russian torpedo?"

PINGPINGPINGPING...

"Nixie's blooming nicely," Bearkiller said.

"Conn, we got more noise on the self-monitors, starboard side somewhere."

"We can make it. Captain, but it'll be either slower or riskier. We can't bob again like we just did, either, no air for it." It would take days to regenerate that much high-pressure air unless they could surface.

"Acknowledged. Sonar we know where the noise is, where is the torpedo, the torpedo!" Too many things!

"Bravo is closing portside rear, bearing two-zero-zero relative," Tullibee said.

PINGPINGPINGPING...

"Russian torpedo is on opposite bearing and will pass to starboard if it holds course. Can you back off the throttle, Conn? Sir that torpedo is singing."

Singing? "Singing? Helm, throttle back. Put us back at ten knots. Sonar, feed that to First. Ed, listen to this." Why did it seem important to him? "Bravo status?"

"Angling behind us, sir, at high speed. He's closing the angle."

There was a very high pitched and very rapid pinging coming through one earphone. The cycling was so fast it was almost keening. It changed slightly in pitch as they listened.

"Be advised, Russian torpedo has passed us, is steering toward Bravo. It looks...stand by, Conn, Bravo is crossing our stem, passing, we've—"

"—lost Nixie!" Bearkiller said, finishing the sentence.

The pursuing submarine had chosen the clearer signal put out by the towed decoy's amplifiers and had rammed it instead of them. That was the last one, though. There were no more decoys to stream behind them, and precious few left to drop in their wake.

"That Russian torpedo is turning behind Bravo. I don't get it, Conn, it passed and turned back. Looks like pursuit."

Pursuit? Why steer for a stern shot? Are they crazier than he is?

"Be advised, Conn, Bravo is turning back for us."

* * *

Multiple returns from the American's countermeasures suite, partially but not completely filtered out by Molniya's electronics, had confirmed their survival. For the moment. Arunov ordered the active sonar turned off, but otherwise he did not react. There was, they knew, something wrong with the American, some damage or a mechanical problem. The Brazilian was moving twice as fast as it turned and pursued. Molniya was still just outside of standard torpedo range, and even then it would take over eight minutes for a torpedo to reach the target. Arunov ground his teeth and received two reports.

From Sonar: "He's hit! Something...stand by...sir, he's overrun and eliminated a noise source. Not, I repeat, not the American."

"A towed decoy," Marsilov said, "He'll cross back and get them now."

Arunov nodded and continued to grind his teeth. There was nothing else he could do. Curse them! The bureaucrats! Damn them all!

From the weapons officer: "The wire's snapped! Captain, we've lost direct guidance!"

Aumov's head snapped around. "What was the last indication from the torpedo?" he demanded.

"It had turned on track," the weapons officer said, "and had reported a lock on trail. That was the last feedback before we lost command."

"Sonar! Can you hear our torpedo?!"

A lock on trail message meant that the torpedo's decision circuitry was getting enough assurance from its passive seeker so that it didn't need to turn on the terminal guidance system, a medium-frequency active sonar. That was good. But whose trail had it lock on to? The American, especially in his current condition, left a far larger trail than the Brazilian. But the Brazilian was moving very fast, and the torpedo had been instructed before launch about what target characteristics to look for. There was still a chance that it would find the wrong target, however.

That would be very bad indeed.

"Captain, we lost track of the torpedo when it passed opposite the American. We think it is somewhere behind them."

It would turn. It would sense the wakes, and it would turn. It would most likely turn to follow the one it had first. That would be the Brazilian.

Maybe.

Arunov stopped grinding his teeth, but he didn't smile.

* * *

Delamadrid felt something, barely, and saw the image on his sonar monitor change. But it wasn't what he had been waiting to feel and see. He had missed again. He did not curse, or sigh, or even feel pride in his behavior any more. He simply started turning toward the one remaining target.

Automatically.

* * *

There was still a danger, in addition to the very obvious one of the Brazilian submarine that was trying to ram them. Ed Simmons pointed it out to everyone.

"Wake-follower!" he shouted. Had it not been for the restraint, Bearkiller would have come out of his seat at the sound.

"My God, he's right!" the weapons officer said when he had resettled his consciousness.

"What?" J.T.'s head came up and around, aiming at his first officer.

"The Russian," Sirrmons said, "the torpedo! It's a Type Sixty-Five! That singing we heard was leakage from a VHF sonar!"

"Jim?"

"I think he's right," Bearkiller answered, "It's got the range, and our system would interpret the wake-seeker that way, I'd think."

"But that's surface-capable only," J.T. said, meaning that the torpedo was only rated for use against surface ships.

"Not anymore," Simmons said.

"They've upgraded it," Bearkiller said, "That's the only explanation that fits. It's the wake-seeker, it has to be."

The Russian-made Type Sixty-Five torpedo was big—it was fired from a twenty-seven-inch torpedo tube—and a bit slower than most others, travelling at either thirty or fifty knots for anywhere up to fifty nautical miles. It had the longest range of any modem torpedo. It also had a unique primary homing system. The Type Sixty-Five would find and then follow the wake of a target, the faint trail of turbulence that was left behind by any propeller- driven vessel. It apparently used a very-high-frequency sonar for that purpose. It was known that such units could detect wakes at short range. What had not been known with certainty was the Sixty-Five used that method to find the wakes that it followed. The intelligence types would be very interested in such a fact.

"It's behind us both," J.T. said.

Provided that they could survive to tell the intelligence types about it. Alabama, especially damaged like she was, would have a bigger wake than an intact Two-oh-nine would.

J.T. looked from Simmons back to the chart display. Bravo had actually passed them after ramming the Nixie (somehow, without either ripping off or becoming fouled in the towed array). He was turning hard to starboard now, a full circle that would shortly bring him back into line for another approach, this time from about one-three-zero. J.T. didn't expect another miss. The Russian torpedo was still behind them both, probably in a position to pick up either wake or to acquire either one of them if it activated its terminal homing sonar. Was it close enough? And whose wake would it be picking up? He had perhaps thirty seconds left.

Decide. Now.

"Helm, all stop. Course two-seven-zero on momentum. Understood?"

"All stop and two-seven-zero on drift." Petersen brought the throttle all the way back and turned his wheel over. "Sir, engines register all stop, turning to two-seven-zero on drift."

"Acknowledged."

The planesman was whispering. "Hail, Mary, full of grace..."

"Now," J.T. whispered to himself, "it's over. One way or another."

* * *

One of the reasons that a Type Sixty-Five torpedo was as big as it was is that it requires a lot of electronics for its homing system. Finding and following the wake of a ship or submarine amid the many eddies, currents, and vortexes that exist in the open ocean required sensitive sonar receivers and very intelligent processors. Those processors were for a moment confused by the chaotic water that was caused when its target crossed Alabama's larger and more turbulent wake. The torpedo's brain wavered for a microsecond or so before concluding that it had simply hit a cross-current or strong updraft. So that it would not be thrown off, the torpedo turned on it terminal homing system, a strong medium-frequency sonar that had about twice the range of the wake-seeking system.

The torpedo found two targets, one very large one at the edge of the seeker's cone of coverage and one smaller one moving very fast and turning across the torpedo's current heading. Normally the torpedo would automatically turn to follow the larger target because larger targets were assumed to be the more valuable major combatants. But one of the modifications that had been made to the Type Sixty-Five was the ability to specify certain target characteristics so that the torpedo would have a better chance of hitting what the Russians wanted to hit and nothing else. In this case the Russian weapons officer had given the torpedo an upper limit to its echo return size. It was told to ignore any very large return from its terminal homing system, such as the kind that would be given by an Ohio-class ballistic missile submarine.

The fast-turning target that was crossing its line, however, was well within the programmed limits of acceptable targets. So, using the information from its terminal-homing system, the torpedo plotted an intercept course and made a turn to port to close the angle of approach to its target.

A few seconds later it set off an almost-two-thousand-pound warhead after striking Triunfante on the port side, just aft of the attack center.

PRESENT EXTENDED

J.T. looked down at where the starboard hydroplane used to be. Where it had been relocated from the conning tower to the bow there was now the turbulence caused by a tangle of rods and cables and ripped metal. It was fortunate that they had been moved when the experimental modifications were being made. It would have been awkward operating on the surface without a conning tower.

"Conn, Engineering."

J.T. had finally taken off his headset. He picked up a microphone. "What is it, Chief?"

"It wasn't what we thought, sir. It was just a weak spot in a secondary core-flood line. It's not fixed yet, but we can dive anyway if you want. I can even give you full speed, if you don't mind your teeth rattling."

The Russian torpedo had done more than disintegrate the center third of the Brazilian submarine. An almost one-ton warhead had gone off not very far from where Alabama had been drifting. The shock wave had cracked a weak weld in one of the systems designed to flood the reactor core with coolant in case a full and fast shutdown was required. And it had thrown the propeller further out of line as well. Fearing a pressure hull breach, J.T. had brought his boat up, using what was left of the hydroplanes, far enough to draw air in through the emergency snorkel tube and pump out the ballast tanks. The Russian attack boat, Molniya, had also surfaced and offered assistance, which had been politely declined.

"Thank you, Chief. Conn out." J.T. looked at the Sierra. It was riding very low in the water about a mile away. "Communications, Conn. Raise the Russian for me." It looked dangerous. J.T. was glad to have it close by.

"Ulanovitch here, Captain. What may we do for you?" Captain Arunov didn't speak English. For some crazy reason it comforted J.T. to know that.

"You may inform your captain that we have completed repairs and we will now continue with our mission." There was no use lying about it. The Russian wouldn't have been here at all if they hadn't known what was going on to begin with.

"He will be pleased to hear that, Captain. We are all sorry that we weren't able to help you more quickly."

"That you were here at all was significant enough. You have our appreciation for that."

J.T. made a mental note to confiscate the sex organs of anyone who said that they had been doing all right without the Russians. He didn't think he would need very many jars, though.

"We will continue to watch over you until your own escort forces arrive, of course, or at least until the other adversary units are accounted for."

That meant that the last Brazilian submarine, which was supposedly patrolling around the missile firing point, would probably get a torpedo up the stern if the long range antisubmarine aircraft that were heading toward them didn't get to it first. There was also a small chance that other units of Brazil's navy would attempt to stop them, but it was only a small chance. The Russians had other reasons to hang around besides simple altruism, and they all knew that.

"Thank you." *Might as well say thank you, I can't say go away and make it stick, now can I?* "I assume that all of your recording devices are in good repair?"

Ulanovitch laughed. "Of course, Captain, I have checked them myself. And we have extra sensors on the masts just for this." It was good to be dealing with a realist. They would get a great deal of information out of this. "My captain repeats his invitation to you: a cup of tea before you go?" *A full firing sequence. Twenty-four missiles. It will be incredible.*

J.T. raised binoculars toward the Russian. Arunov, wearing a headset like J.T. had been, raised a mug toward him, drank, and said something into the microphone.

"It's a very good tea, he says. A personal blend."

J.T. made an exaggerated shake of his head. "My apologies, but I still have work to do. Some other time, perhaps."

"Perhaps. Let's hope so. He says good luck and good sailing, Captain. We are both very pleased to have made your acquaintance."

Arunov saluted them.

"Thank you, Mr. Ulanovitch." Ulanovitch had mentioned no rank. J.T. returned Arunov's salute. "Good sailing to you." He racked the mike and turned to the lookouts, the only other men who were with him on the tower. "Clear it." There were down the ladder within seconds. J.T. took one last look at the Russian. Her bridge was empty, and there was already less of her visible than there had been a moment ago.

Show off. But he smiled.

He checked the hatches carefully as he went down the ladder. "Take her down," he ordered, "Make your depth one hundred feet. Ed, instruct Atchison to take a careful look around before we go any deeper. I want to be sure of this. How long to the firing point?"

"Three, maybe four hours," Simmons answered.

"Good enough. Helm, ahead slow." He felt very tired. He was sure that he wasn't the only one who did. "Have the missile crewmen stand down." The launch control and missile maintenance people had other jobs during battle stations. No one was every totally idle on a submarine. "I want somebody to be rested by the time we get there, even if I'm not. Any word on the rendezvous?" Two attack submarines were boiling water toward them. A surface escort group was coming together on the fly not far behind, and a submarine tender was farther back but making its best possible speed in their direction. Long-range antisubmarine aircraft would be there first to clear the firing point and then form an airborne barrier between them and the coast to screen against further attacks.

"We'll have two Orions on a racetrack west by the time we launch. And Seawolf is chasing Atlanta to see who gets here first. They should arrive about ninety minutes after we empty the tubes."

"When you care enough to send the very best, I guess. Who are you putting money on?"

"It's close. Seawolf's faster, but Atlanta had the head start. A tossup. What do you think they'll do with the Russian?"

"Shake his hand, I hope, if he's still around. I don't expect him to be." J.T. put his headset back on. "Sonar, Conn. How does it look out there?"

"Not as bad as we thought, Captain. Molniya is pulling ahead of us slowly, about zero-four-zero at four thousand yards now. We're getting some degradation from our own noise, of course, but the ears are still pretty long."

"Thank you. Conn out." J.T. racked the headset. "First officer has the Conn. Ed, I'm going back to talk to the missilemen. I want to make sure that the birds are ready to take flight on time."

But for what? Okay, we bust their nukes. We do something that we couldn't really do before. Eighty or more men dead, hundreds of millions expended, relationships disrupted. The money is still there, the names will change, the location might change, or it might not. Either way, the merry-go- round starts the next ride. I'm being too pessimistic. Aren't I? Aren't we accomplishing something, at least? Would we even be doing this if we weren't? But what, really? What?

* * *

Delay. Extra time for negotiation or for SDI/ORBIT SHIELD deployment or for simple common sense. Maybe a temporary or partial disruption of drug supplies as a bonus. Maybe.

Making some kind of geo-military-political statement was very much secondary to him. Time was what he wanted. Time, maybe, was what had been bought today.

Was it enough?

The President turned away from the window. On the desk in front of him were two folders. One contained the statement that would be read at the press conference in a few minutes. The other contained the up-to-date log of HAMMERSTRIKE from the time of the original idea development to the preliminary strike evaluation. It was a synopsis, not very thick. A little less than one inch, that was all.

The operation had gone well, just like the one on the other side of that continent—the one that would never be acknowledged—had. SCARLET COBRA reported at least twelve of the twenty-four smart rocks to be exactly on target, with most of the rest falling more than close enough to do the job. There would be no more South American nuclear programs for the near future. They had made sure of that. What wasn't as certain to him was whether getting it into the open as he had done was the smartest thing to do. For all the good that would be recognized as having come from the operation, there would still be a great amount of weeping and wailing and gnashing of teeth over what had been done. Maybe that was part of the price for the eventual elimination of the damn bombs.

Then why did it bother him to pay it?

It bothered him because it was an imperfect solution that was why. It was an imperfect solution constructed by imperfect men who were trying to deal with an imperfect world where the only alternative to an imperfect solution was to have no solution at all.

SDI was an imperfect solution. ORBIT SHIELD was an imperfect solution. The special detectors being installed at transit points was an imperfect solution. HAMMERSTRIKE was an imperfect solution, and making this part of it public was an imperfect solution. Far better to have men and nations see no need to have nuclear weapons, to have no wish throughout the world for their possession, much less their use. Far, far, better.

The intercom buzzed. He pressed the button.

"Yes, Nancy."

"It's time, sir."

"It most certainly is. Thank you. I'll be out in a moment."

As to drugs-well, the Russian move would help, some, though it wasn't really targeted to that. But it wasn't a solution of any kind, much less an imperfect one. It would help only if linked to everything else, to the assistance to producer nations, to interdiction, to law enforcement, to education, to treatment, to everything else that had to be linked together still. All a chain. All imperfect. All still better than no solution at all.

Would there be a day when no man or woman, or at least only a pitiful few, would neither need nor want such things?

He stood up, picked up the folder with the statement in it, and stood for another moment looking down at what was left of HAMMERSTRIKE.

Time. Time to come up with less imperfect solutions, and to make current solutions better than they were before. Time paid for with blood.

Time.

"Memo to God: Please allow us to use it wisely."

He went out to meet the press.

* * *

They had been there for a long time, and they were very glad to be on the way out.

SCARLET COBRA was a thirty-man SEAL team, an extraordinarily large unit in a service where four-man groups were nearer the norm. The numbers involved made those who knew about it nervous for reasons other than the increased risk of discovery run by a group of that size. What really made those who knew nervous was the reason that the team was so large: A strong guard was needed for the ATMs, the Atomic Demolition Munitions, that the team was carrying.

SCARLET COBRA had been mounted for three reasons: First, to provide certain assistance to the targeting of the Trident D-X missiles if needed. Second, to observe the impact and effect of those missiles once they were fired. Third, so that they could act in case a problem developed in the first operational deployment of the D-X. SCARLET COBRA was an insurance policy in case the missiles didn't work.

Fortunately, no claim had been made on the policy. It would have been much more difficult to set up something that would look like an accidental detonation of a stored weapon than the men in the air-conditioned offices thought it would be. They would have had to work for that one. Heavy as the ADMs were ("man-portable" never meant the same thing to a weapon designer that it did to the soldier in the field), there was much less of a problem carrying them out than there would have been in setting them off. A glass-sided crater would not have been a desirable addition to the landscaping anyway.

The missile warheads had dropped in so fast that the first sign of the fire mission had been a geyser of dirt and trees erupting from the side of the mountain that covered the target. Warheads had landed at regular intervals for thirty minutes, "walking" up and down the slope. If their information about the location of the facility was correct, the warheads were very much dead on target, and certainly not more than twenty or thirty yards off at any point. The mountain had collapsed on that side somewhere around the tenth or eleventh inpact, the many tunnels and chambers in the rock giving way to create a giant trench, a cut in the slope that looked like someone had run a giant plow blade from the base to the summit. The men who watched and made records of the strike were struck silent by the sight of it.

The last warhead fell. Rock and earth and dust settled, and the ground stopped trembling from the shock of repeated hammer blows. It was over.

So the watchers shouldered their equipment and picked up their weapons. Starting with the point man and the forward flank guards, each man then turned his back on the cloud of fine dust that still hung in the air above the devastated facility. There was nothing more for them to do here. And it was a long walk back to the submarine.

* * *

They helped Eric and Morana move in—a half-dozen wiry, muscular, very fit-looking men, some with very short haircuts, who looked to be in their mid-twenties to perhaps the early thirties. All of them looked around a lot. None of them seemed to miss much of what was happening around them even though they were concentrating on the loads they carried into the house. A few of the people who watched or who went to welcome the new arrivals made remarks about this, but not to anyone in the group. No one remarked on the fact that there was always more than one member of the moving team with a free hand, mostly the right, because no one noticed it. They didn't notice the sidearms that everyone carried, either. They weren't meant to. If someone had been good enough to notice, and dumb enough to ask about it, they would have met with one or both of two reactions: Multiple copies of the appropriate paperwork to cover the possession of such weapons, and/or genuinely blank looks. Asking anyone there why they were armed would have been like asking them why they were wearing underwear.

At close to mid-day a break was called. Because the TV wasn't hooked up yet, everyone gathered around a radio to listen to what the President had to say, even though every one of them was pretty sure that they knew what he would be talking about.

"Good afternoon, ladies and gentlemen of the press, and to my fellow citizens, good afternoon. Thank you all for coming. I have a short statement to read, and then the floor will be open for questions. We'll even untie Craig and take the tape off his mouth, if he'll promise to behave himself."

(Laughter.)

"You are all aware of the continuing difficulties caused by the overturning of the democratic government of Brazil such a relatively short time ago. You are also aware of the linkage between the current government of that nation and a loose coalition of drug cartels that came to light just a few months ago. This revelation, along with ongoing questions and, yes, disputes over such things as human rights and environmental concerns ultimately resulted in the repudiation of debt payments by Brazil and the subsequent suspension of loan agreements with that country by both the World Bank and the International Monetary Fund.

"As if all this was not enough, the leaders of the Brazilian government also revived a program to develop nuclear weapons that had been canceled in 1989. At a time when nuclear disarmament was not only underway but gaining momentum, the government of Brazil elected instead to further isolate itself from the community of nations and to further enlarge the atmosphere of apprehension and fear that it was already creating among its neighbors.

"After consultation with representatives of the Organization of American States, and after direct consultation with the leaders of several of the Central and South American countries that were involved in the developing situation, the United States made it clear that we did not consider such a capability to be conducive to regional stability and security. I, and other members of this administration, further stated that certain measures to counter this threat would be considered if such a capability became evident or if we had sufficiently strong evidence that such a capability was in fact close to becoming real.

"Unfortunately, the government of Brazil has not chosen to take these statements seriously. Not quite two days ago, a two-thirty p.m. Eastern Standard Time, they successfully detonated what they termed a demonstrator, a nuclear device with an estimated yield of between one hundred and one hundred and fifty kilotons, at an underground site. They had thus demonstrated an evident capability and capacity to produce and deploy nuclear weapons. There was also very clear evidence of a decision to enter series production and actual deployment of at least two types, and possibly more, of aircraft and missile-deliverable weapons of this type.

"So—acting in the interests of regional peace and security, and to some degree in the interests of world peace, I reluctantly ordered the Secretary to initiate a contingency-response operation. About three hours ago, at about nine a.m. Eastern Standard Time, the Brazilian bomb production and storage facility was taken under fire by submarine-launched ballistic missiles mounting special non-nuclear warheads. These missiles were fired by the Trident submarine USS Alabama, marking the first time in history that a nuclear ballistic missile submarine has conducted an operational launch.

"That concludes my statement. The floor is now open for questions."

* * *

He was already in the secure communications room, so all the technician had to do was tear the sheet off the clear-text printer, the end point of the double-encryption process, and hand it to him. He had been there since the fire order had been transmitted almost twenty-four hours ago. He might, might, be able to sleep in another hour, when he knew that Alabama was on the way home with her escorts. He was glad that it was finally over, and that everyone would be able to return to their regular missions now.

Brad:

Details of encounter and missile firing transmitting concurrently. Damage is significant but repairable. Minor casualties among the crew. It was close, but we made it. You'll never believe the part about the Russian. Crew performed well throughout. We can all be proud of them.

Now, a personal favor, if you please: Call Diana.

Tell her to rent a limousine.

CR Williams works a day job as a professional geek administrating server systems and helping to keep networks running. Otherwise, he writes books and conducts defensive firearms training through his company In Shadow In Light. This is his first foray into fiction but there will be others before he's through with the concept. He can be reached with questions or comments and for queries about firearms training through his website www.inshadowinlight.com or directly at crwilliams@inshadowinlight.com.

Other books by CR Williams:

Gunfighting, and Other Thoughts about Doing Violence
Volumes One throughThree
Facing the Active Shooter

All available in print and Kindle format through Amazon.com.

Planned future releases:
Nonfiction-
Bare-Bones Gunfighting

Gunfighting, and Other Thoughts about Doing Violence

Volume Four

Fiction-

An Even Break 1: Concerning the Construction of Heroes